The Se

Zipacna Dragons

A Tale of Adijari

by

S.P. Jayaraj

Dear Jean,
Fly as high
as you can

[signature]

outskirts
press

PRELUDE

With her baby against her breast, Bamay lowered to her knees before the Fire Spirit Ta'ar. She relaxed the child into her forearm, his dark brown skin and coal black hair illuminated by the Fire Spirit. He was not crying. She always thought her first son would be a crier, but he was not. She wondered as she looked at him, if it was due to the essence of the Fire Spirit within him. He was looking back at her, before he rolled his eyes towards the Fire Spirit who floated closer. Bamay obediently also gave her attention back to her lord.

The moon had been out for hours, though it was easy to forget that with Ta'ar before her. The whole of Aristahl was able to see his light through the square openings of his ziggurat. Amesha nations were jointly ruled by a shah and a spirit, and Ta'ar had been the spirit ruler of Aristahl for the reign of three mortal shahs. It was said that his fiery aura was fueled by the belief of those who worshipped him. Ta'ar's skin was made of orange flames while red fire formed his square molten crown and his rectangular beard. Layered over him were sheets of lava that formed his patterned clothes. Of late, the brightness of Ta'ar's presence was inconsistent. It had been gradual, but the flames of his aura were in flux due to the rivalry of rulership with Shah Zahk.

Bamay had expected that due to their shared interest in the nation that the two rulers would work well together, especially since the Fire Spirit Ta'ar had appointed Zahk to be the new shah. Zahk had been the general of the army of Aristahl, and so Ta'ar anticipated him to act with strong resolve against the dragons that inhabited the surrounding forest. But Shah Zahk defied the spirit after he assumed power, by redirecting Aristahl's resources into infrastructure instead. Before Shah Zahk, Aristahl had been dedicating so much to the battle against the dragons that its people were barely able to survive. Troops of Aristahlians were sent out regularly to slay the dragons in the forest, many of whom were not even soldiers. Resources were spent on making weapons and armor or were sent to other nations battling different species of dragons. What had always troubled Bamay, even before Zahk had assumed the throne, was that Ta'ar had convinced the last two shahs to send resources to nations that were not even amesha. Aristahl couldn't afford to make such sacrifices, and it could afford even less what Ta'ar did next.

In skirmishes against the dragons within the surrounding forests, Aristahlians discovered that the olive tree was resistant to fire. Since then, they started cutting down the trees in masses under Ta'ar's orders. They cut down all the trees in Aristahl and then moved on to the forest. Spears made from these trees were sent to the dev nations to aid them in their war against the sesha dragons, dragons that resembled giant cobras and had the fangs to match. Later, Aristahl sent trees by the cartload to the elves who used it to build their base of Delthurk. To those who were not amesha, it seemed like the perfect plan. They were taking away the dragon's habitat as well as making weapons that were used against them.

But ameshas were magically bonded to the earth around

them. By defiling the trees, they also harmed themselves. So Shah Zahk put an end to all that. He stated that it was heresy for ameshas to desecrate the trees that nourished them. He went further and devoted resources toward re-seeding the barren parts of Aristahl, and banned the harvesting of forest wood. Bamay remembered the day when she stepped outside her home, and saw grass sprouting from the ground again. Compelled, she took a walk, and did so barefoot the way ameshas were supposed to. Every step gave her strength, and by the time she returned home her good health was reflected by the renewed brown color in her skin.

But as a priestess of Ta'ar's temple, Bamay still went along with the Fire Spirit's suspicions that the shah's leniency against dragons was a cause for concern. That was until Shah Zahk completely changed her life. Eight months ago and late at night, Bamay was running from a group of men. It was foolish for her to be at the graveyard at so late an hour, but it was only in the privacy of night that she could mourn for her dead lover, a man she now cursed for not being there to protect her and their unborn son from certain death.

The men cornered her, and Bamay fell to her knees and prayed that the Fire Spirit would save her. But it was not the Fire Spirit who pounced between her and her would-be murderers; but Shah Zahk. It was dark and so she saw little, but after a minute of screaming and the sound of weapons tearing through leather and flesh, only the shah remained standing. He sheathed his bloody sword and calmed his ferocious breathing before putting his hand out to her. Without thinking, she forgot that he was the shah and bawled into his chest. She said things within her tears that she would later wonder if she had. As priestess to Ta'ar, she was supposed to be devoted entirely to the spirit and not be involved with another. The Fire Spirit had just asked her to become a high priestess earlier that day. It was disrespectful to refuse, but by accepting, she was lying to the entire order about her complete devotion to Ta'ar, a lie that time would reveal as her child continued to grow inside her.

The shah took her to her home without saying a single word, and she cried herself to sleep. She cursed herself for foolishly laying her burden on a shah who had a nation to run.

But the next day, two royal guards came to her home to bring her to the palace. Confused and in the shah's debt, she went with them. When she saw Shah Zahk, he did not say anything of what had passed the night before. He just said that he needed a new diplomat and offered her the title of Ambassador of Aristahl.

Still confused, she accepted, and since then had lived within the luxury of the Aristahl palace. She maintained her title as high priestess, while also engrossing herself in her new diplomatic responsibilities. She was surprisingly good at it too. She worked often with Zahk's primary advisor, Minister Sheemu, and personally thought that alongside her, they were better at their duty than the other Aristahl court diplomats. Zahk never once mentioned the night on which Bamay disposed her secrets to him, and so she did not either. She simply served him happily, and while she did, no one dared to ask about the father of her child.

Furthermore, Shah Zahk had no child or even wife of his own. He always asked about her baby. Bamay could tell that he too, was hoping for it to be a boy. She knew that when the time came, he would proclaim that the child was his son, and secrets had been kept to protect her and her child from the shah's enemies. Why else would he be so protective of the two of them?

But that was a long time ago, before Ta'ar took bolder action against Shah Zahk. As denoted by his dimming flames, Ta'ar was losing followers weekly. As a spirit, a being that was not of flesh and blood, he was always limited in his ability to act, a limitation that was aggravating him more and more with Shah Zahk's growing popularity.

So the Fire Spirit Ta'ar started looking for a human to share his power with, power that would physically manifest within the inheritor, that could then be used against Zahk and the dragons. A month before Bamay's child was born, the Fire Spirit told her that he had chosen her son to be that vessel.

A gurgle rippled under Bamay's caressing fingers and out of Erdūn's mouth. She shook him gently, and whipped her liquid-like strands of hair away from her face to see him clearly. Everything she did was for him. She used to wonder if he would ever understand all that she had gone through and would sacrifice for his sake. Today, as the blue flames of Ta'ar's pupils burned through the dark inferno of his eyes, she knew he never would. *'Chosen her son'*; she was no fool, though she only figured out the truth after being approached. She had been coming daily to Ta'ar's ziggurat since even before she was pregnant with Erdūn, thus bonding him at that time with Ta'ar's aura. Erdūn had not been chosen; he was the only one possible.

Still, she could not allow herself to deny what that meant for her boy. Erdūn was going to be a man with the power of a spirit. He would not just be a hero, but the one who would lead the world against the dragons, and be forever known as the hero king who put an end to the dragon threat. Such greatness; no mother could deny their son that honor. So when she learnt that Ta'ar had brought devs into Aristahl to *deal* with Shah Zahk and his fondness for dragons, she did nothing to stop it. These devs were part of an order known as the Disciples of Gaorda. She knew little about them, except that they were obsessed warriors who were responsible for the extinction of the sesha dragons in the Dev-Sesha War. Across their sash was the order's insignia—a rukh, or giant eagle, which held a sesha dragon hanging lifelessly from its talons. Right now, while she was here before Ta'ar, these devs were hunting down her shah.

"He is my son, great spirit. I want him to be everything you say he will be. I just do not understand why there is a need to leave Aristahl? Surely the nation will need you more than ever now? You can reclaim what was taken from you, and bring up Erdūn here amongst his own people?"

"Zahk's stain still remains on this nation," Ta'ar stated, his flames pulsing with anger- his voice like an ongoing explosion. "Though dead by now, there will always be some who are loyal to him here. For the savior to fulfill his destiny, we must raise him away from any interference."

Bamay hid her tears of guilt by looking down at her child. "Great Spirit, forgive me for doubting your word, but I am afraid. This all depends on the shah's fate tonight. Will he truly be killed?"

"It is done." The answer came from behind her.

Bamay turned around and instinctively cradled Erdūn. It was the dark blue of a deva who answered her. Beside him were two other devas and devis. That was how the devs were; they divided themselves, the men were known as devas, and the women as devis. Bamay did not trust them, especially now in the late night when their skin was such a dark blue that it was almost black. The more prominent the moon, the darker they were, and the more they could blur into the night at will. How was she to trust such beings that were so tied to shadows?

Yet trust was what they demanded. They would all go to some place they had not yet told her about, and while Ta'ar would invest his magic into her son, the Disciples of Gaorda would train him to become the ultimate dragon slayer. The deva who spoke continued to come forward. His face became clear and she saw it was the one named Yagura. She noticed that only a handful of them were in the ziggurat. The disciples always traveled together. Yagura came so close to her as he passed, that she smelled the blood that was sprayed across his body.

"Where are the rest of you?" she asked.

Yagura ignored her, and walked toward Ta'ar whom he eyed accusingly. She had never seen him so angry as to face the Fire Spirit so directly. Bamay brought her son up to her face to hide an unwilling smile. Five Disciples. Her shah had slain five of the Disciples before being butchered by them. She had thought he had not the skill with a blade to even kill one.

"Bamay!" the Fire Spirit erupted suddenly. "We can wait no longer!"

"Where are we going, Lord Ta'ar?"

"You still wish to come?"

"Yes, Lord. I wish to continue to serve." There was nothing left for her anymore in Aristahl. Things were already in motion. Her place was with her son.

"He cannot know that he came from you," Ta'ar said. The devs looked in her direction. This idea was theirs, to shield Erdūn away from his mother so that they could do with him what they wanted.

"I know." she said.

She became aware of the sound of hooves traveling to

the entrance of the ziggurat. The devs moved aside so that they could follow her into the carriage.

"We are going to the borders of the dev lands," Ta'ar said, "a place only the Disciples of Gaorda know of. The shah's supporters will not be able to reach us there. Come now if you wish. Otherwise hand Erdūn to us."

Bamay turned and walked steadily down the shallow stairs of the ziggurat, free for several moments to shed some tears while no one could see her face. With the crackling of Ta'ar's flames becoming distant, she could once again hear her son gurgling. He would become legendary; sacrifices needed to be made to ensure that that would come to pass.

For four short seconds, she felt invigorated as her feet touched the grass between the ziggurat and the carriage. The devs followed and crowded beside her. Suddenly, Erdūn began to cry as the carriage rumbled out of Aristahl's gates. Squeezed in between a deva and a devi, Bamay tried bouncing him up and down, but she was unpracticed in consoling him. She wanted the carriage to slow down, but knew not to ask. She held him for the entire journey, despite the devs eyeing her incriminatingly. Immediately upon arriving they took him from her. She never held him again.

Book One

CHAPTER 1

G radni traced his fingers along the stone corridor of the orphanage as he made his way to the man by the exit. The fat caretaker grunted as he pushed the door open.

"You have three hours," he said to Gradni with his nose turned away.

"Why the extra hour?" Gradni asked distrustfully.

"It is for you to bathe. Now hurry. Your smell is unbearable."

Gradni scratched the back of his neck as he purposely stepped right under the caretaker's nose and into the midday light. His hair that fell around his narrow face and nose was chestnut brown with slivers of green running through it. The green was almost invisible right now. He hadn't bathed in the lake in weeks, so it was more a mess of maroon tentacles that oddly matched his hazel eyes. Dirt had darkened his skin from its natural pale elf color, and it was becoming tedious trying to find the itchy spots behind his triangular ears. He would bathe today, but only after he did everything else he wanted to with his three hours of freedom.

Two soldiers were training against each other on the practice field when Gradni got there. He hiked up to his usual place on the grassy hill that shadowed the field. His father's pendant was dangling from his neck. Gradni held it between his palms with his knees huddled in as he studied the two men. It was not often that the soldiers of Scandar took their duty seriously enough to train. It was a hand-to-hand fight, which Gradni enjoyed watching the most—the way they ducked, kicked, leapt, and punched, trying to defeat each other with nothing more than their hands and feet. The smaller of the fighters moved faster when he attacked and further when he dodged. Elves had the innate ability to turn the air around their bodies into wind that augmented their movements. It was called wind channeling, and the smaller of the two fighters was clearly better at it.

Gradni liked watching fights with practice weapons as well, but the closest he had come to owning a sword of his own was a splintered wooden stick. Maybe tomorrow if he was let out again he would get a proper branch from the forest. He had never been to the forest before, but assumed it wouldn't be difficult to find a branch there if he looked.

His left ear twitched. Heavy footsteps were coming down the hill behind him. Gradni turned to see who it was.

"Hullo," the younger boy said.

Gradni turned back to the fight. He knew nothing about this nuisance, except that he was fat from his mother's cooking. He readjusted his knees away from him, but the nuisance spoke anyway.

"We noticed that you spend your time here instead of on the playing grounds. You can join us if you want."

"I'm fine where I am."

"Are you sure? We would really like you to join us."

In the two seasons Gradni had been coming here for, no one had ever invited him to join them. Gradni was suspicious. "Why all of a sudden?"

The boy stuttered. Gradni then noticed that there was more noise coming from behind them on the other side of the hill where the grounds were. He stood up and walked to the top of the hill to see what was happening. The younger kids, friends of the nuisance, were huddled along an edge of the field while the older ones dominated the center. The two groups were trading jeers.

"How long has Ferklen and his friends been pushing you *have* off the field?" Gradni asked.

"It has been almost a week now. We could really use your help. Everyone knows that Ferklen won't bother you anymore."

Ferklen and his group were three years older than Gradni. They used to bully him as well by surrounding him and pushing him to and fro like he was a ball. He had been an easy target for them because he had no friends, and his father was never in Scandar to protect him. That all changed when Gradni's father died, and they mistakenly thought that he would be an even easier victim of their harassment. While two of Ferklen's friends held him from behind, Gradni struggled viciously against them. He kicked out wildly toward Ferklen and missed his face by a hair. Gradni fell back onto his captors and lashed out like a rabid dog till they scrambled out from under him. They yelled insults at him as they ran away, but never attacked him again. Gradni had never been satisfied with the way the harassment had ended. Even today, he yearned to do Ferklen damage.

"You want me to help you fight them? That's really why you came here."

"Yes, but we'll play with you if you do, and we won't stop once they leave us alone either, promise."

He wanted to say yes. Yes, for all the times Ferklen had embarrassed him, but he was not going to do it for this boy and his friends. Ferklen still yelled insults at him from a distance and others always chimed in, including, Gradni was sure, this boy and his cowering friends.

"Too bad you never helped when he was bullying me. You can deal with them yourselves. He is your problem now."

"T'nas said you would say that, so she said to offer you something else. Ferklen is afraid of you, so we don't mind sharing our sweets to make him go away. And you probably don't get anything nice to eat at the orphanage. Have you ever even had cake before?"

Gradni pushed the boy away. "I don't want your cake. Leave me alone and don't bother me with this again!"

The boy stumbled back a couple steps before running down the slope. Gradni watched him huff all the way off the hill before turning back to the soldiers. An hour later the soldiers finished training. Gradni stood up, still angry from being interrupted. His right ear started itching again. He miserably tried to find the troublesome spot before giving in to the fact that there was more than one. He started trekking toward the lake. The market was on the way. Maybe if he hung around long enough, a fruit vendor would toss him an apple for his persistence. He didn't even know what was in the bland gruel they served at the orphanage, and fruit would serve him better than cake did the out-of-breath nuisance.

Halfway to the market, a creaking of heavy wheels caught his attention. The carriage was a fair distance from him, but the insignia on its door was clear—an upside-down drake dragon with its wings spread out, and a spear through its center. Gradni sprinted after it. He had never seen a drake, but he was familiar enough with the emblem that he would have recognized it at twice the distance. It was the insignia of Delthurk—the elven base where his father gave his life three seasons ago. The carriage was parked by the stables when he caught up to it. He circled around a wagon and peered at the elves stepping out of the carriage. Four of them were dressed in plates of steel that marked them as soldiers. The fifth was Mogurn, a senator from Delthurk. Gradni had seen him often enough. He came regularly to recruit for the war against the dragons, sometimes successfully and sometimes not, but never this far from the Scandar Castle. He wondered why they were meeting all the way out here.

Mogurn was dressed in the usual attire of a senator. He had a loose fitting sepia robe that was tightened at the waist by a maroon rope. Today, he had chalk-white hair down to his shoulders that ran parallel to the indented lines in his cheeks. On previous occasions when Gradni saw him, his hair was silver, gray, or white with a bluish hue. Like the thickness of Gradni's green slivers, and other elves' hair, its appearance was dependent on the changing seasons and weather. Mogurn sat on a bench and intertwined his fingers in front of his frown. A horse came galloping from across a hill. Gradni's heartbeat quickened when he saw the rider. Mogurn had come to get S'freed, the Drake Slayer of Scandar.

S'freed had always been one of the biggest men Gradni had ever seen. If there was any elf who looked able to slay the humongous drakes, it was S'freed. But Scandar had never allowed S'freed to join the war against the dragons at Delthurk. They found him too valuable to send away.

Gradni shifted nervously as S'freed got off his horse in front of the senator. The knight had long blond hair down to his shoulder blades. Gradni liked him best in summer when his hair was a lustrous red.

Mogurn stood up. He shook S'freed's large hand with both of his and bowed.

Gradni strained to hear them, but even with his elven ears, he was too far away to make out what they were saying. He skipped to a haystack that was closer and poked his face around. "...you are not going to send me to the Zipacna Mountains?" S'freed suddenly yelled.

Mogurn was smiling, a contrast to his demeanor a couple minutes ago. S'freed was not returning the gesture with any measure of kindness, and only became more agitated as the conversation drew on. The Drake Slayer said something final to the senator, and stomped into the carriage. Gradni twitched. As wide as the smile on Mogurn's face was during the conversation with S'freed, it was now as tight a scowl. The senator looked to either side before spitting through his thin lips. He put on his fake smile once again, and climbed into the carriage before it rode away. drove

It was already past the time Gradni was meant to return to the orphanage by. He plodded back, his father's pendant bobbing up and down with each lazy step. Mogurn's scowl stuck with him. While trying to figure out what it meant, he didn't realize that he was cutting through the playgrounds until he was halfway through it. There was a commotion to his left. Whatever was happening earlier had escalated. Gradni kept his eyes in front of him when he heard the raised voices of Ferklen and the nuisance. The words were unclear, but the tone changed as he passed by. Gradni fought down the urge to acknowledge that everyone was staring at him. What had the nuisance told them? Gradni made sure not to change his pace as he walked off the field, to make it seem like he wasn't aware of them.

It was very late now. Even when the caretaker could see him coming, Gradni continued to walk.

"You missed dinner. And you did not bathe!" the caretaker said as Gradni got to the gate.

"I know."

"Do you expect me to feed you?"

Gradni's stomach felt hollow, but he knew the answer.

"You are not special," the caretaker declared.

Gradni raised his head and looked the man straight in the eye. He was a large man with round facial features and a shabby red beard. "We'll see. At least I will not be a fat pig."

The caretaker grabbed Gradni by his greasy hair and yanked him across the threshold of the gate. "Get to your room! You are not special! You are like everyone else!"

Gradni found his footing and walked along the jagged stone path. He threw his head up so that the caretaker could see it as he sauntered onward into the ugly stone building.

Years ago, before even his late father was born, Scandar built a new prison to deal with the town's increasing development. Several years later when the growth led to the need for an orphanage, they rebuilt the metal fence around the old prison and put up a sign. It was a hollowed-out rectangular block of black stones. Along the single corridor were torches that were fastened to the wall every four doors. Even though there were no other orphans living here right now, Gradni's room was at the very end. It was the closest room to the confinement space that was used to punish orphans who became too rowdy. The caretaker figured that he would save himself a lot of trips by placing Gradni as close to the confinement space as possible, and Gradni had little argument to say otherwise. He stepped into his room and closed the wooden door behind him. He bent his hands against themselves before stretching his arms, legs, and back. The caretaker had lied when he said Gradni was like everyone else. Orphans in Scandar were less than anyone.

They were taken care of not out of compassion, but out of reluctant debt. Beyond that, they did not care that he was the son of the heroic Yorn the Dragon Slayer.

Gradni lifted the pendant from his neck. It was the only thing in his entire room that was spotless. Engraved upon the gold disc was a detailed sword upon a background of low mountains. Heavy rain was falling at a diagonal, and a streak of lightning cut everything except the sword in half. The sword signified the warrior's valor, while the storm represented the furious strength in which elves thrived, because it enhanced their ability to wind channel.

The pendant was a medal that was awarded to Yorn for having slain so many dragons on the border of Scandar. It was that achievement that led him to leave several years ago for Delthurk, the elf base that had been built specifically to kill the dragons in that region. It was all that came back from there, and it was given to Gradni minutes before he was moved to the orphanage. Gradni kept it with him always.

He let it fall back around his neck. He wrapped a layer of cloth around his hands, and then threw a fist against the door. He shook the pain off while removing his tunic, then threw his other fist into the wood in exactly the same way. He collected himself and began to assault an imaginary foe, using front kicks and straight punches that he had seen the soldiers using.

When his father was alive and at war with the dragons, Gradni lived under the care of those who served Scandar. That all changed. When the dragons killed his father, Gradni was thrown into the orphanage. Now he was forgotten, in a nation that did not care of the atrocity that the dragons had committed against him. His breath was heavy as he danced around his room. He hadn't learned to pace himself, nor had he been taught how to wind channel properly. He tried a hook kick but it left him off balance. He had seen a soldier lose a fight for doing the same thing, so Gradni tried it again and again until he did it without staggering.

His father was a great Dragon Slayer. No one ever disrespected him and no one equaled him in battle. Scandar had taken care of Gradni out of fear of what his father would do to them if they did not. He sidestepped left and right before he bent low, and rammed his knuckles against the wood harder than he intended. He stumbled and fell on his back. He would be Yorn. He would avenge his father and show Scandar and the dragons what they had made, and S'freed would be in awe of him. Gradni imagined the door to be a drake and fiercely elbowed it. The vibrations of the attack rattled through his entire arm. He yelped and fell to the floor again. The light of the corridor went out.

"Enough noise, boy. Go to sleep!"

"Come in here and make me!" Gradni yelled back at the caretaker while crawling onto the stiff straw mattress. He rolled deeper into the bed, wearing a painful grin as he cradled his knuckles and elbow in turn. The caretaker would doubtlessly tell others as always what he had seen and heard. That would keep the other boys afraid of him. He rolled onto his stomach, and continued to toss and turn till he fell asleep.

CHAPTER 2

EDGE OF THE ZIPACNA MOUNTAINS

The sun was just coming up over the Zipacna mountain range east of the lake. It illuminated the surrounding forest, and even the pebbles that formed the shallow bed under the water. S'freed was hiding in the branches that over shadowed the lake. Below him were twenty other elves, who had also covered themselves in mud and leaves to camouflage their scent and pale skin. They had been waiting for several hours already, and S'freed was becoming irritated. Patience had always been a necessary trait when he lied in wait for drake dragons, but it had been more than a year since his last kill, and he had been dormant in Delthurk for a whole week already.

He glanced upward. He was so close to the Zipacna Mountains that it seemed more like a wall than the mountain that he would conquer, especially with the foliage above shielding him from the sky. By right, he should be up there leading an army, instead of waiting to ambush a measly group of dragons here.

Delthurk was a necessary but still imperfect place. When people began to take the threat seriously, and waged war upon the dragons around their land, the beasts gradually left their lairs and united here at the Zipacna Mountains—the supposed birthplace of their kind. S'freed, like other dragon slayers, was suddenly of little value in his home nation. He became an honored heirloom that Scandar was proud to have, but never used. It was fine for a while to be the hero, but with the dragons gone, they gave him a shameful place within the army. They treated him like a regular soldier instead of the knight that he was.

Fortunately, elves from various nations took the initiative against the dragons of Zipacna. They built the military base of Delthurk on the mountain range beside the dragons. Its sole purpose was to wage war upon the dragons until they were gone forever.

After many years of waiting, Delthurk finally came for S'freed. Scandar was reluctant to let him go, and it was through Senator Mogurn's underhanded politics that S'freed had escaped the life of an ordinary footman. He was originally pleased at the news, until he discovered on the day of his departure, that instead of thrusting him into battle, Delthurk was going to 'ease' him into the war. They argued that even though S'freed had killed mighty drakes, that the smaller dragons were skilled in other diabolical ways that needed to be learned. S'freed knew the truth. Other Dragon Slayers who ventured passed the exterior mountains of Zipacna to the inner ones were never seen again, and it was difficult for Delthurk to justify more recruitment when they could not even return the bodies of earlier knights to their homes. But for him, they should have put aside their paranoia. He was the Drake Slayer of Scandar. No matter the species of dragons, he would return from the Zipacna Mountains victorious.

S'freed held his breath when he heard rustling. Dragons came out of the green on the opposite side of the lake. The first was the length of a wolf and half the height. It looked almost like a giant lizard, except for the muscular mammal like legs and four inch-long claws at the ends of its feet. The creature dipped the lower half of its emerald head into the lake, and began to drink over its prominent long teeth. *A salamander*, S'freed recalled from his distant past. He had seen some hopping around several years ago when traveling to other elf nations. It was the first dragon he had seen in a year, and other shades of green followed.

One dragon, taller than S'freed, shuffled forward on its wide legs. Its tail was several feet long, and it balanced out the beast's thick and lengthy snout. Thick scales covered its body, and four rows of protective spines lined its back from the neck to the tip of the tail. He recognized the species as sobekian from the amesha people's accounts of them.

The sobekian came to the shoreline and flopped onto the lake, splashing the salamander, which leaped two meters away. The salamander rasped at the sobekian, but the sobekian did not seem to notice as it guzzled the lake water. S'freed's eyes shifted from dragon to dragon as more of them emerged. This blend of sinful creatures was exhilarating in itself, but then a serpent dragon arrived that was as red as blood.

The red dragon slid so smoothly across the grass and into the lake that it was as if it was laced with oil. The leaves below S'freed rustled fearfully. S'freed showed the other elves his hand, assuring them that this horned dragon would be his conquest. These rare dragons were much fiercer than the regular green ones. Apart from their horns that were as strong and sharp as swords, their scales were finer and tougher. The serpent's length was thrice S'freed's height, and its width was three times that of his thigh. This kill would be the perfect way for S'freed to begin anew his destiny.

S'freed gave the command with his free hand. The Delthurk elves raced forward through the bushes, creating the disturbance S'freed desired. The dragons immediately lurched toward the noise. With his sword in one hand, S'freed leapt forward. Wind channeling, he swung ape-like on a thick branch above the lake, and as he came down, drove his sword into the sobekian dragon's neck.

Teeth and claws bared, scaly backs arched, and fire foamed at the dragons' mouths. S'freed ignored all of it as he removed his shield from his back, and wrenched his sword out of the dead sobekian. The other eight green dragons would be dealt with by the Delthurk soldiers rushing forward on either side of him. S'freed focused on the red serpent dragon that was already meeting his gaze.

It came toward him, its lower half on the shallow surface of the lake, its upper in an *S* position with its slit eyes, horns, and snout vivid against the green background. The head began to whirl in sideways eights before springing toward S'freed fangs first. S'freed pivoted and arched himself backward, evading the head that flashed in front of his face. There was no time to be distracted by the burning breath. The coils were coming toward him from behind. He backflipped over it while swinging his blade to ward off his prey. The serpent reacted by shooting a burst of fire toward him. S'freed stayed low where he landed in the water, and held his shield above him to divert the blaze. He shuffled quickly on his haunches toward the serpent as his shield burned, and gashed the dragon's middle with his blade.

It slithered back, hissing a cry that S'freed had all but forgotten. There was no time to celebrate, even for a moment, not against a horned dragon. As succesful as the cut was, it was not enough. The blade would have cut twice as deep against the scales of a green serpent dragon. S'freed ran forward to keep up with his prey. As if ignorant to its wound, the serpent launched itself at him again. S'freed leapt toward it in response, his shield supported by his shoulder. The red snout and shield collided; the dragon rebounded to the right, S'freed to the left. S'freed rolled onto his feet, saw red coming toward him, and slashed upward with his sword—tearing through the flesh of the bladed tail that was whipping toward him. The serpent hissed again while coiling away. It left a trail of blood so thick around S'freed's ankles that it blanketed the pebbles.

S'freed exhaled a grin of triumph. The serpent was exhausted, weak, and bleeding from two wounds. One more slash to its throat and he would have killed a horned serpent dragon. He ran toward it. The serpent stopped backing away and rasped, not even bothering to use its fire against him. S'freed yelled as he got up close. He swung his sword over his head to strike between the serpent's horns, but the weapon jarred to a stop while still high above him. Then, a flash of green, a sudden force against his chest that winded him, and he found himself flying several feet from the serpent.

S'freed immediately stood up. He readied his weapons to face the new dragon that had gotten in the way of his kill.

But this was no dragon; this was something else. It was holding a sword that had a greenish hue to it, holding it with two green scaly hands while growling past inch-long canines. There was no time to study it. S'freed launched himself toward it while swinging his sword. But in spite of S'freed's proficiency at wind channeling, the creature blocked his blows with its own, and darted around him faster than the serpent had. S'freed fought with rage, but the creature remained too quick for him, and was skilled enough to use its strength against him. For the first time in a long while,

S'freed desired help. He broke away and looked around, but there was none to be found. Most of his support was already dead, cut down by the sword that was now pointing at him. While he had been fighting the horned dragon, this strange creature had decimated his men.

Had it been a ploy? Were the dragons capable of such a scheme? The horned serpent was no longer huddled pathetically in a corner either, but was shooting its flames alongside the other dragons toward the last remaining elves. S'freed growled and rushed the abomination again.

He was twice the size of the creature. Reasoning that he had more strength, S'freed hammered both sword and shield down upon it, but it blocked the blow with its sword. They stood locked in that position—S'freed trying to use his height over the creature to bear it down as he stared at the black pupils of its eyes. Suddenly, a conflagration came to life around his opponent's blade. S'freed was thrown several feet backward. Blinded by the blade's sudden flames, S'freed swung his own sword madly in front of him.

Still he was stunned - when the fiery sword slid into his own chest, and out his back.

CHAPTER 3

Gradni was concerned when he saw the Delthurk carriage riding back into Scandar a month later. He followed it all the way to the courtyard of the castle. Mogurn came out with S'freed's sword in his hand. He held it like an offering to the Scandar senators before him. Gradni left before seeing the exchange that followed. He shuffled back to the orphanage with his head hanging low. He would not be allowed to attend the funeral without an escort, and the caretaker would relish in his misery if Gradni asked him. Gradni went to bed early on the day of the ceremony. He woke up to the sound of heavy rain during the night, and decided that now was as good a time as any to pay his respects.

The lamps of the corridor were out, but he could hear the caretaker's obnoxious snoring in the room beside the entrance. He used it to guide him to the main door.

As he neared the exit, Gradni automatically placed his hand on his chest. There was nothing to grab on to. He had forgotten to put it on. Cursing himself, he crept impatiently back his room, and dragged his father's pendant off the stand.

Safely outside the gate with his father's pendant dangling from his neck, Gradni ran toward the garden. It was not as late as he thought. Only the orphanage and its fat lazy caretaker were asleep. Still, he had not been out this late for a while. Gradni breathed in the nourishing wind as he ran. It gave him strength, as it did all elves due to their magical alignment with the atmosphere. The more violent the weather, the better their ability to wind channel, though it was also more difficult to stay focused. With the energy of the harsh winds churning within him, Gradni moved so fast that he passed the cemetary garden. He backtracked and passed it again before realizing that he needed to either calm himself, or keep missing it all night.

Once in the garden, Gradni approached S'freed's sword. It was cast in a stone dais and was decorated with carved lilies and vines. The blade was hidden in the stone. Gradni wanted to know if there was still dragon blood on it.

He knelt before the stand and clenched his father's pendant. The winds picked up. It pressed Gradni's cold wet hair on one side of him, and pulled it from the other. He became increasingly restless, but he was here to offer his respects. He bowed his head, and closed his eyes.

It was too small a memorial for S'freed. Scandar had lost its respect for Dragon Slayers. The way Gradni was treated despite all the dragons his father killed had proved that. It would have been better if Delthurk kept the sword with them, where S'freed would have received real respect from fellow knights. When his father used to visit from Delthurk, he told Gradni what an honorable place it was. The finest Dragon Slayers came together at Delthurk, and not just elven knights, but warriors of the other people as well. Amesha, qui-lahk, and dev dragon slayers all called Delthurk home. S'freed's memorial should have been there, where he would receive proper tribute.

Gradni started walking back to the orphanage. He pushed aside the strands of wet hair that were blurring his vision. The year was getting away from him. He did not even realize how far into spring it was till he saw the thickness of his green locks.

Ferklen and three of his lackeys were standing right outside the garden entrance. The violent winds were within them as well. They must have spotted him running into the garden earlier, and were eager to dispense some of their fury. Gradni clenched his fists as he walked toward them. Ferklen was hanging back, yet looking directly at Gradni. His curly brown hair with yellow locks was not as affected by the rain as everyone else's. He seemed annoyed; as if this confrontation was one he did not want either. Yet as Gradni came closer, Ferklen smiled vindictively. There was only a couple feet between the two of them when Ferklen spoke.

"I wonder what your caretaker would say about you disobeying the orphanage rules. Shouldn't you be inside, sleeping like a dog in your snug bed of sticks?"

Gradni ignored the comment, prompting one of Ferklen's flock to stand in his way. Gradni shoved the older boy. There was almost a retaliation, but Ferklen motioned him aside and took his place in front of Gradni.

"There are rumors that you are planning on fighting me, so that you and your friends can have the field to yourselves?"

The other three stepped away to give them space. Gradni waited for them to be far enough before unclenching his fist. He was invigorated by the weather, but for some inexplicable reason he did not want to fight right now. It was not a good time.

"They are not my friends. They are lia—" A sudden movement flashed in front of him. Gradni felt his jaw shift violently before he fell down.

He was on his back with a throbbing mouth. There had

not even been a warning. The rain was hitting his eyes. He raised his head off the ground. Ferklen was rubbing his fist as if to get the filth of Gradni's skin off of it. Gradni rolled slowly onto his feet so that he was facing away from Ferklen. His hair dragged up mud while everyone laughed at him.

"Look—his hair doesn't look any different with dirt in it!"

Gradni clenched his fists tightly when he heard Ferklen begin talking again.

"I am glad to hear that they are not your friends, Gradni. Because now you know tha—"

In one motion, Gradni whirled around and struck Ferklen in the chest- the pent-up energy channeling through his fist as he made impact. Ferklen fell onto his rear and tumbled backward through the mud.

Gradni had never lashed out like that before, at least not successfully. When Ferklen didn't move right away he was afraid he had hit too hard, but Ferklen found his way back to his feet, though it was a struggle for him. No one spoke when he turned a fierce eye toward Gradni. Remembering the soldiers he watched, Gradni put himself into a fight stance. Other children who saw the first couple punches came running to watch the show. They formed an arena around Gradni and Ferklen. Gradni focused on Ferklen and welcomed his glare.

Ferklen lunged toward Gradni. As he had seen the soldiers do, Gradni stepped forward and swung his fist against Ferklen's jaw, then bent low and drove his other fist into Ferklen's stomach. Ferklen keeled over from the double blow. Gradni hesitated, and it was all the respite Ferklen needed. Ferklen rushed Gradni in the chest, and knocked him down. He pinned Gradni against the muddy earth. Again emulating the fighters he had seen, Gradni swung his elbows around to knock aside the attacks to his upper body. He made contact with something. Ferklen scrambled to break away, and Gradni helped him by thrusting him away with his foot.

Ferklen shuffled away with a bloody hand pressed against his nose. Gradni rushed over and shoved him onto his side. The older elf boy fell with a splash against the mud. Gradni moved to kick Ferklen while he was crawling away, but backed away after seeing his opponent cupping his bleeding nose. Gradni let his fists lie and stood straight.

There were around twenty boys and girls of various ages surrounding them. Gradni took a step toward them to move through their barrier. But the crowd's attention suddenly diverted behind him. Gradni turned. Ferklen was taking a heavy branch from someone.

"Put it down!" Gradni yelled. Ferklen stood up as if rejuvenated and swung his branch twice in the air, the fierce weather giving him extra momentum.

Gradni readied his hands once again while backing toward the wall of boys who did not give way. Ferklen approached him warily this time. There was no need for it; nothing Gradni had learned from observing the soldiers would help him against an armed foe.

Another branch flashed through the rain and landed at Gradni's feet. There was no telling who had thrown it. It could have been the fat elf boy whom he swore he would beat later, or just one of the spectators looking to see a good fight. It didn't matter right now. Gradni picked it up.

The crowd cheered as Ferklen charged at Gradni and swung his branch overhead. Gradni lifted his branch with both hands to meet the blow and almost fell from the impact. Ferklen did not pull back after contact. He was forcing Gradni down with his strength. Gradni arched a foot back to balance himself. It would be over if he fell now. With his back foot sinking into the slippery mud, Gradni's mind raced through all the fights he had seen. He leaned to one side and stopped pushing with his branch, causing Ferklen to stumble forward into the perfect position for Gradni to elbow him to the ground. Gradni did so twice, and then for good measure, raised his arms high and hammered his branch against Ferklen's back. Ferklen screamed.

Gradni dropped his branch and stepped back. Ferklen was cringing. The crowd was silent. They glanced over at Gradni, but turned away before he looked back. None of them expected him to be the one standing. Ferklen's three friends just stood there, stunned.

"Are you not going to do anything?" Gradni yelled toward them "Come on! Come on!"

Suddenly, something large knocked Gradni off his feet. He landed with a hard splat against the ground, where the grimy taste of mud corrupted his victory.

"What have you done to my son?" Gradni heard, as he rose onto his hands and knees. The weight around his neck was missing. He looked ahead and saw his father's pendant shimmering in the softening rain. Still on all fours, Gradni scrambled toward it, till Ferklen's father drove the jut of his foot into Gradni's stomach.

"What did you do to him?" Gradni heard above his own gasp for air as he rolled onto his back. He looked blankly at the moving mouth yelling above him. Another shot of pain broke from his shoulder, before the old man left to tend to his son. Gradni remained still for a minute, the pain paralyzing and simultaneously fueling him with fury.

It was meant to be clear to all of them now. Things were not as they were months ago.

Gradni stood and picked up the branch. Everyone

thought the fight was over, including Ferklen's father, who rolled his son onto his back. Gradni stepped toward the old man. With both hands holding the branch, Gradni bent low and swung, smashing its center against the old man's knee. The scream from the father mimicked the son's. Gradni tossed the branch away and raced toward his pendant, but was grabbed by soldiers before he got to it. He struggled viciously, trying to bite wherever possible with his arms restrained. He kicked and screamed, and reached hopelessly for his pendant as they dragged him away.

CHAPTER 4

G radni sat on the damp wooden floor of the confinement room. Glimmers of firelight were coming in through the cracks in the door. He had been awake all night, his mood in constant flux as his thoughts switched between his actions and their consequences. It was still unbelievable to him what he had done, and the more he thought about it, the more the screams of the father and son outweighed whatever punishment was in store for him.

That idea faltered again when the jail door swung open.

"Get up!"

Gradni obeyed. There was something strange about the caretaker's demeanor. He was not as angry as he was bitter. It became more apparent when Gradni's hands were not tied together as harshly as he expected them to be. Something had ruined this moment for the caretaker; perhaps the oaf was being blamed for Gradni getting out in the first place? He grinned at this, till the caretaker yanked him by his binds.

He was led out of the orphanage. The moonlight was weak. Hours had passed since the fight.

"Where are you taking me?" Gradni asked, when led into the Scandar Castle.

"Hurry up," was the response, as the rope yanked at Gradni's wrists.

Gradni followed without question up the spiral staircase.

The caretaker pulled him into a room and untied the rope. Without a word, the caretaker doubled back and left, closing the door behind him. Bewildered, Gradni looked up from his loosened binds. Mogurn, the Delthurk senator, was sitting on the opposite side of the table in front of him.

"Have a seat," Mogurn said.

Gradni did. The torch in the room was badly lit. The only reason Gradni could tell that it was Mogurn was from the shine of silvery white hair, and the outline of knotted fingers over a mouth. The fingers lowered.

"You are in a lot of trouble, Master Gradni." Gradni had never been close enough to the senator to make out his voice; he pronounced each word distinctively. "Feroles, whose knee is still being attended to, will demand that you be punished severely for what you did. If you are lucky, he will say that you are too savage to ever leave the orphanage, or to even leave your room. Do you have anyone here who will argue for you?"

"I did not start the fight, sir," Gradni blurted. "I was only defending myself."

"Whether you did or did not is irrelevant. Your father, Yorn, a great knight who fought for us at Delthurk, is no longer with us. So is there anyone else here who will vouch for you?"

Gradni said nothing. He did not know how to react to Mogurn knowing that he was Yorn's son. He had always wanted to be acknowledged by Delthurk, but this was strange, to be questioned this way after a life time of barely even being seen.

"No. There is no one."

"Well then," Mogurn continued, "what are you going to do?"

"Sir, why have I been brought to you?"

Gradni wanted answers. What was happening was not normal. There was no reason for a senator to be involved, never mind a senator who was not of Scandar.

Mogurn smiled as he dug into his sepia robes, reminding Gradni of the scowl he saw him wear on the eve of S'freed's departure.

"There is no future for you here," Mogurn said, before placing Gradni's gold pendant on the table. Gradni stared at it. It had been cleaned of mud, but had a dent in it from the scuffle. "I know what you want. Scandar is not the place for you, Sir Gradni. Like many of the others, this nation refuses to believe that people like S'freed are still needed, and will be needed in the future. I saw you from the castle balcony as you went to pay your respects to the Drake Slayer. He was a decent warrior, though sadly not good enough."

"S'freed slew countless drakes! He was a great knight!" Gradni shouted back. He surprised himself a little, but he couldn't allow his hero to be spoken about in such a way. He remembered again Mogurn's untrustworthy scowl.

"That he did, but that he did not survive his last bout attests to the fact that we need someone better. The problem we face is that Delthurk is the only force still fighting the dragons. We alone understand the importance of future dragon slayers. I am here to offer you the chance to come with me to Delthurk to train to become the best dragon slayer we have ever had. We will start training you now, and by the time you are done you will be better than S'freed was, better even than your father. Do you accept?"

Gradni forgot his anger. His feet were swinging from the chair that was too big for him. He felt like running around the room, but thought he would awaken from a dream if he did. Maybe he had fallen asleep in the confinement room? It was too much, and it was unreal. Gradni looked toward the senator but said nothing. Mogurn was cunning. He needed to remember that.

"You hesitate," Mogurn said. "Is there reason for it? Is there much that you will miss by leaving your life here, like the punishment you are sure to receive because of your actions this night?"

"Why me?" Gradni uttered. There was something very wrong with this. He just assaulted an older elf. He was an orphan, a nuisance who was hated by everyone except those who ignored him. Simply put, this could not be happening.

"Because you have already been training, have you not? Because this is what you have always wanted? Or is everything you have been doing just for attention?"

"No!" Gradni exclaimed suddenly.

Mogurn sighed. "The war is ongoing, Master Gradni. I cannot waste time returning here for no reason. This opportunity is only available to you now. If I leave this room without an answer, then I will find someone else more willing. Do you accept?"

"I do," Gradni said, exhaling. "I accept."

Mogurn smiled, and it sent a chill up Gradni's spine.

"Good. Come along, then. Preparations have already been made."

⸺ ◈ ⸺

The carriage was waiting for them outside the castle. Gradni had only to bring the pendant that was around his neck. Everything else, he was told, he would find at Delthurk. It still seemed like it could not be happening. He looked back at the orphanage and the crooked gate that surrounded it.

"Quickly, Gradni. There is little point in waiting till morning."

Gradni stepped into the carriage and Mogurn followed. The horses neighed and the carriage jolted into a race. He had always wanted to leave Scandar. He was now beyond its border and getting farther away still. Would he see any of it again? Would he see the caretaker, whose name, he realized, he didn't even know. Mogurn was staring at him from the seat opposite him.

"Why are you looking at me?" Gradni asked.

The senator took his time in answering. It seemed to Gradni that he always took his time when speaking. "Do you think you will miss Scandar?"

"No. Why are you doing this for me?" He was getting farther away from what was familiar, and he was afraid. The odd questions, the strange looks, the senator was studying him like he was an animal.

"The reasons I gave you were not enough?"

"You've told me nothing. I deserve to know why you picked me. I demand it!"

Mogurn again took another agonizing moment to himself. The carriage rattled over uneven ground. "You demand it? Good. You are intelligent. That is good. No one takes the dragon threat seriously anymore. Delthurk is not enough. When the dragons left to gather at the Zipacna Mountains, all the nations that they used to haunt thought their problems were over. They think that just because the dragons left their lands that the threat is over, that the dragons do not need to be eradicated for us to be safe. We need more support from them than we are getting, or else everything that your father and S'freed fought for will be for nothing. You, however, know unquestionably of their evil, don't you?"

"Yes."

"It takes courage to face dragons. You have courage, Gradni, and you have determination, and you have respect for those who fight for the cause. It is in your blood. I saw it all from the castle when you visited S'freed's memorial, and I saw you fight those that you should not have beaten, and yet did. Once I found out who your father was, my task was clear." Mogurn extended his hand. "It is truly an honor, Master Gradni, son of Dragon Slayer Yorn."

Gradni sat forward, hesitant to take the hand being offered. Even when his father was alive, Gradni had never gotten real respect. The little good treatment he did receive was purely because of who his father was. It had never been because of his own actions. He reached out and took the resolute hand in his. "The dragons killed my father. They ruined my life, and I want to avenge him."

Mogurn shook his hand firmly. "Yes, you will have your vengeance. I will make sure of it! It will not be easy, but I and others will guide you along. Scandar is in your past now. I hope that you will embrace Delthurk and not let us down."

"No, sir, I will not."

Mogurn rested back in his seat. "I have confidence in you. You should rest. We have several days' journey ahead of us, and there will be much to see once we reach Delthurk."

Gradni sat back and looked out the window. The morning light was breaking through the shadows. It was all actually happening. His father would be proud of him.

Gradni woke to the sound of galloping horses around him. This place felt different. The warm wind slipping in under the curtain window was soothing. They had traveled a great distance from the cold winds of Scandar. Throughout the journey he had been slipping in and out of sleep, and wasn't sure if it had been three or four days since they had begun traveling. He drew the curtain on his right to see the four elf riders who had woken him. There were another four on the other side as well. They were dressed in layers of steel over leather. Each of them had crossbows strapped to their right thighs, and a sword and quiver of arrows crossing their backs. Gradni watched them. In all his time in Scandar, he had never seen soldiers so prepared for battle.

"What are they doing?" Gradni asked without turning away.

"Escorting us. We are passing the Zipacna Mountains. They are here in case the dragons attack."

"The Zipacna Mountains?"

Mogurn pointed to the other side of the carriage. Gradni bounced to it and drew the curtain. He had been picturing them all wrong. From here it looked like several flames that had solidified into a mass of rock. They were not as jagged or uneven as he had come to believe, but were much more spread out. He had heard that it was twenty-five mountains in all, but there was no way of telling where one mountain ended and another began. He had to turn his head to see all of it. Each spire was a different shape and size to the one next to it. From any other angle it might look like a different mountain range altogether.

"I heard that it looked different," Gradni said.

"It did," Mogurn stated. "We did not know ourselves until we could watch it from Delthurk. The mountain changes; it takes years, but we know that it is constantly changing shape, from one wicked fire to another."

"How does it do that?"

"It is their land. Their unholy site. Once we annihilate them, then perhaps the fire of Zipacna will also be extinguished."

Gradni looked back out the window as they moved farther away from the dragons' home.

There were sparks dancing around the peaks, but the colors were wrong, and they were moving independently from the solidified flame beneath them.

"What are those green things floating around?"

Mogurn answered without following Gradni's finger. "Winged dragons, mostly wyverns and some longues. You will learn all about the different species while here."

Dragons. They were actual dragons that he was looking at.

The horse riders shifted to the front and back of the carriage as they rode into the thick of the forest.

"Do they attack carriages often?" Gradni asked.

"No. The escorts deter them from doing so." Gradni did not react. He sat back. A half minute went by before anything was said. "What are you thinking, young Gradni?"

"I wonder what it will be like to kill such a beast."

Mogurn smiled at him. Uncomfortable with being looked at in this way, Gradni stuck his head out the window again as the carriage started to climb uphill. Though the forest was not in a valley, it almost seemed that way to Gradni as they rode between mountains. Behind him was the outer edge of Zipacna. Ahead was a wall that squared around a mountain peak and hid it from view. This was the Delthurk base, where his father was a heroic martyr. As they got closer, Gradni saw that the wall was built upon the jagged crust of the mountain, so though the top of the square wall was aligned, the bottom moved along with the uneven stone. He saw a spire protruding up that must have been part of a castle, but as the carriage got closer, he lost sight of that too to the overbearing wall. It was so high up that Gradni was barely able to see the elves on top of it.

He heard a deafening creak as the massive wooden doors of the wall started to open. The wood was lighter colored than any he had seen, and from the way it creaked, it was much heavier as well. Gradni swallowed. In Scandar the caretaker never locked the door to the orphanage. Gradni had thought often about accepting the caretaker's unsaid invitation to run away. The only reason he hadn't was because he had nowhere to run to. He heard the great door close behind him. There was no way to escape that obstruction.

Gradni flopped back into his seat before anyone saw him. The carriage travelled uphill for a while before rolling to a stop. Mogurn stepped out.

"Why are you just sitting there? We are here," Mogurn said.

Gradni stepped off the carriage and into a circle of soldiers. Curiosity tugged his chin into looking up at them. Their faces were scarred. The soldiers of Scandar did not bear any such marks. These soldiers had seen real battle, and had probably killed during them. His admiration of them was so complete that it took him a while to discern that it was returned with disappointment. A twelve-year-old boy was not the hero they were hoping their senator would return with. Their eyes still upon him, Gradni turned to Mogurn. But the senator was in conversation with someone else. Gradni gazed idly back at the gate.

The soldiers dispersed when Mogurn told them to, and the elf whom he was whispering with came toward Gradni. He was wearing a smile and carrying a heavy brown leather tome under one arm. His hair was pale orange, short, and matted.

"This is Lays," Mogurn said, "my assistant. I have matters that need my immediate attention. He will take you to your new quarters."

Gradni let himself be led by the assistant Lays as they walked toward the Delthurk castle. It was made of black stone bricks, and formed a giant block with towers at each corner- the closest one Gradni had already seen when peering from the carriage. It occurred to him as he trudged into the castle, that till now he was haplessly following Mogurn's instructions. A twisting within his stomach urged him to rebel against the claustrophobia, but the narrow staircase did not give the thought room to flourish. He tripped twice. The steps were just slabs placed on top of each other. They were wide and mismatched his stride. There were no other children in this place. There were no families either. Only senators and soldiers lived in Delthurk.

Lays opened a door and moved aside so that Gradni could walk in first. The room was large. The bed in front of him could fit three of him, and the room itself could fit five of the beds. A chest of drawers was in the corner, and the entire floor was covered in sheep wool carpet. There were two windows on the opposite side, and even though he could only see halfway out of them from the threshold, they were large enough to allow the nourishing wind to flow through.

"Sir Gradni?"

Gradni whirled around, remembering that he was not alone. He looked closer at the assistant this time instead of the tome that he carried. He was short and thin, and the tip of his narrow nose curled a little too much toward his mouth. His sticklike arms were somehow able to hold the giant book.

"I hope you find your room comfortable?"

"My room?"

"Yes, Sir Gradni. This is your room. We were not expecting someone as young as you, so we were unprepared some. Allow us some days, and we will make sure that you have everything you need."

"Like what?"

"Well. Clothes, furniture for your size, proper shoes, a servant. Mogurn said to make sure you get all the provisions that all our knights receive."

"But I am not a knight?"

"You will be. I will leave you alone now. Mogurn advises you to get some rest. You have had a long journey, and tomorrow you will meet your trainers."

Lays blew out the lamp as he left and closed the door. Gradni stood still for a while in the darkness before succumbing to the unfamiliar bed. It was softer than any bed he had ever been on. The ceiling was high. He would never be able to use all that height. Outside the window opposite the bed were the Zipacna Mountains. It would be the first thing he would see every morning, and the last thing he would see at night. Someday he would be there, and whoever was in this room would be able to see him, as he slew dragon, after dragon, after dragon.

"You will not amount to anything," the caretaker had said to him back in Scandar. *"We'll see,"* Gradni had said back. Gradni smiled as he turned onto his side. He smiled for a very long time.

CHAPTER 5

Mogurn watched the boy train from the arena stands. He had brought in a specialist, Cluthan, to exclusively teach him. Mogurn stroked his chin as Gradni thrusted his blade forward. The boy was almost too eager to prove his worth. Something desperate was driving him.

"He is mad!" the caretaker of Gradni's orphanage kept saying to Mogurn. To have such energy and anger at his young age, perhaps it was madness, but it was also power. The boy would become a magnificent dragon slayer, as long as Mogurn could control the politics around him.

Taking an unwanted orphan from Scandar had been easy, but introducing him into Delthurk was proving difficult. His fellow senators were not keen on spending their scant resources on a single boy. It had been difficult enough to pay for Cluthan. The others were especially afraid that their main source of supplies, the amesha nation of Aristahl, would find the investment foolhardy, and cut them off. Such as it was, Mogurn needed to persuade the deva Yagura, who spoke for Aristahl, more than he needed to persuade his own elves. Yagura was one of the Disciples of Gaorda, the dev organization of warriors that had eradicated the sesha dragon species many years ago. They had also killed Shah Zahk, the foolish ruler of Aristahl, thus placing the amesha kingdom in their debt. This in turn led to Aristahl's devotion of resources to Delthurk.

Yet for warriors who had done so much, the Disciples now refrained from battling with dragons. Their stance was that they had already sacrificed enough against this common evil, while others remained on the peripheral and reaped the benefits. They served in every other capacity, including advising and mentoring, but they refused fight. The finest warriors- with the greatest success fighting the dragons; now serving as teachers and politicians. Mogurn wondered what had happened to make them sit on the sidelines, besides their blatant arrogance. He resented having to please Yagura, who was fully aware of the power he had over them by being Aristahl's representative. Fortunately, when Mogurn stated his plan to the senate to train Gradni into becoming Delthurk's ultimate dragon slayer, Yagura said nothing in rebuttal. He even left the conference early that day. A lack of disapproval being the best they ever hoped for from Yagura, the senate approved Mogurn's strategy, at least for now.

Mogurn immediately created a schedule for his subject. He made sure that when the boy wasn't training to fight dragons that he was learning about them. The experts Mogurn recruited taught Gradni the dragon's weaknesses, as well as their wickedness throughout history. By adulthood, Gradni would be both knowledgeable about the details of his enemy as well as a warrior who could handle his sword with finesse. This alone would put him ahead of all the brutes they had used in the past.

A loud *clack* brought Mogurn out of his thoughts. Gradni had only been training for three months, and was already hitting much harder than a boy of twelve should be. Mogurn glanced around the circular arena, and smirked at the growing audience. As planned, he had brought attention to Gradni's training sessions by making them exclusive.

The spectators would spread word of Gradni's quick progress, and Yagura would have to take notice soon. As satisfactory as Cluthan was for Gradni now, and as much as Mogurn disliked Yagura, he needed the Disciple of Gaorda to take an avid interest in his prodigy.

"Senator Mogurn?"

His assistant often interrupted his deliberations. "What is it, Lays?"

"The amesha woman is here. She wishes to see you."

Mogurn stood up immediately, his thoughts scrambling. She came so rarely that he forgot to plan for her.

"Where is she?"

"In the same room in the castle where you always see her."

"Has she spoken to anyone else?"

"Just Yagura as always. What is wrong, Senator?"

"Was she here, at the arena?"

"I do not know."

Mogurn walked steadily out of the arena and toward the castle. The amesha woman was the diplomat from Aristahl. Her disapproval could be as harmful as Yagura's. She needed to be handled delicately. It would complicate matters if she discovered the emphasis Delthurk was placing on Gradni. Mogurn did not know if Yagura even thought enough of Gradni to mention him to her, especially since they disliked each other just as much as Mogurn did either of them.

Mogurn forced himself into a calm demeanor before entering the room. He put on his bewitching false smile as he opened the door to greet her.

"Lady Bamay. I am sorry I was not available upon your arrival. I trust that my assistant made sure Delthurk received you well?"

The woman turned away from the window and came toward him. In the sunlight her hair had faded even further from the raven black it had been when Mogurn first met her. She was thinner too, her skin tighter around her face.

"I heard you recently returned from an attempt to recruit a slayer." She said with a delicate voice. "Any luck?"

"No. The dragons killed the last slayer that Scandar sent us. It happened on his first mission with us, so they refuse to send us another. We hope that will change in the future; but for now, Scandar is not going to help us."

Her hollow eyes held his attention as she nodded. "Then who is the boy you brought back with you?" Her voice had lost its softness.

He restrained from answering immediately. She was as cunning as he was. "Just a boy who shows some potential; we are going to raise him to become a dragon slayer."

She nodded, but not out of consent. "The Fire Spirit Ta'ar is raising the greatest dragon slayer ever to exist, Senator Mogurn. Ta'ar will send him here to command an army against the dragons in a war that will end them forever. Yet you have now decided, without our permission, to train a competitor?"

"Lady Bamay. He will not be a competitor. He will serve beside Ta'ar's prodigy."

"Beside him!" she yelled. "Erdūn is being trained by the Disciples of Gaorda. He is being taught magic under the guidance of the Fire Spirit Ta'ar himself. Everyone is to serve under him and not beside. You are now raising an elf dragon slayer, right here in Delthurk. Erdūn is an amesha. He will have enough trouble gaining the loyalty of your soldiers without competing with a native elf."

"With respect, Lady Bamay, we are grateful to receive Ta'ar's help, but it is a long time yet before Erdūn will lead us. We have not even seen this prodigy, and cannot rely on him completely."

"I have seen him, Senator. I know what he will become, and I will not have his skills wasted. An army must follow him, and protect him, and not be divided by following another!"

"Of course, but we must make sure that there is an army to follow him when he is ready to lead. We are entrusting so much to your savior, Lady Bamay. Entrust us to do what we have done since the dragons started coming to the mountains."

There was a moment of silence.

"Very well, Senator Mogurn, but I will be reporting this to Ta'ar. Whatever your plan for this elf boy, it had better not conflict with Erdūn's destiny! We provide for you. Do not forget that."

Mogurn relaxed his tone. "Lady Bamay, Ta'ar and Aristahl provide for our joint cause. I believe fully that the Fire Spirit will appreciate us doing our part. I would be happy for you to report to Ta'ar of our Gradni."

She paused. Perhaps she was not as conniving as he thought. She smiled after a moment. "I guess we will see, Senator Mogurn, how far this champion of yours will rise. Good day to you."

Mogurn watched her through the window as she left the castle. Yagura was by the carriage. He bowed to his three fellow Disciples of Gaorda who accompanied Bamay, but said nothing to her as she stepped into the carriage. And yet, Yagura had mentioned Gradni to her upon her arrival. The boy was making an impression on the deva after all.

CHAPTER 6

In the week that it took to return from Delthurk, Bamay was for once grateful for being the Disciples' messenger. It was seven years ago when she fled with her son to the Disciples' base. She had had so few moments alone with him, even in the early years when she bathed, fed, and did everything else for him that the Disciples considered beneath them to do. Even then there was always at least one of them with her at all times, watching to make sure she did not overstep her boundaries. It was increasingly difficult for her as he got older. All it would take was one sentence for him to know that she was his mother.

One time when he was four, the devi watching Bamay and Erdūn was called away. Erdūn was eating methodically. With the fire of Ta'ar being channeled into him, his little hands were already strong enough to tear leathery bread. Still she could not help herself. She reached over and took a big piece of bread. He looked up at her in bewilderment. Caught in his gaze, she smiled back as she tore up the bread for him to eat, not seeing that the devi had returned until it was too late. Bamay put the bread back and removed her hands from the table. Erdūn took the piece and continued eating, unaware of what had just happened. Less than a day later, it was decided that Bamay would spend her time traveling between the tower base, Aristahl, and Delthurk, as the Disciples' messenger.

On the day she left for her recent visit to Delthurk, the deva training Erdūn swung his staff so hard into Erdūn's face that blood spewed from his mouth. Even Ta'ar's aura rippled from the attack, but he never challenged them. Ta'ar agreed long ago to trust the Disciples, provided that they trust him. Bamay had turned away from seeing her son's blood, as if struck by the blow herself. She walked straight out of the tower and into the carriage. They would only take her even further from him if she criticized their wickedness.

Nor could she deny the progress of their vicious ways. Erdūn was able to swing his weapons and block attacks with a precision and skill that no one of his young age was meant to possess. Part of it was due to the great strength gained from Ta'ar's magic. Erdūn was a foot taller than any of the other boys of seven years that Bamay saw running around in her visits to Aristahl. The magic made his skin unnaturally tough as well. None of the boys of Aristahl would have been able to eat properly for weeks if they were to suffer the blows that Erdūn did daily.

Seeing the way he changed every time she returned from an excursion, she convinced herself that they were right about her presence being a weakness to him. It was for the best that she was now the diplomat. Besides, after seeing the elf boy, she knew that her original purpose to protect her son was now renewed. Whether Erdūn knew it or not, she would always be his mother, and she could see threats to him that no others could.

She had gone to see this Gradni as soon as Yagura mentioned him to her. Yagura said they only brought this boy to Scandar one season ago. That much showed. The elf boy lacked skill that Erdūn had from years of training. But there was a vitality and chaotic independence to Gradni that her

Erdūn didn't have. When the time came, she knew the soldiers of Delthurk would follow Gradni and not her son.

The carriage rolled into the jungle. Bamay hated living in the tower which served as the base. It was not just because she was the only other amesha save her son who was living there, or even the way she was treated. That would have been the same anywhere with the Disciples. It was the tower itself, and its location in the unfamiliar jungle.

The trees that suffocated the tower were taller than any trees had the right to be, and the trunks were not even straight like the trees that surrounded Aristahl. They bent in all directions as they reached up high, as if they were intentionally blocking out the light. She could hear the deva ahead of the carriage slashing the vines, which always grew back in the weeks that she was away. She also did not like what this place did to her body. She was full of strength here, but that only aggravated her further, as there was no opportunity to use it. Her arms, as well as Erdūn's, were longer here in the jungle. They reached down to her knees, and her fingers were at least an inch longer as well. The adaptation, she figured, was for climbing and swinging through the curved trees and branches. But she never entered the jungle except to leave it, and such long arms and fingers were just annoyances within the cramped tower.

It was not even a complete tower. It was built eighty years ago for a war that ended a year later. It was meant to stand taller than the trees, but it had been attacked before it was finished. What the Disciples of Gaorda insisted on calling a tower was no more than an orange stump of broken clay.

When they left Aristahl seven years ago, her one small hope was that they would be moving from one palace to another. Instead she found more reason to not trust the Disciples.

During the Dev-Sesha War, many dev nations had offered the Disciples sanctuary at their palaces. All the Disciples' provisions were taken care of. But once the seshas were exterminated, the dev nations had no more use for the Disciples. They were cast out and needed to find a new place to live. This abandoned tower was the best place they could find. It was almost amusing to Bamay that the once high and mighty Disciples of the great Gaorda were now living in a broken abandoned tower with guards stationed in trees for protection. But she was too closely tied to them now. Laughing at them would be laughing at herself.

It was after coming here that she realized why the Disciples had reached out to those foreign to them - her own nation of Aristahl, and the elf base, Delthurk. At the time of the Dev-Sesha War, there were almost five hundred Disciples of Gaorda. There were now less than a hundred. It had not been difficult for the Disciples to entice Aristahl or Delthurk in spite of the dev nations rejecting them. They never did stop boasting of their undeniable success in ridding the world of the sesha dragons. She wondered if the elves hated dealing with the Disciples as much as she did.

Fourteen guards were surrounding the tower in sets of two. It was midday, and thus the devs were only beginning to turn a darker shade of blue as the carriage rode into the tower. Bamay did not wait for it to stop before getting off.

Ta'ar was illuminating the center hall from the border when she walked in. She followed his line of sight to see Erdūn swing his steel blade in a vicious arc against his trainer. The deva dodged the attack and swung his staff around and into Erdūn's chest.

She fought down the urge to run and protect him from those she had given him to, and reminded herself that his destiny could not be achieved without a price. She turned back toward Ta'ar.

"My Lord Ta'ar, I have vital news. The elves at Delthurk have taken in an elf boy. They are training him to become their champion Dragon Slayer."

Without facing her, Ta'ar nodded his head approvingly. "Good, that they are doing their part," he said in his fiery voice.

Bamay panicked and silently cursed Mogurn. "But my lord, the races are tied together by thin strings. When Erdūn goes to Delthurk, they will follow their own slayer instead, for Erdūn is amesha, and not elf like they are."

Ta'ar continued looking ahead as Bamay spoke. She once again followed his burning blue eyes. The trainer knocked Erdūn to the floor with a slap across his face. Erdūn immediately got up and ran toward the deva— sword in hand. There were even more bruises on him now than on the day she left. They were not even allowing him time to heal.

"I will address it," Ta'ar boomed. "Once they see him, their loyalty will be his." Erdūn leapt forward and brought his sword down on the trainer's staff. Bamay felt the heat of Ta'ar's aura as it pulsed happily. "They will know that it can only be Erdūn and I who will finish this war for them."

Bamay nodded in fake concession. It was not enough. She would have to act on her own. Her thoughts were interrupted when four devs marched into the auditorium. They headed straight for the center as if no one else was there. Two of them carried a net with an unconscious beast inside. The creature started to move, sending shivers down Bamay's back. It was a wyvern dragon. Though once native to Aristahl, she had never see one before. It looked to have the shape of an eagle, except instead of feathers it had green scales, and its wings were more like a bat's. Upon a closer look, she saw it had a long snakelike neck and an elongated wide beak. Bamay waited for the others to surround the dragon before following suit. Its similarities to the sobekian were unmistakable.

"It followed them back from Delthurk," said a devi, referring to the carriage that Bamay just disembarked from. "How did it know to follow their carriage, and not any of the others that pass through the elven barracks? How did it know that this carriage would lead them to the savior?" No one had an answer for her. The wyvern grunted as it began to awaken. Bamay trembled at the sight of the beast's wriggling claws. Each of those claws could tear out her throat.

"Did you look for others?" Ta'ar asked.

"There are none."

Ta'ar floated closer to the beast than even the devs dared. The wyvern awoke immediately and snapped toward the spirit, but the ball of fire that began in its mouth died as the Fire Spirit put out his palm. Ta'ar stood in front of the dragon as it heaved air at him before it lowered its head in futility. Bamay looked toward the spirit once the large eyes of the dragon sank back down. Ta'ar's fiery aura had softened slightly. The moving lava-like clothes were more orange than red right now. As omnipotent as he was, the presence of this defiant dragon was harmful to him.

"Erdūn. Come here," Ta'ar commanded. Bamay looked back toward her son. She did not notice that even he was keeping his distance. "Come here now, Erdūn." Ta'ar repeated. "Bring your weapon."

Her son did so slowly, dragging the point of his weapon upon the stony ground. The wyvern saw him and reacted, but the net allowed it only inches of movement. Erdūn hesitated, his small eyes blinking repeatedly. The aura around

Ta'ar grew warmer, and no fire came from the dragon's open mouth. Erdūn continued toward them.

"Hold it," Ta'ar demanded of the wyvern's captors. The four devs wrestled the netted dragon and exposed its neck to Erdūn. Wyverns were flying dragons. Unlike the rugged sobekians, their skin was lighter and more delicate to facilitate their flight.

"Lift your sword, Erdūn."

Erdūn did so, first by only a couple inches, and then higher when the devs scrutinized him. It stopped there. Bamay crept around her son and put her hands upon his shoulders. She gently pressed away the tension while Ta'ar's aura became warmer and his voice fierier.

"This is your destiny, Erdūn. Show us. Show yourself what you will become."

Bamay watched as the devs twisted the beast further so that its exposed neck glinted in the light. Its suffocated caw could be heard from under the arms of the devi that held its jaw. Erdūn turned his head toward the wyvern's eyes as the creature glared at him. Impatient murmurs arose from the devs.

"Now, Erdūn!" the Fire Spirit bellowed. Bamay pressed her nails deep into Erdūn's shoulders. He lifted the sword some inches higher, and then brought it down, slicing the wyvern's neck completely to separate the head from the body.

Erdūn dragged the sword backward while Bamay backed away with him. His fingers were frozen around the handle. She wanted to hug him, but she settled with keeping her hands rested upon his shoulders.

The devs dropped the beast. Bamay saw them smile for the first time. She wanted to lift her son's chin so he could see it too, but he was too focused on the lifeless head.

Bamay tucked her head into her sleeve to wipe away her tears before they were seen. One of the devas bent onto one knee in front of Erdūn. The deva untied the sash from his waist and used it to wipe the blood off Erdūn's sword.

Ta'ar backed away from the blood. "We are done for today. Bamay, take Erdūn and get him ready. This place is not safe for him anymore."

Bamay tugged her son gently. There was no emotion in his young face, but he was still looking at the dead dragon. She brought her hand to his rough cheek and softly turned him away. He followed her to his room which bordered the hall. Erdūn said nothing as she changed his clothes. She wanted to let him know how proud she was of him. He had done something that she never could, but somehow the awareness of that stopped her from saying anything.

Light rippled into the room as Ta'ar floated in. "We will leave here as soon as the Disciples are done bathing. We are fortunate that the scouts trapped the dragon before it could escape and reveal our location to Zipacna."

"Bathing! They are bathing now?" Bamay asked.

Ta'ar paused. He too did not understand their timing.

"It is due to the wyvern. They bathe in water that has been exposed to the sun to cleanse themselves after encountering a dragon."

Her eyebrows narrowed. They never did this when they fought the sobekians in Aristahl years ago. This was some new ritual.

"Where will we be going?" Bamay asked.

"The Disciples know another place where we can stay temporarily, but we will have to move to Delthurk sooner than planned. You will go to Aristahl first to arrange provisions."

"Of course, Lord Ta'ar." She would have to act quicker

now to secure her son's destiny. The elf boy needed to be dealt with before her son was taken in by Delthurk.

Ta'ar turned from her to Erdūn. He had still not said anything. The Fire Spirit floated toward him, illuminating Erdūn's emotionless face.

"They are coming for you now, Erdūn. They know you are a threat to them."

Erdūn returned Ta'ar's burning gaze with an intense glare.

"I know, but I will kill them all first."

CHAPTER 7

Gradni studied the diagram of a drake while a scholar explained the details to him. This scholar was an elf who was supposedly an expert on the history of drake slaying. This was part of Gradni's daily routine. Scholars on the different dragons would teach him in the early morning, while warriors would train him to fight in the evening. This particular scholar had also spent time with the late S'freed.

There were random paragraphs of information written all around the image of the drake, and dotted lines connecting them to the wings, feet, and other key points of the dragon. The markings were all in different toned ink, indicating that the parchment had been worked on at multiple times by different people. He learned today that except for the giant rukhs and a few other known species, drake dragons were also one of the largest creatures ever seen. Their mouth alone was large enough to chew up an entire human body. Yet they were also able to fly higher than any other dragon. But, as the scholar was pointing out to him, as monsters of the air, they were vulnerable when on the ground. Their scales were light and thin so as not to hinder flight, and thus did not serve well as protection. One of the more faded paragraphs was beside the drake's neck, indicating where the creature was most vulnerable.

S'freed, it seemed, would creep up to the monster

while it slept, and with one broad swipe of his long sword he would slash the drake's throat, cutting as close to the hilt as possible.

Gradni listened with reticence to the scholar. S'freed had been so large himself. Gradni never imagined that most of his killings had been done this way. He was not as much a warrior as he was an assassin.

The drakes did sometimes awaken before S'freed got to them, but the battles the scholar told Gradni about were still not the grand fights he had hoped them to be. Due to the intensity of their flames, drakes needed several seconds to prepare their fire, and they could not immediately lift themselves into the air the way the smaller wyverns could. Their only resort in such circumstances was to lash out with their teeth. But they were slow lumbering beasts. When a drake would awaken when S'freed was still several feet from his prey, he would run toward the dragon, maybe evade a single drive of teeth, and thrust his sword into the monster's jugular.

Gradni thought the battles went differently, that dragons came into villages breathing their terrible fire, and that drake slayers like S'freed battled them there to the death. The scenario made little sense now when he thought about it, but he had still expected there to be more actual fighting. Even S'freed's most *valorous* conquest, according to the scholar, was a large drake that had already killed several slayers. After a troop of soldiers rustled the dragon into chasing them, S'freed hid inside the drake's cave and slew it sometime after it returned—again, in its sleep.

Gradni looked at the diagram. There was a figure beside the dragon's wing that showed the size of an average elf. Gradni felt consoled by the comparison. Even though S'freed was an assassin who killed drakes in their sleep, it still took courage to face such large beasts, so he still deserved respect for having slain so many.

After finishing the lecture, the scholar rolled up the parchment. Their time was over for today. Gradni nodded and quickly scuttled out of the castle room and toward the arena. He had learned more than he cared to. It was now time to fight.

Gradni strapped on his armor and was already swinging his wooden sword before Cluthan arrived. A few hours of this was just what he needed to forget what he had learned about S'freed. Mogurn was right. Delthurk needed someone better.

"Harder," Cluthan yelled.

Gradni reared his head up, his sweaty arms drooping as his hands loosened around the sword handle. He had been swinging his weapon for three hours now. As usual, he was so caught up that he had not saved any strength to make the last half hour bearable. But he could not stop now. Mogurn and Lays were watching him from several rows up. Gradni pulled his wooden sword over his head and hammered it against his trainer's ready weapon.

He carried on until the time was done, swinging and sidestepping across the sand while wind channeling as commanded. His last strike barely connected. Even breathing was a task now.

"Very good!" Cluthan said.

Gradni tried to be nonchalant as he turned away from his trainer and rotated his neck to look around the arena. He immediately looked back to where Mogurn was. The senator was not there.

"Go bathe and eat," Cluthan said from behind him. "We will do new things tomorrow."

Gradni grabbed the jug of water that a servant had left for him and gulped it down. Two streams leaked from either side of his mouth until there was none left. He dropped the pitcher down and left. He was very hungry. Along the way to the castle dining hall, he wondered how much the senator had seen before leaving. It had been seven months since Gradni was brought to Delthurk by Mogurn. Yet the senator had not spoken to him since. These were the only times that Gradni ever saw him, as Mogurn only talked to him through Lays. Mogurn and Lays were always talking while they watched him train. After all these months, Gradni wanted to know what they were saying about him. Mogurn had told him that he was going to be Delthurk's prodigy, and he wanted to know if he was meeting those expectations.

Gradni carried his tray of bread and venison stew toward the exit. He was stopped by two soldiers.

"I always eat in my own room," Gradni said to them. He had never been stopped before.

"Not anymore. You will eat here like the rest of us."

"Why?"

"Senator Mogurn's orders."

Helpless and starving, Gradni turned to face the rows of seated soldiers. None of them were paying any attention to him. If anything, it seemed that they were avoiding seeing him. Gradni found an empty table and sat down. Soldiers filled up the tables beside his. They talked loudly and banged the table with their heavy mugs of mead. Gradni ate quickly. He guzzled water from his jug to force down what he did not chew, wiped the brown liquid from his mouth with his sleeve as the soldiers did, and left the hall. Gradni did not stop till he got back to his room. Normally, he would go to the top of the castle after dinner, but that was when he'd already had some quiet time eating alone. Instead, he sat for several minutes- his fingers intertwined in his lap.

There was no reason for those guards to stop him from bringing his dinner here. Mogurn was keeping too much from him. Gradni left his room and headed for the western staircase.

He was not expecting anything grand from the senators' floor, but it was still a surprise that this top corridor was almost exactly like all the others. The only difference was the sepia colored carpet that ran down the center. There were two armed guards a step from each side of the corridor, protecting the two flights of stairs that were on either side of it.

Gradni cleared his throat. "I wish to see Senator Mogurn!" he demanded.

The two guards looked at each other. "It is late. He is resting now."

"I wish to see him," Gradni repeated.

Another brief look passed between them. One of them walked down the corridor and knocked softly on Mogurn's door. A couple seconds later the soldier was let in.

Gradni paced for five minutes in front of the remaining guard until Mogurn's door opened again. The soldier came out of Mogurn's office and went down the east staircase instead of coming back to Gradni. Gradni looked up at the remaining guard but received no acknowledgment.

It was a couple minutes before Gradni realized whom the soldier went to get.

"Sir Gradni." Gradni turned around. Lays had come up the dim staircase behind him. "What are you doing here?"

"I am here to see Senator Mogurn."

"I have an important meeting with the senator right now. Tell me what you need, and if it is something I cannot aid you with, I shall pass your concerns to the senator."

Gradni held his tongue. The guard had just said that

Mogurn was resting. Lays was also suspiciously not carrying his log book. "I wish to speak to the senator directly. I want to know about my father." Gradni figured that his father was someone whom Lays knew little about.

Lays fished within his clothes. "That may not be possible, Sir Gradni. The senator is a very busy man. In the meantime, here is my key to the record hall. You can now find out all you need to know whenever you wish to." He was holding out the iron key. "If there is ever anything else that you need from the senator, then it would be best if you tell me so that I can relay your issue to him."

"No," Gradni said in a raised voice. "I wish to talk to Senator Mogurn, not you!"

Lay's lowered himself to Gradni's level and edged his hand out to rest on Gradni's shoulder. He leaned forward to speak softly. His hand on Gradni's shoulder tightened enough for him to feel it.

"Sir Gradni. As important as you are to the senator and to Delthurk, you must be aware that Senator Mogurn has other matters that need his attention apart from you. If you two are to meet, it is because he will wish it. Is that understood, Sir Gradni?"

Gradni stood motionless. "Why can't I eat in my room anymore?"

"You will be leading these men when you grow older. It is important that you do not run from them." Lays stood back up. "Do you still want the key?"

Gradni took it without saying anything.

"You have a long day tomorrow," Lays said in his regular, polite tone, "and you had best get some rest."

Gradni nodded and left the senators' floor. Determined not to listen to Lays, he went to the top of the castle instead of back to his room.

There was never anyone on top of the castle at this late hour. Due to the number of archers and ballista operators on the thick walls that surrounded the base, there was plenty of time for them to ring the giant corner bell in case of an attack. A gust of wind ran through Gradni's hair as he leaned over the edge. The weather here was as docile as it was in Scandar, though it was somewhat warmer. Gradni's green streaks of hair were still going through its regular cycles, but they were noticeably darker here. Gradni flicked it back and looked out the north-west corner.

The castle was surrounded by blacksmiths and stables. Around them was roofed housing, - all of it only interesting because of the rippled mountain rock underneath it. Each structure was built specifically to fulfill its purpose and nothing more. There was barely even any street as every passageway was suffocated by stone from all sides. The edge of Delthurk suffered the worst due to the unforgiving wall that surrounded the entire base. It was like a dam that was barricading what was pushing to get out. The only release to this was the wooden gate that allowed the trickle of supplies and soldiers to enter and exit the encampment.

Delthurk was not a real nation like his home of the past. It was just an area which was built into a base to fight the dragons. Gradni looked toward the gate. Elves were loading up a carriage that was preparing to leave. He watched them load it for another minute before leaving the castle. The wall was preventing him from seeing anything outside except the Zipacna Mountains. Though he was not allowed out of Delthurk, he could at least catch a glimpse of the world that surrounded it when the gate was opened.

While waiting for the carriage to finish loading, Gradni sat against a house with one knee bent and the other sloping down the angled ground. Above the wall and on either side of the gate stood five soldiers who were looking outward. Gradni would not have been able to see them if not for the lamps that lit the top, so it was doubtful that they could see him.

The loud creaking of the gate rapped against Gradni's ears. He stood up and arched on his toes as the portal widened. All he could see was darkness. He was not close enough. Gradni walked ahead to get as good a view as he could. The horses of the carriage four meters ahead of him neighed when the creaking ended in a clang as the gate opened fully. It was too dark to see anything. The rider whipped the horses for them to go.

An idea began to stir in Gradni. No one was even aware of him. The few that were around could barely see themselves at this hour. There was no time to consider it. The horses were already trotting and would soon be in a gallop. Gradni ran forward and sprung off the sloping ground into the back of the carriage. He landed as the wheels below him rattled against the wood of the path. He smiled. Mogurn was not going to like this.

Once the rattling settled, Gradni peered outside the curtain. Neither Delthurk nor Zipacna were visible within the thick forest growth. The horses slowed—probably to cross a river. Gradni leapt out, landing on his shoulder which he rolled upon. Falling was the first action Cluthan taught him. Hands first, Gradni left the path and delved deep into the thick foliage of the forest.

The leaves, gentle yet rough, stroked his arms as specs of water splashed against his shins. He pulled off his tunic and tied the sleeves around his waist before venturing farther in. With his thumb and forefinger, he stripped the leaves off a needle-thin branch and brought its scent to his nose. He had never smelled anything like it. He closed his fist tight, then opened it again for its full flavor. He wondered how many other scents were out there that he had not experienced.

His other hand rippled down a rough bark. He threw the leaves away and grabbed the trunk with his other hand and revolved around it. It wouldn't do; it was just a trunk with all its branches on the top. Right by it, though, was a tree with branches more vertically spread out. He put his foot on one such branch and pushed himself off it to reach a higher one, and went higher still from there. From this new position there were three options. He chose the one that would take him to the highest point, and pulled himself up.

He rested himself against the trunk while sitting on a thick branch. The back of his neck flopped against the trunk, and a smile opened from within him. He had no idea what this feeling was, this feeling of stillness that left him thoughtless and happy. He was perfectly balanced, with different parts of his body against different parts of the tree. Gradni took another deep breath of the forest air, and closed his eyes.

His foot slid down the branch and kicked him awake. His hands scrambled to grip something solid as he recollected where he was. He gasped when he was unable to recognize his surroundings. The rising sun had removed the familiarity of the forest darkness. Hours had passed. It was probably time for him to begin his morning training. He located the river before starting the climb down. His throat was dry and he needed to drink in case he would have to train immediately after getting back. Going down was more difficult. For that alone he was grateful for the light as he tested the strength of the branches below him. He bounded for the river and dropped to his knees to greedily cup water into his mouth. The taste made him realize how thirsty he was.

After several scoops he stood up. A brownish-green dragon was less than two meters from him.

Gradni's feet dug into the mud of the riverbank. The dragon had been drinking from the same river. It had been staring at Gradni while he drank. The scaly creature was the size of a lion, with four paws, and a set of wings from its back that stretched out and shadowed the bushes it stood between. Its snout was short when compared to the pictures of the other species of dragons that Gradni had seen, as if it had been scrunched to half the normal size. He recognized it as a piasa, known for its unique ability to travel by air and fight on land.

The piasa arched itself like a cat and drew its lips back from its teeth. Gradni focused on its large eyes. He had had only six months of training—not enough to face this animal. He drew his feet into a better position to leap away should the dragon lunge at him. Flickers of red and yellow danced around the dragon's broad teeth. Maybe Gradni would be able to grab a stone or a branch after diving out of the way? It was possible. It had to be. The dragon's front feet moved. Gradni readied himself to leap. His throat was dry again. The dragon's back feet moved as well. Left, Gradni thought repeatedly. He would leap left, away from the river where there was a greater chance of finding something to use as a weapon.

The flickering stopped, and the lips closed over the teeth. Gradni was so focused on the eyes that he did not realize till now that the piasa was moving away from him and not toward. The staring continued as the piasa backed away, and ended only when it outstretched its wings fully and leapt into the foliage.

Gradni remained frozen.

He lay on his bed wide awake. The archers on the Delthurk wall had seen him coming back long before he got to the gate. In less than an hour he would begin his daily routine.

Mogurn had reprimanded him for his actions. He had yelled for a long time and Gradni had heard little of it.

"What is wrong with you? What happened while you were out there?" Mogurn had asked. "Nothing," had been Gradni's reply. He realized now how badly he handled it. Mogurn would remember this.

But it was difficult to be concerned about that now. The piasa knew he was an enemy. All dragons were evil. That much had always been true. It could have easily killed him. Why didn't it?

CHAPTER 8

Bamay's hands sprung to the walls of the carriage as it sped over one of the potholes that peppered Aristahl's entrance. Nasphir, the deva accompanying her, grumbled as the chest Bamay held in her lap almost dropped onto his feet.

"When you see her, tell her to fix this road. We cannot stand to lose the horses to such idiocy."

Bamay nodded. It was Aristahl that provided the Disciples of Gaorda with the horses. They provided so generously for the cause that they could not afford to even repair the damage to their entrance. Still, she was expected to ask for more. Minister Sheemu would oblige. She was the standing ruler of Aristahl. She had been an advisor to Zahk before he was killed by the Disciples. Sheemu was the strategic choice by Ta'ar. As a woman, she could not assume the role of shah herself and would always be second to Ta'ar, leaving him as the undisputed leader, even in his absence.

The Aristahl Bamay remembered was fading. The sturdy houses that the old Shah Zahk had left them with were surrounded by dying land. The grass was not as green, and even the tree trunks were not as brown. Sacrifice, she reminded herself. She was sacrificing every day for her son, and it was Aristahl's duty to their champion to sacrifice for him as well. But for Aristahl's earth to blacken and die for some green-haired elf boy instead—that was unfair.

The deva huffed as the carriage rolled to a stop. "Make sure you tell her we are relocating and need extra supplies."

Bamay stepped off the carriage after the deva did. Her bare foot took little invigoration from the earth. Minister Sheemu was waiting for them with a guard on either side of her.

It was painful to see them. As much as Bamay disliked the jungle tower, the earth there was full of energy that filled her skin with a rich brown. The land of Aristahl was so worn that even Sheemu was hiding the gray in her skin. Her face was coated with an excess of mud-based cream, and she had long sleeves that Bamay had never seen her wearing before.

"Lady Bamay," Sheemu said in greeting.

"Minister Sh—"

"The weapons," Nasphir interrupted, "where are they?" Sheemu attempted to smile as she raised her silk wrapped arm to point toward the blacksmith entrance. Gray- skinned ameshas in ragged clothing were pulling on a loaded carriage, followed by a heavyset blacksmith. Bamay could barely stand to look at them. There were almost twenty of them, and yet they still looked like they were about to fall from exhaustion.

"Thank you all," Sheemu said to them.

They dispersed without responding. 'Sacrifice', Bamay reminded herself as she turned to the weapons. All she knew about them was what she heard from hearsay. Yagura at Delthurk had asked for them to be made to exploit a weakness in the dragon's defenses.

The blacksmith removed the heavy sheet from the carriage. Bamay immediately understood why Aristahl was in a worse state than ever before. They were giant wooden spears. The weapons ended in steel pointed arrowheads.

Like good arrowheads, they were made of the perpendicular cross sections of two sharpened triangular blades, each of which was the length of an entire arm. The wood was from olive trees. The cutting of these trees had been banned by the Shah Zahk so that the land could heal. The last use of them had been to build the great gate at Delthurk. It was no wonder that Aristahl had gotten worse. The war against the dragons was once again taking Aristahl toward ruin.

Nasphir rubbed his hands against the spears as he inspected them for any weakness. Bamay's stomach started to churn. She shifted closer toward Sheemu. "We should discuss gold."

Sheemu nodded. "Excuse us," she said to Nasphir, who continued to rub his fingers across one of the spear's edges.

Bamay and Sheemu got into a carriage that took them to the palace. Bamay looked up at her old home as she walked upon the sandstone steps. The once proud central dome was covered in dust. Her observation did not go unnoticed by Sheemu.

"I had to reassign palace workers to help cut down the trees."

The inside was better, good enough for Bamay to remember living here without thinking too much of how things had fallen. Sandstone pillars holding up the palace were still engraved with images that told the history of the kingdom. Stories of heroes, and kings, and conquest, revolved around each tower. Some pillars were still smooth, - waiting for grand stories to be carved onto them. Bamay had long ago picked out the one that would have Erdun's.

"Watch your step," Sheemu said on their way up. "A couple of these steps are cracked."

From the palace room window, Aristahl did not seem as bad as it was. The clusters of mismatched sandstone buildings still looked beautiful, as long as she avoided looking at the stumped trees and cracked pavement between them. She left the window to sit down after seeing the speckled crops. There was a time when the crops were so high that they completely hid the earth beneath them.

The two women sat at the table. Sheemu placed a bag of gold coins in front of Bamay. Bamay poured it into the chest she carried with her. They did not even fill it halfway.

Again, Sheemu noticed Bamay's disappointment. "That is all we can spare today. Creating the weapons took much out of us."

Bamay rubbed her fingers across the surface of the coins. "How are the people without their spirit?"

Sheemu leaned back. "They endure, but naturally they are suffering, Bamay. For them to sacrifice for him when he is not here, it is difficult without his presence."

Bamay nodded compassionately. "When Zahk betrayed us, Ta'ar thought it best to lead others to fight the dragons. All that is left for Aristahl to do is to help them do so." Bamay picked up some gold coins from the chest and put them back in front of Sheemu. "You need to fix the road at the entrance of the nation."

"It will be done. There is no need for so much," Sheemu said.

"Keep it. If we are to regain Ta'ar's blessing, we must show that we are ready to fight for the cause itself. We can no longer sit on the sidelines, but we need some of our own resources to do this." Bamay picked up another stack of coins from the chest and placed them beside the others she had already removed.

Sheemu glared at it. "I do not know if this is wise, Bamay. The spirit demands that we give everything we have to you and Delthurk."

"The spirit demands that we do what needs to be done for the cause. We are amesha, Sheemu. You, me, and Erdūn. The Lord Ta'ar has lost faith in us, and we cannot show our worth if we give everything we have for the elves and devs to thrive on. We have resources from our lands that the devs and the elves do not. Use this money to discover something that they cannot get their hands on. If it is something that Erdūn can use, then Aristahl will once again gain Ta'ar's favor."

Sheemu placed her hand over the pile. "It will take more than this."

"I know. You will need to save our money going forward."

"Should the spirit find out that we are not giving him everything…"

"He will not. I will always be the one to collect."

"What about the Disciples?"

"I will deal with the Disciples. They will not know what we have done until we have done it, provided, Sheemu, that you invest it properly."

"This money will go into helping Erdūn and the cause, Lady Bamay. I give you my word on that. But only if you can assure me that our spirit will return to us if I do. There are many things I would rather spend Aristahl's money on. Ta'ar does not even need to acknowledge our achievements, as long as he comes back. That we have survived this long in his servitude without his presence is remarkable, yet shameful. Amesha nations must have a ruling spirit, Bamay!"

"I will make sure that Ta'ar remembers Aristahl, Sheemu. The next time I come, after you have looked into possibilities, we can discuss how to go about reclaiming our pride."

Sheemu's fingernails tapped the table before swiping the coins back into her bag. "I will do my best."

Nasphir grunted when he looked into the chest on the

ride out. "This is not even worth our trip here? Did you tell her we are relocating? How are we to make do with this?"

"It is all they had. The nation is dying without their spirit."

Nasphir locked the chest and pushed it away. He rubbed his brow with his fist "This is pitiful. What can be done about it?"

"It has been years since Ta'ar has visited Aristahl. They need to see their guiding spirit to produce for us, but it would do little good for the spirit to hear it from me."

Nasphir smiled smugly. "We will tell him then. He listens to us."

Bamay hid a wince through smiling as the carriage rattled over the road.

CHAPTER 9

Mogurn left to intercept Yagura at the black-smith's when informed that the deva was inspecting the new weapons from Aristahl. He needed to plan his words carefully, but he was distracted by other news. Along with the new weapons, Aristahl had sent a trivial amount of gold. There were barely any provisions coming from any other nations as it was, and the lack of support would make it even harder to maintain that the investment in Gradni was worth the effort. Yagura's involvement in Gradni was now essential for it to go any further.

Mogurn walked into the blacksmith's back room where he caught someone trying to pull the metal and wood of a spear apart. He realized seconds after making eye contact that it was Yagura testing their strength. It was not that the Disciple did not have distinguished features. He had thin eyes, and a long flat nose that led to a finger-thick divided moustache, all on a long triangular face. His dress code was unique as well. Most of his hair was caught in a giant halo-like gold ring above his head, and his waist and legs were wrapped in a large gold-colored cloth that ended in a sash from his left hip. Mogurn had trouble recognizing Yagura because he had never seen him this early in the day before, and though Yagura was still blue, he was as pale as most elves. Such was his way; Yagura took Mogurn's instant of ill recognition as disrespect. It was not the start Mogurn wished for.

"Disciple Yagura," Mogurn said, with one hand against the rough wood of one of the spears.

"All the senators approved my newest strategy of attack. All except for you," Yagura said coldly.

Mogurn continued to feign interest in the weapons. His insides churned at the commanding tone of Yagura's voice. His fellow senators had failed to tell him that it was Yagura's plan and not one of theirs.

"I did not disapprove it, Disciple."

"No. So should the plan succeed, everyone at Delthurk will get credit. Should it fail, you will stand out for not agreeing to it. The rest of us are more concerned for the cause than we are for personal glory, Senator." Yagura walked out of the forge. Mogurn followed a couple steps behind. He allowed a moment of silence to soften the deva.

"I did not know that it was your plan, Disciple Yagura. I would have no qualms against it if I did. I just generally fear that a simple plan will have a simple counter."

"A simple plan leaves less room for error. How many spears do we have?"

All the spears were inside the same forge they had just left. Yagura could easily have counted them himself if he didn't already.

"Fifty, by my count."

"Your plan of rearing a symbolic hero, Mogurn, is long and complicated. Many problems are already taking place. He is disobedient to start with."

Mogurn skipped forward to keep up. "Indeed he is. He has not been performing as well as I hoped. I believe it is because he lacks inspiration from true warriors such as yourself."

Yagura stopped and faced the senator. "He has been here for a year now. He is progressing at a pace acceptable to you perhaps, but your prodigy has not earned my attention."

"His pace would quicken if he were to receive guidance. Disciple Yagura, you have a history with dragons unlike any other here. Gradni does have potential. You've seen that for yourself. Give him some of your time and he will do wonders for our cause."

"Yes. I have seen your servant watching me when I pass by the boy. I will not be spied on Mogurn. Regardless, your boy does not yet deserve to be trained by me."

"I apologize for Lay's nosiness. I am not asking you to train him until you wish to do so. I merely wish for you to speak to him, to inspire him to become like you." The words fell easily out of Mogurn's lips despite not believing in them. Gradni was already rebellious. He did not want the boy's arrogance to match the deva's.

"I will consider it. Keep your servant away from me."

Mogurn thanked him apologetically and left the deva in peace. It had not gone as he had hoped, but he realized from the conversation that there was no way it could have. From the detailed information that Lays had accrued from watching the deva, Yagura was more than intrigued by the boy's prowess. Despite what he had just said to Mogurn, Yagura wanted to train Gradni. But he wouldn't, not while Mogurn was around to take the credit. Mogurn realized what he needed to do, and it felt almost like relief.

"You are leaving sire, so suddenly? What about Gradni?" Lays asked.

Mogurn stood beside his assistant as others loaded up the carriage with heaps of supplies.

"I have put off my travels to find support for too long already. Besides, my presence is holding Gradni back at this juncture. Yagura will not make his move while I am here to watch over him. If he is to train the boy, he will only do it if I am not here to interfere." He looked up toward the castle. Gradni was looking out his window toward them. Mogurn turned back to Lays as the last of the supplies were being loaded.

"Besides, we have been doing this all wrong, appealing to the governments of nations. I will speak of the evil of dragons to our fellow elves directly. I will tell them of Gradni and how a boy is shaming them with his determination. I will try recruiting from non-elven nations as well, including the qui-lahk. We are fools to depend solely on Aristahl. Make sure you record everything while I am gone. I will demand to see the logbook immediately after I get back."

He risked another glance toward Gradni. The boy was still watching them. Mogurn turned away and got into the carriage where he could resume his thoughts in private. He hoped that this gamble would pay off, but either way, distancing himself from the boy was necessary.

CHAPTER 10

G radni's history tutor had left Delthurk the day before after some argument of no longer being able to pay him. Lays had informed the senate that Mogurn had opposed the motion to cut the tutor's pay despite the lack of funds, but it passed nonetheless. Gradni was to read the books in the Delthurk library until another more dedicated tutor could be found.

The tiny library in the castle's basement was shabby. With only one table and chair with a single torch above it, it made the Scandar Library look like a treasure trove. However, there was a long shelf on the ground of unlabeled tomes that were like the one that Lays always carried with him. In the record hall that was right above the library, his father's name was hung high for having slain thirty dragons, including horned ones. These record books would tell him about each of those kills.

For now though, he desired something simpler, and so turned to the higher shelves. Though he expected as much, it was disappointing that there was not a single book that was not about dragons. After a quick scan he found a small book beside the intimidating larger ones. Gradni slid it out and sat at the table. The pages were feeble, but most of them were covered in pictures and diagrams. The book was simply titled *Zipacna*.

Gradni began to read.

Before the lands were plagued by today's multitude of dragons, there was just the one dragon, named Zipacna. Zipacna was so monstrous in size that a single claw of his four terrible feet could unearth a whole village.

Zipacna's very breath was made of dark magic that corrupted the good nature of the races, and wherever he roamed his breath would infect people with discontent. Rebellion began against the perfect order that was, because of this evil dragon. Unsatisfied with the harm he already caused, Zipacna then turned to complicate the ground itself. He gathered mounds of earth together with his great claws, and fused it into stone with his fiery breath, thus making mountains that no civilization could build upon. This could not be ignored, and so some of our people, the qui-lahk, decided that it was time to unite against the dragon. There were five hundred in all who committed to this. Warriors, sorcerers, village leaders, toolmakers, and even thieves and assassins were part of the summit that conceived the end of Zipacna.

They acted while the monster slept. By aid of the magic of the sorcerers, the thieves and assassins silently moved past Zipacna's ears, and across his flesh. They used rope that was lined with steel, and giant pegs of iron, to immobilize the mighty dragon.

But in their haste, while they tied the knots around the dragon's jaw, they became careless and clumsy, and created disturbances that the sorcerers' tricks could not disguise. The great dragon started to wake. The warriors attacked immediately, and despite Zipacna's early wakening, his fate was already sealed. But he was about to lay one final curse upon us before passing.

His mouth bound, Zipacna turned his cursed fire inward, hiding his magic within him where it could not be seen by the five hundred qui-lahk who surrounded him. The dragon exploded in a burst of flames that consumed it, and all those around him. The fire, made of Zipacna's dark magic, solidified as quickly as it had begun into a mass of stone.

We thought that Zipacna's evil was at an end. We mourned the valiant death of the heroes and celebrated the death of Zipacna, all while the true evil legacy of the dragon was hatching.

Portions of rock within the Zipacna Mountains shifted and came to life. From what used to be Zipacna's back sprouted the wings of the mighty drakes. From the front legs came the salamanders, and from the back legs came the sobekians. Serpents wriggled free from what used to be Zipacna's tail, and the monster's infinite teeth broke off to become wyverns. The shell of his tongue transformed into the wicked seshas, the heart unfolded into the lethal piasas, and the intestines broke through and flew into the air as the longues.

The dragons dispersed to the farthest regions of the land, making their containment impossible.

Gradni breezed through the rest of the book. It was the words that now interested him, and the many pictures had become a hindrance. They were not even well drawn. It was clear not just from the state of it, but by the content that it was an aged book. Bored by the rest of it, Gradni put it back and looked through the other titles.

The Dev-Sesha War. A History of Delthurk. The Kshatriya Gaorda. The Serpent That Returned from a Winter Death. . . .

He hopped up and climbed onto the higher shelves to peruse them. There were no other books on Zipacna itself, or even on the qui-lahk and their history with dragons. There were some of dragons and elves, and a few on ameshas and dragons, but none that would give further insight on what he just read.

"Sir Gradni." Gradni turned to see the familiar tome of Lays. "I hope you have learned something today and have not just been climbing all over the shelves?"

Gradni hopped back down. He brushed off the dust that he had accumulated and half slid out the book on Zipacna. "I read this one," he said.

"Ah, and which one is that?"

Gradni pushed the book back in. "It is about the dragon Zipacna and the creation of the mountains."

"Ah, you mean according to the qui-lahk?"

"Yes. Is it true that this is how the Zipacna Mountains and the dragons came to be?"

"Doubtful, but it is what the qui-lahk believe. It is their way of explaining the dragons' evil, as well as the dragons' attraction to Zipacna. That is all you should take away from that book."

Gradni nodded out of habit. As always, Lays' answer was the expected one. He wondered what perfect answer the assistant would have for the piasa that had not killed him.

"Why are the qui-lahk not fighting the dragons anymore?"

"We do not know if they ever did. They are afraid of the dragons and see no reason to become involved."

"But they believe their ancestors are the ones who killed Zipacna? They have to see some reason?"

"We have approached them many times before and have given up. Not since Delthurk's conception have we received help from any qui-lahk nation. They have done the very least in dealing with the threat even in their own lands. That is how afraid of them they are. It is why we doubt the validity of the story of Zipacna's creation. Clearly, such bravery does not exist in their kind. Now, we have wasted enough time. I came to tell you that it is time to train."

Gradni headed toward the arena. He was done asking Lays questions of any kind. First the piasa, and now this clear breach of knowledge. He was beginning to doubt Delthurk's professed intellectualism on dragons.

Cluthan attacked him with his wooden blade three times. Each time Gradni blocked it.

"Good, now attack,"

Gradni thrust his blade twice toward his master's chest and swept toward his legs. They were the exact same moves he did yesterday, yet he received no criticism for it. It went on for an hour with periodic breaks. Gradni put in the physical effort but allowed himself to fall into habitual movements. It was no less than what he had seen other soldiers do, and Cluthan did not seem to mind today.

"Very good, we will end early today. Tomorrow you will—"

But Cluthan never finished his sentence. Gradni followed his line of sight. The deva was standing at the edge of the pit and was piercing Gradni with his gaze. His dark blue frame contrasted with the pale sand. Gradni had only glimpsed him on the edges of the arena before; this was the first time he was standing inside it.

Gradni had been here long enough to know that the deva was to be respected. He stood up straight. The deva walked softly toward the training equipment, passing Cluthan by a hair without acknowledging him.

"Do you know who I am?" the deva asked while facing the weapons rack.

"Yes," Gradni answered. The deva picked out a wooden disk and turned toward Gradni; the answer was unsatisfactory. "You are Yagura. You are one of the Disciples of Gaorda."

"Do you know who Gaorda was?"

It took Gradni a moment to realize that he did not. He shook his head. The deva suddenly whirled around. Before Gradni knew why, a disc curved into view and clipped his forehead. Gradni stumbled and fell. Dazed, Gradni pushed himself onto his knees with one hand. A strand of his sweaty brown and green hair was discolored by blood. He shook it aside. Yagura was looking back, expressionless—his thin eyes seemingly deepening Gradni's wound.

Gradni grinded his teeth as he looked for the weapon he had dropped. He grabbed it and stood ready to fight.

"Lift your weapon against me and I will break your hand," Yagura said plainly.

Fuming, Gradni froze with his sword tight in his grip. Yagura said nothing more. Gradni let go of his weapon. He shook another bloody strand of hair from his sight.

"Wash yourself and come to my quarters," Yagura said as he left the arena. Cluthan simply watched him go and left by another exit. All the spectators were still watching from the stands.

Gradni stood alone and humiliated in the middle of the arena.

When Gradni walked into Yagura's room, it felt like stepping out of Delthurk and into an unknown world.

The floor was covered with a thin, soft-yellow carpet. Naturally the walls were still made of the stone brick of the castle, but there was not much of it that could be seen. Yagura had covered one wall with paintings, and another with a huge cloth depicting a large gray eagle. Hanging from the eagle's talons was an upside down and lifeless cobra. It had to have been a sesha dragon; the dragon that he had heard little about save that it was extinct.

"Close the door," Yagura said.

Gradni obeyed. Two other items were on either side of the room entrance. The one on the right was a stone bust of someone from the waist up. The figure's muscles were huge and shaped under fitted armor. The helmet was shaped like an eagle head, with its beak hooked over the forehead and wings on either side that reached three inches higher than the rest of it.

The item on the left was even more attractive than the tribute to Gaorda. It was a sheathed sword, resting on the forks of a stand of thin interweaved lines of gold. The handle was wrapped in a soft material for the sake of grip. It was not like any elven swords Gradni had seen. The knob under the handle was silver in color like the hilt, and was shaped like a closed rose flower with short flames imitating its petals. The guard of the hilt was also shaped like a fiery flower, except it was in bloom. The blade that presumably emerged from it was hidden within a sheath. Gradni moved to remove it. An inch would do, just enough to see if the metal matched the beauty of the hilt.

"Do not touch that." Gradni turned immediately to face Yagura while straightening his hands beside him. "That sword was made for a Dragon Slayer. It was wielded with such perfection, that it is disrespectful for anyone not of her greatness to touch it."

Gradni took a step away from the sword. He was back in Delthurk, and back to hating Yagura for treating him like a child. "This was not Gaorda's sword?" Gradni said through pressed teeth.

"No, not Gaorda's. Sit and listen to who Gaorda was before you make any more stupid assumptions." The deva had been looking out the window the entire time. Even now he did not turn around, though Gradni guessed he was watching him through the reflection of the glass. Begrudgingly, Gradni inched toward the chair and sat down to listen.

"A hundred years ago, when there was friction between the races, the capital dev nation welcomed the sesha dragons into our society. We knew they were evil, but we were unafraid. It was the other races that were afraid of them, especially you elves, and we knew we could use that to our advantage. For a long time we were successful, for no one could withstand the combined might of dev and dragon. Even rebels within the capital nation were quelled.

"But we underestimated the evil of the dragons. We thought we tamed them, but evil as theirs cannot be tamed. They fooled us into thinking it so, and we allowed them to roam freely within our nations.

"It was a young Gaorda who realized that they would be our end. He trained and became a kshatriya in his own right. Do you even know what a kshatriya is, boy?"

Gradni shook his head, wondering if he would be berated again for not knowing this culture that was not his. "They are the finest warriors in the dev nations. Ten times the warriors that have ever come from this place. Kshatriya Gaorda recruited others whom he educated on the threat. All this was done initially in secret from the government, for the seshas had infiltrated even the rulers of the nation. Gaorda's disciples slew seshas and began taking our nation back from their influence. Kshatriya Gaorda himself battled their lord, Irath, a sesha dragon that had already killed seven Disciples. He killed the snake, but died soon after from wounds. His sacrifice was not in vain, for the death of the sesha king signaled the end of the sesha dragons.

"Because of his achievement, the second generation of Disciples of Gaorda were able to make allies in government, and we studied the dragons with more freedom and support than before. They learned their habits, their life-style, and their weaknesses.

"The third generation, my generation, used the information to enact their end. We killed them with more ferocity than our predecessors used, and once the sesha's true violent nature surfaced, the capital agreed to their extermination. The seshas' plan had left many of them trapped within our cities instead of the other way around. We struck them there where they could not escape. Some managed despite this, but we lined our borders with soldiers. They killed every dragon that approached. Other Disciples went to the heart of the seshas' base outside of our reign, and annihilated them there. I was one of these. I slew fifteen dragons some days, and killed vicious horned ones on others.

Yagura turned around, "Because of me and mine, not a single sesha is alive. But Gaorda's purpose is not complete, for where the devs have triumphed, others have failed. Serpents, piasas, drakes, salamanders, sobekians, wyverns—they are all alive still!" Yagura pointed accusingly at Gradni. "You are supposed to be the solution, the one who will lead us against them, yet you cannot even evade a discus. You are nothing more than an angry child who thinks he can fight!"

"I can fight!" Gradni yelled back. "I've fought boys older than me and won!"

"And what are boys compared to dragons? You compare your skills to other children and I am supposed to believe that you will be the next Gaorda? You shame him by even thinking it."

"Give me a chance, and I will be greater than he!"

"I give you nothing, just as Gaorda was given nothing!"

"Show me!" Gradni yelled. "Show me how you killed horned dragons and I will do the same. It is what I am here to do!"

"I will not waste my efforts on you. Your master does nothing for you, and you accept it like any other regular soldier. I see no Gaorda here. If you think you can take my training, show me what you can really do. Now leave. We are done."

Gradni's steps were hard as he marched through the castle. He circled the perimeter twice before going to the mess hall where he knew he would find Cluthan.

"You!" Gradni yelled. Cluthan and those he was conversing with looked toward him. "You're meant to train me for three hours today; you owe me at least an hour and a half!"

Speechless, Cluthan got up and followed Gradni to the pit.

For a month Gradni tried to defeat Cluthan, instead of listening to him. Gradni just wanted to be better than him, and he attacked his master at different angles than he was instructed too. Had Cluthan been doing what he was meant to, Yagura would never have embarrassed him. It was Cluthan's own fault for taking him at too slow a pace.

Gradni faked a high strike and twisted the blade to thrust low. Cluthan's hands barely managed to move fast enough to parry it away from the side of his hip.

Gradni was about to swing again when he saw the dark blue of Yagura calmly walking into the arena. He had been training for hours and it was late. A servant had already lit the torches that surrounded the arena. Yagura stepped between Gradni and Cluthan. It took Cluthan a second under Yagura's look to understand that he was no longer needed here. Yagura turned to Gradni.

"Throw that thing in your hand away!" Yagura said. Gradni did so, and took the wooden sword that Yagura handed to him. It was made of a lighter colored wood, and looked similar to the sword in Yagura's quarters. It fell a little once he took it, revealing that it was the same weight as a real sword as well.

"No!" Yagura yelled. "The blade must never touch the ground!"

Gradni nodded as he fought against the will of his aching muscles. "What is it?" he asked.

"It is an imitation jian sword that is mostly made out of bamboo; it is vastly superior to any of your elven weapons. Position your feet apart like this."

Gradni mirrored Yagura's stance, barely in time to defend himself against an attack to the head.

CHAPTER 11

The past was the past. The present was the dragons. The naga grabbed the deer leg from the fire and ripped at the flesh with his top and bottom canines. His friends had used their breath to light the stack of dead wood which they had collected along with the deer.

He longed for the thrill of the hunt, but could not risk being seen by their enemies. Much of their survival rested on the elves not knowing that he existed, and it would take just one look for them to know who his allies were. The naga's skin was made of the same scales as his brethren, though several shades darker. His hair was as black as it always had been, though not as barbarously unkempt as it was now. Only two blade-shaped tufts of hair that grew on either side of his chin gave the illusion that he groomed himself.

Seconds after he consumed his meal, a longue snaked its way through the wind into the crooked entrance of his cave. Though they were not much smaller than wyverns, in many ways longues symbolized better than the other dragons the reasons for the hatred against them. They were creatures naturally of the air the way fish were of the sea. Along the length of their snake like bodies were four wings that were twice the width of their bodies. Even after seeing these wings up close, the races still feared this ability of theirs to remain constantly in the air. The longues also had a natural spade-shaped blade at the end of their tail. They were thought to be evil because of this weapon, as if the various unicorn species did not have a single defensive weapon as well.

The longue hissed. The naga bowed his head. "He will not be coming back," the naga said in his deep voice that overlapped a roar. "We cannot send any more. Too many have died this way already."

The first wyvern who was sent out a couple years ago had been killed; it was clear when they followed his trail that he had discovered the Disciples' then whereabouts. The naga had agreed to let other dragons, either wyvern or longue, try and track their new base, but it was for naught. Dragons either returned after following an artificial trail, or not at all. The Disciples needed to be stopped, but time was running out, and if he could not even find them there would be no chance of stopping their or Ta'ar's influence on Erdūn.

The longue had left without the naga noticing—longue wings didn't even flutter. The naga left his own cave to visit his friend. The dragons watched him as he bounced over them from spire to spire. His feet had adapted to Zipacna by becoming tough and able to bend over rock. This combined with his strength made him faster over the mountain than the salamanders.

He arrived at a cave entrance. A wyvern, serpent, and piasa were keeping his friend company. They were relieved to see the naga. They could leave now that he was here, and no longer have to put up with the salamander's grumbling.

The salamander was covered in a thin veil of blood that was dripping down to the scales that had been shed. He grunted annoyingly as the naga tossed a slab of meat in front of him and sat down. The transformation was painful and time consuming. The naga grinned as he wiped away the fallen scales that the other dragons could not. They all knew that it was coming. Dragons transformed into horned dragons by the decrees of fate, but it was often possible to discern which dragons would undergo the transformation. It was just a question of when. The naga lay down on his back. His friend released a bitter grunt at the other's comfort, letting him know in his own way that the company was appreciated.

Just as the naga was settling in, the wyvern returned, screeching. The salamander growled viciously, but the naga laid his hand upon his back to settle him.

"No!" he ordered.

The salamander growled again, but settled down in admittance that even that effort was painful. They would do without him for this battle. The naga followed the wyvern out of the cave. He watched the phalanx from Delthurk that was at the base of the mountain. For the sake of secrecy he rarely engaged the elves when they first stepped onto the mountains. He was their secret weapon, and that meant that he could not rush into battle. Only when the enemy were at the inner mountains and there was no chance of any of them surviving his attacks would he enter the fray. It was something he had needed to adjust to. Until he did fight himself, it was his duty to observe the enemy, and decide how to command dragons against them. His answer came quickly this time when he saw what they had brought with them. He roared commands to his brethren as he leapt from ledge to ledge toward the charging elves.

The elves never attacked from this mountain ledge before. It was a glacis slope flanked on both sides by high spires and guarded at two places by separate lines of sobekian dragons. Fifty sobekians were all that was ever needed to guard the ridge. As the naga bounded toward them, the elven commander in the front motioned for the entire first line of attackers to weave to the back, and for the lance holders to come forward. There was one seven meter lance for each sobekian, each held by five elves. The sobekians let out their fury. With their arms around the leather bound wood, the lance holders rushed their weapons into the flames. The naga felt a pang of hope when he got closer, as he saw the lances shift momentarily under the pressure of the fire. But with five elves to each lance, the steel points stayed steady enough. The lances pushed through the flames and ripped through the lungs, throats, and hearts of the first line of sobekians. The naga removed his sword from his back and called forth the fire of its blade.

New spears were handed to the lance holders as they realigned themselves for the second line of sobekians that guarded the ridge. They had not seen him yet, so he could still pounce on them from above. Other dragons were coming as well, but would not get there before the attack. The naga was meters from them, yet still not fast enough to stop the hundred and twenty-five holding the lances. He would have to pick which dragons to save.

The elves lifted their spears and began to rush the second line. With their eyes closed to the expectant flames, the naga saw an opportunity. He growled for the sobekians to blow softly, instead of using their full fury the way their fallen brethren had. With his sword surrounded in its own sheath of fire, the naga landed between the sobekians and the oncoming blind elves.

With single powerful sweeps, he moved across and attacked the lances instead of the elves, turning them into short burning stumps. Their eyes still shut; they ran right past him toward the waiting sobekians. The naga turned toward the sobekians as their chests expanded.

The dragons released the full fury of their flames,

blowing all a hundred and twenty-five elves and their ruined spears over the naga. The bodies landed before the last waiting elven phalanx.

It was not just the death of the comrades that held their gaze, but the naga himself as he stood before the smoldering bodies. He shook the more resilient splinters from his fire soaked blade as the elves stared at him. He glared directly at the elven commander. Compelled, the commander came forward, brandishing his sword loosely. With two simple swipes, the naga knocked the other's sword away, then burned a hole into the commander's chest. The elves stood grounded. The naga waited for them to move first.

When they finally attacked a half minute later, The naga knelt down and leapt over the three lines of soldiers to land in the middle of the rattled battalion. He swung his blade mercilessly. No matter in what direction he attacked, his enemies died. His fiery sword traveled entire circumferences around him, cutting through armor and tearing into flesh. When the elves finally began to attack instead of backing away, he was ready for them. He parried their swords and broke their bones with his fist and heels. An elf came toward him shield first; the naga tore the shield from his grip and rammed it edge first into the elf's neck.

There were many of them, but that was their problem. With their leader dead, and their actions hurried by fear, the naga used their disorganization against them.

But he was still one against many, and his fury prevented him from pacing himself. An elf that was calmer than the rest held back and waited for the opportune moment to strike. The naga saw him try to sneak up behind him, but let him be. A red head hooked over the elf's shoulder and sank its fangs into him before yanking him to the ground. A laugh coughed out of the naga as he swung his blade with newfound strength. This was what he was waiting for. The elves were so distracted and afraid of him that they had not watched for the other dragons that were now upon them. The dragons fought furiously. The salamanders, serpents, wyverns, piasas, and he, bit, burned, clawed, and crushed their enemies. Then, all of a sudden, the naga roared for them to retreat. The line of sobekians scrambled away first, then the wyverns and piasas flew away, followed by the serpents, who slithered up the mountains. The naga leapt over the soldiers with the salamanders behind him, and bounded further away from the battle. Flabbergasted, the elves watched them go. The battle was far from over.

The elves regrouped. They could not fathom why the dragons would retreat, unless something had happened that put the dragons at a disadvantage. As the naga hoped, the elves stepped over their fallen comrades and charged up the mountain. The naga leapt onto a high spire to fully reveal himself to the elves coming toward him. Too much had happened for them to still be afraid of him.

But it was not to inspire their fear that he stood before them. His sword was back in its sheath. He surrendered to sadism as he imagined their view, of the two giant horns coming up behind him, followed by the head of the red drake. The red drake rose to the sun and revealed a wingspan that shadowed the Delthurk platoon. The elves in front stood hypnotized, before yelling for their longbow archers to step forward to bring the great beast down. It was strangely anticlimactic for the naga when the elves realized, as green drakes flew up to unite with the red one, that all of their longbow men were already dead. The naga and the other dragons had targeted the archers in the fray. Crossbow archers remained, but their arrows were for the low-flying wyverns, longues, and piasas, and could never reach the height of the drakes. The elves turned and rioted down the mountain as the drakes swooped down. The conflagration fell upon them like a tidal wave.

He stepped toward the split spears and picked up a piece. The wood was different from what Delthurk normally used. Fire burnt out quickly on this material. He threw the shaft down. Olive wood. It was years since he'd seen this in use against dragons. Aristahl had returned to its old habits.

The naga turned away from the stench and walked back up toward his friend's cave. They had lost many- more than they could afford to in the continuing war, but at least they had defended themselves for one more day.

The salamander arched his head as soon as he entered. A couple green scales dropped down from the salamander's cheek. The naga sat down and told him about the battle. Outside the cave, dragons collected the bodies cut by his sword so that his presence would stay a secret.

CHAPTER 12

Mogurn walked between two of his guards toward the Scandar garden. It was important that those gathered here see him formally approach this way. Organizing the two hundred people waiting to hear him had been done by word of mouth from messengers who arrived a week beforehand. Care had been taken to keep the Scandar senators ignorant of his visit.

There were woman and children within the crowd. This was good—for mothers to be afraid for their children because of the dragons. Mogurn's guards took two steps away from him as he stood in front of the audience. Silence spread over the crowd. Mogurn loudly cleared his throat.

"Citizens of Scandar. Thank you for your audience. I come to your nation in part to honor your contributions to our war against the dragons. Without the great warriors that your nation has provided, the dragon threat would be even more dire than it is now, with no hope of it ever ending. Therif, Banten, Yorn, and of course S'freed, whose sword I stand beside—the number of dragons they slew has saved the lives of countless others.

"When the dragons left these lands, they made your rulers think that they were no longer a threat, but those dragons united with others. Though our race understood the need to follow them and build Delthurk beside their new base, and though we have had great heroes who have helped keep their evil at bay, we have made little progress in hurting their numbers. Of late the support of your government and the support of others has lessened. The dragons' scheme to seclude themselves is working too well.

My friends, you have always known of the evil of drakes. Imagine that evil now working with wyverns, sobekians, and the other dragons. Imagine that day when they will return to Scandar in numbers so great that they will not be conquerable, when your children will suffer for our negligence. One of your children has even taken up the fight. Gradni, son of Yorn, has taken the mantle of his father's honor. Of this, you should be proud, elves of Scandar, because I say with all seriousness that this young lad is proving to be a slayer greater than any other we have known. He was wise even at the age of twelve for understanding the great evil we face. Gradni of Scandar fights, and learns, and trains, to be the one who will lead the army that will destroy all the dragons of Zipacna!"

The crowd applauded. Mogurn saw a Scandar senator with eight guards standing behind the crowd. Her arms were crossed.

"It seems my time is over," he declared, gesturing his supporters toward the Scandar senator, "They wish to deny the evil that faces us all, not thinking of how that denial will lead to your slaughter."

That was too much for the Scandar senator. "This gathering is unlawful," she announced suddenly, "disperse, all of you, and go about your business immediately." Her soldiers began urging people to leave as she walked through the center of the dividing crowd toward Mogurn.

"As you are forced to leave," Mogurn yelled, "I ask for you to consider this great evil, and to take action with Delthurk and Gradni to save your legacy from the dragons' fire."

"You are quite the politician." The Scandar senator said to Mogurn as she stood before him."

"Senator Loiree isn't it?" Mogurn said calmly.

"You are going behind out backs now?"

"The last time I was here you said that Scandar does not take the dragon threat seriously enough for you to support it. So I am simply making our people aware."

"We need our soldiers here, Mogurn."

"We need to destroy more of the dragons, so much so, that we are forced to ally with the other races. It may not be ideal for us to fight alongside devs, ameshas, and hopefully qui-lahk, but what choice do we have when our own nations are disillusioned enough to think dragons are not a threat?"

"Do not try these tricks on me, Mogurn. I know your ways."

"Either way, Senator Loiree, I have said what I needed to say." Mogurn got into his carriage.

"I should never have let you take him. Gradni is just an angry boy. Nothing you have been saying about him is true."

"To you that is all he ever was, an angry orphaned boy. I am turning him into something profoundly useful. Good day, Senator."

Mogurn had his rider stir the horses to drown her rebuttal. He was on to the next town. Delthurk elves would infiltrate Scandar in two days, and recruit as many as they could from whom gathered here to see him.

CHAPTER 13

Gradni looked out his window. Drakes were circling above Zipacna. From somewhere deep within the mountains a billowing red smoke was rising into the air. By the books he had read from the library, he knew this was how the dragons celebrated after a successful battle. It was said to be their way of warning others from attacking them. It only made Gradni more determined to fight.

On some days it felt like yesterday when he had first arrived at Delthurk, but as he looked at the drakes through his window without having to stand on his toes, he realized that that day was three years ago.

The three drakes disappeared behind the crooked mountain as the red smoke continued to rise. Gradni took hold of his wooden jian sword and left his room for the arena. Yagura had been his master for almost two years now and still had not given him a real jian. Several other dragon slayers had come to Delthurk in that time due to Mogurn and his recruitment efforts. Gradni had watched them all train. They all had specialized weapons depending on which dragons they fought in their respective homeland. Some used spears, others used axes, and some even used knives. They were all better fighters than the soldiers, but just by observing them Gradni could tell that though they might be marginally better than himself, they were no match for the skill and speed of Yagura. Gradni had still not managed to lay a single successful attack against his deva master, and Yagura never let him forget that. But Gradni still had more respect for the other slayers. At least they were ready to march into battle. For how much Yagura boasted on his past fights with the dragons and how much better he would always be than Gradni, Yagura had not yet battled on Zipacna. Too much was done on Yagura's whims to keep him happy. Gradni's training sessions changed times almost daily. They could be in the morning, afternoon, evening, and sometimes even at night. It all depended on the deva's mood. Two months ago when Gradni was with a tutor, Lays burst in and told him to rush to the arena. By the time Gradni had run up to his room for his weapon and then down to the arena, Yagura had already left. Gradni kept his sword with him all the time after that.

Yagura glared at Gradni when he arrived.

"Hurry! You are late."

Gradni calmed himself with measured breathing. He wasn't late at all. "I am sorry, master."

"My time is not something to toy with."

"It will not happen again."

Yagura took out his weapon. "Let us see if you have at least learned anything from yesterday." He drove his sword forward. Gradni parried it away and attacked back.

Gradni bent his back leg and leaned back in time to avoid Yagura's sword, barely able to keep his balance through a concentrated effort of wind channeling. He directed the wind through his arm as he swung his own sword forward forcefully. Yagura was not there to get hit by it, and before Gradni knew it his master was behind him. Gradni felt a thud against the base of his neck. His head snapped forward as he fell on one knee from the blow. Gradni gritted his teeth as he reaffirmed his grip. He swung his blade back around him, but it was blocked at the hilt almost immediately into his swing. Then, Gradni felt both his feet fly upward as he fell onto his back, winded. He had repeated the same mistake he did yesterday; his anger made his moves predictable.

The curved wood of Yagura's sword dug beneath Gradni's chin. Practice sword or not, the deva could kill him with a single thrust. The wooden tip itched against Gradni's chin and stayed there for what seemed like an hour before Yagura pulled it away.

Keeping his sword close to his body so that it would not touch the ground, Gradni rolled onto his knees and steadied himself with his free hand. Yagura was already walking away. As it had been for the last six months, the lesson ended whenever Gradni let his anger control him.

Yagura knew what he was doing. On days such as today it seemed that he was more interested in infuriating Gradni than training him. Just once, Gradni wanted a lesson to end without being made to feel like a failure. He knew he was getting better, and heard as such from everyone except Yagura. Even the number of spectators watching him train had increased, and just four days ago he would have never thought to evade Yagura's swing the way he did tonight. Why was there a need to humiliate him in front of a crowd?

Gradni rested on a window ledge above the castle entrance and watched the league of carriages entering the main gate. For the past couple months more and more people were coming to Delthurk. Most of them were young-not as young as Gradni, but young enough to not have been soldiers for long. Gradni watched the current batch of sixty walk from the gate to the castle entrance below him. It was something to do before having to meet with his history tutor.

His session was a half hour away. There was always plenty of time to bathe and make his way to the basement library where his lessons were held, but Gradni was consistently arriving later and later. He still had not told anyone of the piasa he had seen some years back, and was glad of it. They would twist the incident into something that it was not. The history classes he was forced to take had not been believable since. He was already training to become their dragon slayer; there was no need for them to bore him with details as to why it was important.

He wanted to remain here and gaze upon the new soldiers, but no excuse would work this time as the historian had already spotted him from below. It was still grating that Lays had managed to find a replacement.

Seeing the new people coming in was always interesting to Gradni. They reminded him of when he arrived and was still fascinated with this place. He wondered if they would lose their admiration of Delthurk as quickly as he did.

It had fallen to Gradni's old master Cluthan to work with the new soldiers to keep their skills sharp. Whatever Mogurn and the other senators were saying on their visits, it was working. The new soldiers looked up at him as they passed below. Some even pointed. Gradni realized that they knew of him before coming here. Everyone at Delthurk knew of him—that much Gradni took extreme pride in, but for newcomers to know him as well? He had no idea his fame stretched that far.

The gate started to close. The grating of the heavy wood reminded Gradni to leave for his lesson. He was already late, but there was a limit to how much he could stretch that. The historian's only purpose for being here was him, and trouble could start if he went too far. He eased off the ledge, when a whisper of familiarity rubbed against his ears. He leaned out again much further, and searched with both ears and eyes until they met on someone that caused his heart to skip a beat. Gradni ran for the stairs.

He pushed his way through the new soldiers to close in on his mark. He pushed with such ferocity that others turned toward him, including the one he was looking for. The young soldier stood up straight and swallowed. Gradni came right up to him and looked back at the familiar small button eyes and short nose. Sadism peeled his lips apart.

"Ferklen? It is you!"

"Gradni," the soldier replied.

Gradni stepped closer and eyed the new recruit from toe to head. There was now only a couple of inches in height difference between them. Gradni took pleasure in not having to tilt his head back as he had to in Scandar. Up close, Ferklen's hair was still the curly mix of brown and yellow that it was years ago when they fought, and though he had some more muscle now, he was still as lanky as he was before. "What are you doing here, Ferklen?"

"The same as you, Gradni," Ferklen stuttered. "I am here to fight the dragons."

"Dragon Slayer, Ferklen. That is my title. You will address me as Dragon Slayer."

There was a brief pause. Gradni continued to smile at the other, challenging him to not say it.

"Of course. Dragon Slayer." Ferklen exhaled. "Scandar is proud of you and the esteem you have brought our town."

"I am sure." An angry shout directed at Ferklen came from behind Gradni. It was Cluthan. All the other new recruits had passed the two of them. "You should follow your orders, Ferklen. I'll find you later. Perhaps in training. I am sure that you have gotten better by now?"

"Yes. Yes, Gr-Dragon Slayer, it will be an honor to train with you," Ferklen stammered. He ran to catch up to the others.

Gradni watched him do so greedily. He only remembered a minute later where he was meant to be. He shrugged it off and decided to investigate the changes that were happening instead. Too much time had passed to meet the historian now anyway.

He bathed before visiting the lower halls of the castle. Mogurn had managed to get more gold from his touring as well as more men. A new barracks was being constructed next to the arena, but until it was ready, the lower halls of the castle was serving as the temporary dorms for the new recruits. Before returning to his own room for the night, Gradni found out where Ferklen was staying so that he could track him down later.

―――――――◦《◉》◦―――――――

Knock, knock.

Gradni's eyes sprung open. It was dark. Even the Zipacna Mountains outside his window were barely visible. All he could see were the tiniest of sparks outlining the mountains' edges.

Knock, knock, knock!

Gradni kicked off his blanket. There was a faint light under his door. Perhaps it was Ferklen, come to settle his debt. He had chosen a terrible hour for it. Gradni got out of bed and pulled the door wide open, eager to oblige.

But it was not Ferklen; instead he saw the reddened hair

of Lays. The assistant backed away a little at the ferocity of the opening door. He was somehow carrying a lit candle as well as his tome.

"Sir Gradni," Lays spluttered.

"Lays? What is it?"

"Sir Gradni, you missed your lesson in history today." Gradni did not know how to respond. This was why he had been woken?

"I don't know how late it is, Lays, but master Yagura could send for me in a couple hours for training. You know how he is! Why was there a need to wake me?"

"You cannot miss your history lessons!"

"That is why you are here?" Gradni yelled. "The lessons serve no point. What difference does it make knowing about dragons and elves who have already died? How can we trust if those stories are even true?"

"Sir Gradni! You must know what has happened, so that you know the importance of your task."

"I am doing my task regardless. I train every day! I have no time for myself as is. You wake me because I did not go for one lesson?"

"They are important, Sir Gradni!"

"Fine!" Gradni spat, annoyed at the argument itself. "May I go back to sleep now?"

Lays nodded. He turned around and started walking away.

"Lays!" Gradni yelled, bringing the assistant back around. "If you ever wake me again, I will tell master Yagura that you interfered with his training of me."

Lays' mouth opened but no words came out. When it was clear that he would say nothing, Gradni shut the door.

CHAPTER 14

While a devi inspected the supplies, Bamay followed the guide that Sheemu sent for her. The Disciple didn't notice that Bamay and the guide weaved around the palace instead of toward it. She had been getting away with it for months now. Each time Bamay came to Aristahl to collect, a different Disciple came with her, so if there was any suspicion, it didn't carry over. But the thought of being discovered was still heavy on Bamay. Ta'ar would not hesitate to cast her out of her son's life if the Disciples wished it.

She and the Aristahl guide mounted the horses that had been left for them, and rode off toward the stables where Minister Sheemu was waiting.

It felt good to return to Aristahl even for this short while. Since abandoning the tower, they had been moving from place to place so rapidly that Bamay did not know what her body was adapting to. She had gone through deserts, forests, and grasslands, and each ecosystem affected her body differently. Right now, her legs were shorter, her hips were slightly wider, and her fingers were extended. Thus, despite the decline of her old kingdom, it was good to come across a place where she recognized the changes that were happening.

She heard the monstrous *neigh* before they reached the stables. She became fearful when the roaring continued. It was only by instinct that she urged her horse forward when he hesitated.

They continued on until the restlessness of their horses convinced them that she walk the rest of the short way. The ground here was even more barren. She felt no life coming into her as she passed the multiple olive tree stumps.

Sheemu was several feet away, her arms folded as she faced the wooden enclosure. Dust reverberated off the fence as the beast inside attacked it. Through the wide wooden bars, Bamay saw an eye that was three times the size of hers. The eye saw her as well, and for a brief moment the beast ceased to move. Sheemu looked back to see what had caused the silence. The beast started trampling again. Bamay could see at least ten big amesha men in the cage trying to control the creature with ropes.

"Bamay!"

"He is perfect, Sheemu. How long do you estimate it will be before he is tame?"

"Bamay!" Sheemu repeated, drawing her attention from the caged beast. Lines of frustration were seeped into her gray face. "We must talk."

Bamay and Sheemu relocated to a meeting room in the palace. Bamay looked outside the window while Sheemu paced. Sheemu had already given Bamay the silver, and the Disciple was waiting. Every minute that went by risked suspicion.

"Seven of our men died capturing that monster. Many others were injured," Sheemu stated.

"That is tragic. Their sacrifice will not be in vain."

"What do you plan to do with this beast?"

"I will ensure that our spirit and glory will return to Aristahl."

"So you have said. How so?"

"Sheemu, after all this time, you should trust that what I do, I do to serve Aristahl."

Sheemu winced. "It seems the more we do for Aristahl, the more we ruin it. You say that Erdūn is growing very quickly with Ta'ar's magic. As monstrous as the karkadan is, by the time Erdūn is ready to go into battle, he will be a giant and too big even for it, and you want the beast ready long before Erdūn will be, so who are we taming this beast for?"

"We made an arrangement, Minister Sheemu. All you need to know is that I will deliver on it. I do not like this sudden suspicion of my methods."

"I am not like the others, Bamay. I do not know what you are ready to do, but I know your real reasons for doing so, and it is not for Aristahl."

"To serve Erdūn and Ta'ar is to serve Aristahl. So far you have not betrayed the Fire Spirit by spending gold on capturing the karkadan. But if you stop now before we finish—and throw away all the effort and lives that have been sacrificed—there will be repercussions from Ta'ar. We have no choice now but to carry on."

"Will Aristahl become more able?"

"If you can tame the karkadan, then yes. Will you do it?"

They stared at each other—each pair of eyes searching for answers within the other—until Sheemu turned to the window. The Disciple was waiting impatiently for Bamay.

"You should go before she starts to wonder where you are. I will continue with the karkadan."

Bamay left the room. In the solitude of the palace corridors she took several breaths. Erdūn and Aristahl were closely bonded, so at least for now Sheemu would not work against her, despite her true suspicions. Bamay would have to act quickly. She was going to Delthurk next. It was her hope to return to her son soon after, but that was now an unrealistic goal. She would have to stay at Delthurk and look for opportunities to bring her plan to fruition.

CHAPTER 15

With a tray of bread and bowl of venison stew in his hands, Gradni passed by all the empty seats in favor for the one person who had been ostracized. The people of Delthurk had come to know about his past history with Ferklen, and were avoiding Ferklen out of respect.

"You do not mind if I sit with you, do you Ferklen?" Gradni said.

Ferklen choked on his bread. "No, of course not, Dragon Slayer! It will be an honor."

Gradni sank into the corner seat beside Ferklen, forcing the other to move his tray away. He tore his bread and shoved the pieces into his mouth with spoonfuls of the runny stew. He was not used to eating this late. For a week he had been coming to the hall at different times, trying to catch Ferklen.

"I knew I would see you again when I decided to come here," Ferklen said. "It is an honor. We hear so much about you in Scandar."

"Why are you here, Ferklen?" Gradni said with his mouth full. "Tell me honestly."

"I am here for the same reason you are here, to slay dragons."

"When did Scandar start to care about the dragon threat?"

"I was not sent by Scandar; none of us were sent by our nations. We came on our own will after hearing the Delthurk senators tell us of the seriousness of the dragon threat. It was the honorable Mogurn, the one who found you, who came to Scandar. You are well known, Gradni. Even before Mogurn came for us, we knew of your success. Many of us are here because of you.

"I am sorry, Dragon Slayer," Ferklen added, "For how I treated you in Scandar. I ask your forgiveness."

Gradni laid down his spoon. "What did he say about the dragons that made you come here?"

The question caught Ferklen by surprise. "Everything that you already know I am sure—of their history against us, their innate evil, and how they will kill you on sight whenever they can."

"You believe him?"

"Yes. I don't understand, Dragon Slayer. Don't you?"

Gradni leaned away from his tray and looked past it for several moments.

"Come with me," Gradni demanded. He rose from his chair and started walking away. Ferklen was still sitting with his fingertips on the table. He looked halfway up.

"I do not want to fight you, Dragon Slayer."

Gradni came back to the table. "I already fought you before and beat you then. I don't need to do so again. Come with me. I want to show you something."

At the far end of the record hall, the names of all of Delthurk's deceased Dragon Slayers were imprinted on plaques and plastered on the wall. By height, they were ranked by the number of dragons they had slain. Gradni lit the torches along the wall with the one in his hand.

"Are you sure we are allowed here now, at this time?" Ferklen asked.

"I am. My day is different every day, so Lays gave me a key." Gradni raised his torch to illuminate the higher names that the other torchlight could not reach. "Look."

"Yorn," Ferklen read. "Your father. I already know that he too was a knight of Delthurk. Mogurn believes, as we all do, that you will be a greater dragon slayer than even he."

Gradni brought the torch down. He spoke softly. "Stop calling me Dragon Slayer for a moment and listen. When I saw that my father had killed over fifty dragons I spent my nights reading the logbooks in the library to find out more. But my father slew maybe twenty dragons, if that. That is all. He did not come close to slaying as many as that plaque says."

"I do not understand."

"They moved the plaque up." Gradni brought the light back to the wall, revealing a gap between the names of two other slayers that had killed twenty dragons. "After I got here, they moved it, not thinking I would look any deeper."

The crackling of the fire from the torch was loud in the otherwise silent hall.

"What are you trying to tell me," Ferklen said, "that because Mogurn lied about this that he lies about everything? That the dragons are not sinful creatures?"

"Of course not! Of course they are evil. I just wanted to show you this. It is late. I have to wake up early tomorrow." With Ferklen following, Gradni left the record hall and locked it behind them. "I haven't told anyone else about this. It would be better if you didn't either."

CHAPTER 16

As Mogurn's carriage rolled into the qui-lahk city, he took offense to the odor that drafted in. There were elephants everywhere in this place; some were even walking side by side with qui-lahk. The qui-lahk had a strange connection with animals. Though they were empowered by all the animals around them, each qui-lahk had an acute connection to a particular species. They called this animal their *totem* animal, and this particular city was built for qui-lahk's who lived alongside their elephant totems.

They were an alien people to Mogurn, but they needed to be brought into the war, and the qui-lahk of the war elephant tribe were the best ones to begin with.

An elephant larger than the others was coming toward them. Mogurn's elf guards became restless.

"Stop!" Mogurn whispered harshly to them before they could take out their shields. They could not show any fear of hostility while here. "Move away from me." He commanded.

The beast stopped, seemingly without any direction to do so. It's rider threw down a rope ladder and descended.

The man's skin was the color of dark bronze, though not as dark as the amesha Bamay's. He was taller than Mogurn by an inch. His hair was dark, but had a bluish tone to it. This was something else that made them strange. Their hair did not change color by the seasons or even by the time of day, and all qui-lahk hair was the same, except for an insignificant discoloration like this one's bluish-gray hue.

"I am Tikal," the qui-lahk stated in his deep voice.

"Greetings, Tikal, I am Senator Mogurn."

"Your guards can stay here," Tikal said before walking toward a hut.

"Very well," Mogurn replied, for the benefit of his guards who were looking up with distrust at the elephant that stood over them.

His back turned to Mogurn; Tikal removed his coat, revealing black tusk-shaped marks that ran down each of his arms. Whenever a qui-lahk came of age, such marks appeared that displayed their totem animal. Mogurn looked away in disgust. He had come across qui-lahk before, but their marks were never so vivid. It must be from being surrounded by their totem.

"I know why you are here, and I know even some of what you will say to convince us." Tikal talked plainly.

"I know that you must recognize that we are from Delthurk from our insignia, but I wish for the opportunity to tell you what new developments there have been. I believe that it will affect your decision to join us."

Tikal sat down on a stool and stared idly at Mogurn. "You have a boy at Delthurk now—I do not know his name, but you are training him to become a dragon slayer unlike any other. He is going to be the one who will lead your army against Zipacna. Is this so?"

Mogurn's eyes narrowed. "It is. His name is Gradni. How do you know all this? I cannot believe that word could have spread this far so soon."

"The places that you have visited thus far—the animals around understood traces of what was said. They communicated enough to us for some to become curious and discover the information ourselves. We have been told by the other tribes to let it be. The crow tribe already warned us that you would come to recruit us first, and that you plan to go to the eagle tribe next."

"This is true. Yours and the eagle tribe used to show such tenacity in dealing with the dragons."

"Going to the eagle tribe will be for naught. They are far too connected with the other tribes who wish to stay out of this conflict."

"And what of your tribe, Tikal?"

Tikal took a breath. "We too should not cross them."

"And yet you did not turn me away upon sight. Why did you bring me here to talk in private? There is some desire in you to join us. You have taken up arms against the dragons in the past."

"Rarely, and each time we were chastised for it. The other tribes are afraid of the retaliation. These dragons are demonic perversions of our totems."

"Then join us, Tikal, so that we may end them."

"The only way we can join you is if there will be no risk of retaliation from the dragons. I will find out who amongst our numbers are willing to join you on Zipacna, but it will only be for the final battle when we do irrevocable damage to them, when there will be no risk of the fight being brought to us and the rest of the qui-lahk. I also want to see this boy of yours in person before agreeing to anything. These are the only terms I offer you."

Mogurn adjusted his robe. "Then I guess that that will have to do. Seeing as how you know the politics of the qui-lahk tribes, would you have any insight at all into how I should proceed with them?"

"Yes. Do not. Do not even go to the eagle tribe. If you do then we will be watched more closely, which will make it more difficult for me to find you allies. There are some amongst my own tribe who will join you. But finding them will be easier without the other tribes' interference."

"Understood, Tikal, but you are asking me to rely solely on you for qui-lahk support, and I do not even have a guarantee. Why shouldn't I take my chances and approach the other tribes directly instead?"

"I am not asking you to do anything. I am advising. You may ignore my advice, but were you even expecting success when you came here, Senator Mogurn?"

"No, Tikal. I was not."

"You will receive none from the other qui-lahk tribes in this area. We are your best chance of bringing them to you. But as a token of faith... confirm this for me; we have done our research into your war on Zipacna. I understand that there is a horned drake that is causing you much trouble?"

"Yes. The red monster has killed many of us and often keeps our forces at bay. We are trying to figure out how to destroy that beast. But have had no success."

Tikal stood up. "Come to me with proof that you have a sizeable army and a scheme, and that this boy is all you say he is, and I promise you a means of dealing with that dragon."

Tikal's last words haunted Mogurn on the return journey to Delthurk. Gradni was going to become a great warrior, but the qui-lahk were now expecting someone far more superior. Gradni's fame had outdone his capability. He was still just a boy, as senator Loiree of Scandar had said. It had never been a problem before, but Mogurn never expected him to also be the key to recruiting the qui-lahk. If they truly had a means of dealing with the horned drake, then that possibility had to be explored. But how was a mere boy going to convince the qui-lahk to fight with them?

CHAPTER 17

Don't do it

"**D**on't do it!" Ferklen shouted. Gradni shoved him aside and marched through Scandar. He saw the Scandar castle, the fields and gardens, and the orphanage. "Leave him alone; he has nothing to do with it! He was only looking out for me!" Ferklen grabbed Gradni's shoulder. Gradni, dressed in the armor of S'freed, whirled around and punched Ferklen in the gut before pushing him to the ground. *Stop. Stop.* He went forward again and kicked the door open. Ferklen's father was inside. Gradni pinned Ferklen's father against the wall, then placed the point of his imitation jian sword against his knee. *This is wrong, stop doing this, stop doing this now.* Ferklen wrapped himself around Gradni's leg. "Please, please, lord Dragon Slayer, he is my father. Please!"

Gradni let Ferklen try to pull him away while facing the father—*stop, stop yourself now!*—and drove the sword right through the knee.

Gradni awoke slowly. He curled up on his side. When that did not help he sat up. Through the whole dream he did not want to do it. And yet he did despite Ferklen begging him not to. No; Gradni knew himself better. It was not de-spite, but because of it. He pulled the sheets over him and closed his eyes tight. An hour later he was still too haunted by the dream to fall asleep. He kicked off his sheets and snuck out of his room.

It was dark, but there were always enough lit torches in the castle corridors to guide him outside. Gradni then made his way to the newly made soldiers' dormitory. He found Ferklen asleep like everyone else, and nudged him.

"Ferklen! Ferklen, wake up!"

Ferklen awoke and jumped away from Gradni. "Gr-Dr— What do you want?" he wheezed.

Gradni looked around while Ferklen caught his breath. No one else had woken up. It was bizarre how Ferklen could sleep with so much snoring around him. Then again, Gradni himself had managed while at the orphanage a lifetime ago.

"Ferklen, I'm sorry for hurting your father."

"What?"

"Your father—I am sorry for breaking his knee. I should never have done it."

Ferklen eased into a sitting position. The light was dim and he had not completely adjusted to it. He looked around before turning his attention back to Gradni. "It is in the past, Gradni. It took some months to heal, but you did not break it. Why do you think that you did? It would have healed quicker, in fact, if he had not stubbornly walked on it as much as he did."

"I remember him telling me that I broke it. I'm sure of it!"

"Who did?"

Gradni backed away from the bed. It was years ago. Had he imagined what Mogurn told him? There was a lapse in the communal snoring. "I still should not have hit him as hard as I did."

"It is in the past, Gradni."

Gradni's lips twitched as he backed away from the bed and toward the exit. Even back then Mogurn had lied to him. What other lies were going on around him that he was not aware of? As he was on his way back to the castle, the gate to Delthurk opened for a single carriage, the same carriage that brought him here years ago. Senator Mogurn had returned.

CHAPTER 18

Since Mogurn's return, Gradni spent less time with Ferklen and more in his room where Mogurn could find him. But the senator had been back for months now and still had not called on him.

When Gradni got to the arena for his lesson with Yagura, there were almost a hundred others in the stands. None of them were Mogurn. Gradni took out his bamboo jian and warmed up as Yagura walked into the arena. He walked slowly toward Gradni, before swiftly sweeping his weapon toward Gradni's feet. Gradni skipped over it and swung his weapon toward his master, while the surrounding elves came to the edge of the stands to watch.

Yagura trained as he always did, teaching through humiliation by sweeping Gradni to the floor. Each time, Gradni flipped back onto his feet and pushed the shame aside. As the minutes and clacks passed, Gradni realized that more and more attacks were being made toward his feet in attempts to make him lose his composure. Yagura was becoming frustrated, and thus predictable.

Gradni did not let on that he was seeing a pattern in Yagura's moves, and allowed himself to be swept to the floor to encourage it.

Yagura would skip to the right while swiping a low arc, the style and fluidity in the move making it look simple and thus all the more humiliating. Each time Yagura did this in the midst of the swordplay, Gradni studied the maneuver to figure out the best way to counter it.

The two danced around each other, bamboo swords clacking rhythmically. Gradni stepped back; from here he could thrust straight or attack overhead. Thrusting would be the usual, better option. Gradni attacked overhead. Yagura sidestepped to the right as Gradni knew he would. Gradni jumped without even seeing Yagura's weapon sweep underneath him. In the air, Gradni turned and wind channeled his sword in a vicious arc.

Finally, after three years, Gradni struck Yagura with his weapon and knocked him back several feet. A sudden yell shot out of Yagura. Gradni stood back with his sword aligned beside his eyes and over his shoulder. Yagura was thrashing his weapon around. Gradni waited for the yelling and angry sword movement to subside.

When it did, Gradni let his gaze wander to Yagura's chest. It was evening, and thus Yagura was already close to being dark blue. Yet there was a streak across his chest that was becoming darker due to a bruise. If Gradni was wielding a real sword, it would have been a killing blow. Gradni reaffirmed his grip and sprung forward.

"Stop!" Yagura yelled. Gradni skidded inches from where he landed. One of Yagura's hands was uncurled in front of him.

"What?" Gradni yelled back.

"Enough swordplay. It is time to move on to our other lesson."

"Now?"

"Yes. Now!"

Gradni pulled back as if his sword was the weight of a mountain. "Yes, master." He scowled.

Yagura walked toward the weapon rack. Gradni took

deeper breaths to calm himself. The discs started flying toward him. Gradni ducked the first few and brandished his sword against the others.

"Use your sword more instead of avoiding. How will you kill dragons if you run away from them?"

Yagura was not even throwing that many discs, or throwing them as quickly as he usually did. Gradni had had enough. It was not a lesson anymore. Yagura was trying to belittle him in front of everyone after failing to do so during the sword fight. He was purposely making it seem that Gradni could not handle a more rapid series of attacks.

Gradni let go of his sword and knocked two discs aside with his leather armbands.

Yagura stopped. His eyes squinted. "I told you to strike them with your sword," Yagura said, bewildered.

"Then you should throw them faster."

Yagura said nothing. He strode toward Gradni, drawing metal knives from his arm sheaths. Gradni smirked and picked up his wooden jian to meet the challenge. With a sudden dash and a movement of each hand, Yagura hurled himself at Gradni, knocked him and his sword to the ground with the blunt end of one knife, and then placed the other knife at his neck. Gradni coughed and looked at Yagura, who moved in closer.

"The discs are the jaws of a dragon, and you hit those open jaws with your arms?"

"If they are the jaws of dragons, then they are too slow to be a threat."

"I am your master! You will do as I say!"

"You told me to stay calm in battle. I have done that. What about you, master?"

Yagura stood up and backed away. By the time Gradni stood up, Yagura was already halfway toward the exit.

"Where are you going? We are not done yet!"

But Yagura kept walking. The entire arena watched him leave. Gradni picked up his sword and rested it on his shoulder. He went back to his room, where Mogurn could reach him.

Gradni followed Lays up the stairs toward the senators' floor. For the past year, Gradni had seen Lays so sporadically that he only just noticed that he was now much taller than the elder elf. Once past the guards, Lays stood aside so that Gradni could enter Mogurn's office alone.

"Shut the door." Mogurn was crooned over his desk in the corner, his bluish-white hair falling around his ears. Gradni obeyed before looking around the room. It was bigger than he expected, larger even than the library. There were no ornaments on the walls. Mogurn apparently did not feel a need to parade his heritage like Yagura did. The desk, though, looked special, a dark wood with curved, sculpted legs.

"So this is where you work," Gradni said, as he strolled toward him. Mogurn's face was discolored. Yagura had probably marched straight here from the arena.

"Sit, Gradni." Gradni hesitated before doing so. The senator had not called him by his title. Mogurn looked up from his desk. "The deva is here by his own will. Apart from being your master, he is a valued ally in ways you do not even know. You will kneel before him and apologize for your behavior."

"I will not!"

"Yes you will!"

"He was wasting my time."

"He is your master. He has slain countless dragons. However he wishes to make you a warrior is his right to do so. If it seems that he is wasting time, then it is his to waste."

"No. I am your dragon slayer, not him."

Mogurn grew angrier. "What you are not yet, and will be is what we are making you," Mogurn stated matter-of-factly, stressing on the word *we*.

Gradni broke eye contact for a second. "It does not matter. New soldiers are coming here because of me. Nations are also giving more for the cause because of me. I know how important I am to this place. I will not kneel to him. The sooner I am able to fight the better. When my time is wasted then Delthurk's is wasted. If he was loyal to the cause he would know that."

Mogurn rubbed his jaw uncomfortably. He spoke a minute later.

"Just do not disrespect him again. Now get out of here."

Gradni strolled out as Lays walked in. The door was immediately shut.

CHAPTER 19

Bamay could not help but admire the elf boy as she stood outside Yagura's room. There was a rebellious fire within him, a burning independence that her son lacked. Ta'ar invested his fire into Erdūn every day to make him stronger and invulnerable—but this fire was not Erdūn's own like Gradni's was.

She had taken more abuse than Gradni had, but never struck back, not like Gradni had just done to Yagura. She thought she was of no use to the Disciples of Gaorda, but like Gradni, she served a purpose. The Disciples had no compassion; they would have discarded her long ago if she was truly useless. They needed her as the amesha link to Aristahl. She knew that fact well enough to abuse their trust. It should not have taken the elf boy to make her aware of it. The audience had been in awe of Gradni. As soon as he left with his wooden sword carried on his shoulder, the arena became noisy with all the talk about their rising dragon slayer. He had angered the resident Disciple of Gaorda. He had done what none of them dared ever do and became an instant hero. When the time came, they would follow him up the Zipacna Mountains, regardless of Erdūn's superior physical strength. She could not blame them after the boy's display of audacity, but she had given up too much to betray Erdūn now by not acting. As worthy as Gradni was to have gained such a following, he just gave her the opportunity she had been waiting months for.

It had only been a couple hours since Gradni had shamed Yagura.

Bamay knocked on Yagura's door. There was no answer. "Kshatriya Yagura, it is Bamay."

"What do you want?" Yagura yelled through the door.

"To talk about Erdūn and Gradni. The elf boy has shown his true nature. He will divide us all unless we act."

The door opened halfway. "What do you propose be done about it?"

"I would rather discuss it in private, away from the elves."

There was another moment of silence before Yagura walked back inside.

"Come in," he said.

CHAPTER 20

One thing Gradni could not bear was standing still. Doing so with his arms outstretched while others fitted him was worse still, and embarrassing. He had heard rumors about this amesha dragon slayer, but this amount of formality seemed ridiculous. Below him were the bobbing heads of elves who were wrapping him like a mannequin in leather and steel. Mogurn was standing a couple feet away with his hand on his chin.

"Is this really necessary?" Gradni spat. Mogurn did not answer. Gradni huffed and fidgeted till the tailors finished. He looked at himself in the mirror and fought an overwhelming grin. Thin leather was strapped loosely around his entire frame to provide him mobility around his joints. They doubled as soft backing to the pieces of steel that were also strapped to him. Engraved upon each plate was the insignia of Delthurk—the drake with a spear through its chest and dead wings outstretched. It was even on the backs of his hands. It was spring, so the dark green of his hair was thicker than ever, and only a shade darker than the images of the drake.

He turned to look at his cape which ended at his knees. It had the same insignia splashed upon it, but on a purple background instead of a sepia one like the plates. This is what he would wear when he would finally go into battle.

"Come now." Mogurn ordered. Gradni grumbled and

followed the senator. An entourage of senators and soldiers crowded around the two of them as they made their way. By the time they exited the castle, there were around twenty people surrounding Gradni. Mogurn spoke again, either just to Gradni or to the entire group- it was harder to read him since Gradni's incident with Yagura almost a year ago. "Do not speak out of turn with these people. They provide us with everything that we need."

Approaching them was a crowd of outsiders as large as theirs. They all had fair blue skin, and hair that was glistening brown in the sunlight. If he had never seen Yagura at this time of day before this moment, Gradni would not have been able to tell that they were devs. Each of them was wearing armor that was identical to the set in Yagura's room. He had never seen so much gold-colored armor. Both groups slowed as they came closer. Central to the other group was a dark skinned young man whose hair was so thick it looked like black liquid. It was the first amesha that Gradni had ever seen. He knew his name to be Erdūn. Erdūn was meant to be younger than Gradni by five years, yet when the two groups stood before each other, Erdūn was less than two inches shorter than Gradni. Part of it was due to how long Erdūn's legs were. From the books that Gradni read about amesha dragon slayers, he knew that ameshas physically adapted to the land the same way that elves took their strength from the weather. But even so, this ability of theirs had its limits. Much of this amesha boy's height was his own. Gradni felt small despite his armor. Erdūn was bulky. He had large and intimidating facial features, except for his lips that were so small and tightly closed, that Gradni wondered if he ever spoke. Surprising himself, Gradni bowed first. The young Amesha did the same.

A devi came forward. Gradni looked toward her, noticing that Yagura was standing with them.

"What is your name, elf dragon slayer?" she asked. Gradni flinched. He had never been referred to by his race before, not even by Yagura.

"Gradni."

"And your age?"

"Sixteen."

"You are old. How many dragons have you slain?"

"None," Gradni said softly, then stuttered an, "as yet."

She nodded. "And you think you can?"

"I know it," Gradni said, now angry. They truly were Yagura's people. Who were they to question him? How could they think that he was already killing dragons? The devi nodded once more and glanced at the senators before falling back in line. Gradni waited for a senator from his side to quiz Erdūn in retaliation. None did. It was possible that they had done this earlier. Either that or they saw no need to test him.

After some forced conversation the two forces stepped back from each other.

"We have had a long journey," the devi began, "and we must retire for today. We thank you for your hospitality, and for allowing Erdūn the sole use of your arena during tonight's late hours."

More words of forced kindness were said as Lays moved to guide the visitors to their quarters. Gradni's group of senators and guards turned and began to walk away. Gradni walked with them before suddenly turning back.

"How many have you killed?" he yelled. After a pause Erdūn faced him.

"Four. Two wyverns, a salamander, and a serpent." He turned back at the ushering of the devi. Mogurn pulled on Gradni. The other senators went their separate ways within the castle. Gradni turned to Mogurn as soon as they were alone.

"How did he come across four dragons?" Mogurn ignored him. "Mogurn!"

Mogurn gritted his teeth. "The first wyvern he killed they caught themselves. The other three- Delthurk captured alive. It happens rarely. In this many years those were the only three we ever captured."

"And you sent them to him? I am your Dragon Slayer!"

"They provide for us; thus Yagura decides what to do with them. He had them all sent to Erdūn."

"I should have gotten them!"

Mogurn winced. "The serpent, the last one we captured, was during our latest skirmish with them a year ago. It was here for days, as Yagura had not decided what to do with it. He sent it to Erdūn right after you were rude to him. You are actually fortunate that he did so. Otherwise he would have found another way to strike back at you. I warned you never to cross him."

"What do they even do, these Disciples, besides send others into battle?"

"Enough," Mogurn whispered harshly. "I must go and make preparations. Our guests will be here awhile. Remember, do not cross them." Mogurn left. Gradni watched him until he went round a bend.

"I'll do whatever I want."

For the past several months, Yagura had been spending less time training Gradni in swordplay and more in evasion. He recruited others to help him. Men held torches while others spat oil into them to imitate dragon fire. It had originally been rather silly, but the exercises became increasingly sophisticated as Yagura made it more challenging each day.

Fortunately they had returned to swordplay for the last month, so Gradni did not feel like he was out of practice.

After doing twenty push-ups he lifted himself on his

hands and rolled his feet under him. Outside his window, the crescent moon was illuminating Zipacna. Gradni grabbed his wooden jian sword and silently left his room and the castle. Luckily the base was quieter than he expected it to be. Despite him being so crucial to Delthurk, the senate would find a way to discipline him if they found out what he was up to. Mogurn made it clear to him that the Disciples were bigger than he was. But that did not matter to him. He had to know about this other slayer.

The arena itself was unguarded; strange, given the paranoia the Disciples had about their slayer. Gradni went inside. The area around the sandpit was pitch black, while the pit itself was lit with torches. Gradni walked into it. Several feet ahead of him, Erdūn leapt and twisted in the air while swinging his wooden weapons. Gradni edged past the torches at the entrance. Erdūn was using two weapons, a sword that was shorter than Gradni's, and a long spear with an axe head next to the blunted point. There were no others with him. He was training alone as the devi had implied. Their eyes met as Erdūn twisted around during an attack. The amesha was sweating lightly. Gradni had timed his arrival perfectly. Both of them were at their peak.

"Slayer Erdūn," Gradni said under the gaze.

"Slayer Gradni. Why are you here? I expected no company," Erdūn said while wielding his sword. It was getting harder to see this boy as being five years younger.

"I was wondering if you wanted to spar with someone?" Erdūn pivoted to face Gradni. He arched one leg back with his spear supported by his forearm, and crossed the spear with his sword. His eyes grew large.

"Yes."

Gradni grinned.

Gradni swung his blade around twice to channel some

wind into the fight. He charged his foe. Erdūn attacked first, twirling before swinging the axe head at Gradni. Gradni parried it with his sword and carried it forward into a thrust, but his opponent backed away in time. Erdūn came forward again, circling to Gradni's right and swinging his sword. Gradni again deflected it. He refooted himself to face the amesha and thrice slashed viciously, each attack deflected by the other's two weapons.

Erdūn backed away once again to be out of Gradni's range, and brought his axe head down. Gradni blocked it effortlessly, realizing that it was a ploy as Erdūn's sword came toward his chest. Gradni shook off the axe and deflected the sword. It brought his elbow in line with Erdūn's chest and he pushed it forward into him. But Erdūn leapt back as Gradni struck, making the attack almost painless. Gradni realized that Erdūn had been doing this from the beginning—moving along with all of Gradni's moves to minimize their impact. He was somehow able to adapt quickly to every move made against him. Again, Gradni could not believe that he was only twelve, the age that Gradni was when he came to Delthurk.

Erdūn came forward, this time unexpectedly slashing with his sword. The variation distracted Gradni, though he managed to deflect the blows far enough to put himself back on the offensive. Once again, Erdūn backed out of range. Gradni stepped forward and kept hammering his sword against Erdūn's weapons. Erdūn was holding his ground. Finally, Gradni used so much force that he knocked Erdūn's weapons away from his body. But by doing so, Gradni had pushed his own sword too far away as well, and so he viciously kicked Erdūn in the chest instead.

Erdūn landed on the sand, and before he could bring his weapons up in time, Gradni pinned his neck with the point of his wooden jian.

Gradni was breathing heavily and sweating profusely. Erdūn, not as much.

"Well done. Do you want to try again?" Erdūn said calmly.

Gradni wrenched his sword away. He took a couple moments to breathe. "No. No, it is late; I must go." Gradni turned around and quickly walked out as he tried not to show his lack of breath.

He had lost the fight. Whether Erdūn knew it or not, Gradni had lost the fight. Erdūn was five years younger, slower, and weaker, yet much more skilled. Each attack and ploy of Erdūn's would have worked against Gradni if Erdūn were only a little older. Gradni could not deny it. He went back to his room and tried hard to forget this night.

Once it was certain that Gradni had left the arena and was back in the castle, Erdūn turned toward the darkened seats and bowed. The large audience—including Mogurn, Yagura, and Bamay—stood up to leave. They had seen all they needed to. Erdūn, before exiting the barracks himself, focused on the torches surrounding the sandpit. He extinguished the fire with a thought.

CHAPTER 21

Gradni spread out the chain of his pendant and clasped it behind his neck before slipping it under his shirt. Five years, he thought to himself.

They brought him here when he was twelve and didn't let a single day go past without preparing him for his destiny. They told him of their history, and of the dragon's evil, and in turn he became even more than they expected—the inspiration and reason why all of Delthurk fought. He looked at himself in his mirror. A few alterations to the armor had been made to accommodate his growing body. Five years, though he still expected it to be longer. He was still only a decent combatant against Yagura and not yet his equal. He would exceed that pinnacle though. This first mission was only the beginning, one that would prove to Delthurk and his followers that he was as capable against dragons as he was in the arena. Yagura had been putting him through the most complex evasion routines, filling the arena with rocks alongside all the regular obstacles to further mimic the chaos Gradni would face on Zipacna. Whatever they had planned, Gradni had managed to evade every breath of burning liquid that was thrown at him. He kept looking at himself. There were still times when it did not feel like five years, like his green strands of hair had not gone through five cycles of thickening and thinning. He left his room and marched toward the senators' council room.

The guards by the council room door bowed as they allowed him in. The senators were waiting for him around the dark semicircle table that bordered the room. Yagura was sitting on one end and Mogurn at the other. Gradni walked in and dropped to one knee in a bow. Some pride would have to be swallowed this day.

"Rise, Dragon Slayer Gradni," a senator said. "You have been preparing for years with us, and we have watched you throughout. You are ready. You can now do what no others can. Our soldiers will follow you in battle very soon, and by the eve of the next great battle against the dragons, you will be a great hero in our cause."

Gradni stood up. Yagura walked toward him. A sheathed sword was in his hand. Gradni muffled the breath of excitement he took. It was the jian sword from Yagura's room, the one he was forbidden even to touch because he was not worthy of it. Yagura held it up for him and Gradni accepted it. All the anticipation he had had on that day returned to him. At his master's approval he removed it from the sheath. The blade was the color of gold and silver, yet it glinted more than the steel of any blade he had ever seen made at Delthurk. Gradni balanced it and checked its weight with two swings. This jian was the exact same weight as the bamboo one. Yagura had planned to give this sword to him since then.

Yagura spoke: "Only a sword forged of dev steel can aid you on this mission. No other metal can cut through the skin of horned dragons as fluidly as this can."

Gradni placed the jian back within its sheath. "You have my gratitude, Master Yagura."

"It was made to slay them. The previous holder of this sword was ruined by their evil. Avenge her by staining it with dragon's blood, and that will be all the gratitude I need."

Yagura backed away to his seat. The senator spoke again. "Senator Mogurn will give you the details of your first mission. Congratulations, Dragon Slayer Gradni. You are the finest there has ever been, and your actions in your first mission will attest to it."

The wings of the drake above Zipacna were stunning, even from Delthurk. Gradni looked at its beating wings. It was such a magnificent beast. He wondered if killing one would thrill him as much as the anticipation had for years. Hopefully it would not disappoint. His meeting with the piasa still haunted him.

Gradni's eyes fell from the distant wings to his jian sword. There was no more room for doubt. Not anymore. He had become what he always wanted to be.

"Are you ready?" Mogurn said from behind him.

"Of course." He followed Mogurn from the castle to the stables. He did not ask questions. This one time he would allow Mogurn to do this his way. But his tune changed when he saw what this stable held. All the horses had been moved elsewhere except for one, and he did not know if it was even a horse.

It was three feet taller than a regular horse, with the build of a bull to match it. The calf muscles were almost as thick as the thighs, and the creature's hooves were wide and bendy. Its head matched the proportions of its gray body, and from it, above the giant yellow eyes, protruded a thick heavy spiraled spire of hardened flesh. It snorted a puff that disheveled Gradni's hair.

"What is it?"

"A karkadan. It is a gift from the ameshas."

It turned its head as if uninterested in the company, revealing even more unnecessary muscle.

Gradni moved closer. "I have never even heard of a beast like this."

"It is rare, native only to amesha regions. With it, and on your first mission, you will do the impossible."

Gradni came closer to it. The karkadan did not seem to acknowledge him, even when Gradni put his hand on the side of its neck. "From the ameshas? Why not give it to their own slayer?" Gradni felt Mogurn's hand on his shoulder. It was anything but comforting.

"Erdūn is not ready for this mission. Neither they nor we know if he ever will be."

That made little sense. When he fought Erdūn two seasons ago Erdūn had been flawless. Either something had happened, or there was some ploy at work.

"You have a plan. You have all had a plan for a long time now," Gradni said to Mogurn. "What is it?"

Yagura had said to Gradni once that the simpler the plan, the easier it was to execute. This plan was simple, but it required an immeasurable amount of faith in the amesha's beast. Gradni was to ride it all the way up the Zipacna Mountains while it dodged and outran the dragons. Delthurk had traced the safest route, but the safest route was by no means safe.

The karkadan would run close to the nest of the horned drake, the single beast that had killed hundreds of Delthurk soldiers with every breath. Gradni would dismount, and like S'freed, kill the dragon while it slept. After everything, he was going to be an assassin like S'freed.

But he would then actually fight, and fight against the other horned dragons in the nest. This he could do. Despite having lost to Erdūn, he was a warrior now who would slay dragons. Gradni could now hold his ground against Yagura after all, but he would be better still against the dragons he was trained to fight. He knew this, and not only because they told him so. All that did was confirm their right to command him. He had read books on every previous slayer who had come to Delthurk, including his father, Yorn. They were honorable warriors, but they simply were never as good as he was. They were not even close. If this mission had been theirs, even if they had managed to survive the trek up the mountain, they would never survive against the horned dragons that would come awake after the first kill was made.

Yet in spite of how he had mastered evading their claws and flames, he knew that he would not survive in such odds for too long, especially once the drakes took to the air. That would take time though. Unlike the smaller flying dragons, drakes needed several minutes to become airborne. By that time the quick karkadan would return to Gradni as it was trained to. Gradni would break from battle, remount the karkadan, and ride back down Zipacna.

The dragons would follow of course, but Yagura and the other Disciples of Gaorda agreed that this mission was worthy of their direct involvement. Eight of them would wait with swords and bows and arrows at the base of Zipacna to take Gradni into safety after his return. He was truly one of them now, as they would never take part in a battle for one who was not their own.

The plan was quick, simple, conclusive, and due to the karkadan and himself, flawless. But because of that, Gradni stayed up at night after training. Nothing could ever be this perfect. There had to be some factors that he still was not able to figure out.

Gradni rode the karkadan for weeks to adjust to its nature. With each ride he realized that this ludicrous plan had a hope of fruition. The beast weaved, powered through, leapt, and curved whenever it needed to. The difficulty arose only with staying upon it. Gradni trained his legs to adjust to it so that his arms were free to defend himself. Even so, he needed ropes to tie him to the beast as it thundered about. Four weeks into it, and he was able to handle the jarring while holding weapons as well. He was ready to ride the karkadan into battle. Any questions he had about the validity of his quest no longer mattered. He was either going to accept his destiny, or not.

CHAPTER 22

Gradni kept looking toward Zipacna between studying every layer of leather and piece of metal of his armor. He wished that he was able to remember what Zipacna looked like when he first came to Delthurk. He partially removed his blade from the sheath. It was strong, glistening, sharp, but unaccomplished. Today he would dress it in blood. He opened his room door when he heard knocking. Mogurn stood at the threshold.

"It is time."

He left his room with Mogurn following closely behind him. The Disciples were waiting for him on horseback by the karkadan. Gradni mounted the heavy beast and took the staff and shield that Yagura tossed toward him.

"Good luck," Mogurn said, before Gradni rode with the Disciples out the gate and into the forest that bordered the Zipacna Mountains.

"There is the triumvirate of trees that we will be hiding behind once their attention is on you," Yagura said, pointing to a distinct looking knot of trees that were close to the border of the mountain. "Good luck." Yagura held out his hand. Gradni rode toward his master's horse and took it in his own. He tried to break away, but Yagura was not ready to let go. "It has been, Dragon Slayer Gradni, a strange honor." Gradni nodded and pulled away from him. The mountain looked more daunting than ever from this angle. He inhaled and exhaled several large breaths to empower himself. Ready, he pulled the reigns of the karkadan.

The karkadan charged forward. It snorted as if angry and accelerated. It trampled bushes and edged past trees; Gradni lifted his staff and shield—the sword only to be used later.

The beast leapt out of the forest and thundered up the Zipacna Mountains. It rode past a salamander, giving it as much attention as it did the rocks it climbed. A serpent jutted in front of them, but before it could spit fire the karkadan knocked it aside. Wyverns flew toward them and breathed fire in their direction. Gradni quickly blocked each burst of flame with his shield. The alarm had been raised. He did not know how high up the mountain they were, but dragons within the area were coming toward them.

There was heat at his right. Gradni turned quickly to a growing set of teeth and smacked the salamander aside with his staff. Behind him, the dragons chasing grew in number, but as of yet none of them could keep up. The karkadan jerked to the right, the ropes preventing Gradni from falling into the flames of a sobekian. Gradni tightened his legs around his fast-moving steed as the flames from the sobekian curled just an inch around his shield.

The karkadan was unpredictable. It would bound to a different ledge even when it was not in danger, and all of a sudden it would slow and then gallop faster than ever. Flames and claws scraped its flesh. Gradni was concerned, but the beast continued to run unfazed.

Gradni rammed his shield against a serpent that leapt at him. They were higher up now where the dragon force was heavier. Fortunately, the invincible and fast karkadan had been running for less than a minute, and the element of surprise was still in effect. The dragons were unprepared. They attacked without thinking, without organization, without even knowing what this thing was that carried him as he defended himself with staff and shield.

A multitude of monsters that Gradni had never seen before was coming at him from every direction, and he did not hesitate to fend them off. But he quelled his pride from rising too high before it distracted him. This was not a training session. If he made a mistake here he would die.

Then he saw it, in a clearing surrounded by jutting spires. Giant red folded wings lying against the ground. The amesha animal had brought him straight to his kill. But the wings were starting to stir: It was preparing to fly. Gradni let go of his staff, and with a knife hidden in his sleeve he cut the ropes that bound his legs to the karkadan. He rolled off the mighty beast, and as he had practiced, he wind channeled to soften his landing. The dragons that were chasing them divided their forces between him and the karkadan that continued to thunder forward.

Whilst still wind channeling and with barely a thought, Gradni leapt over the flames that came toward his lower half, threw his shield against a serpent, rolled under teeth and claws, and then jumped back to his feet in time to defend himself from a swooping wyvern. He could see the head of the red drake now only three meters away; it was larger than Gradni's whole body, but so too was the beast's vulnerable, glossy neck. Its eyes were open. Gradni could hear the wings flutter over the surrounding dragon shrieks. The scholars estimated that it took giant drakes several minutes to gather enough strength to lift themselves off the ground, but the red drake's legs were already primed to leap upwards. There was no time to think.

He hurled the shield away and unsheathed his sword. A head-sized eye turned toward him a moment before fire blocked his path. Both hands on his sword, Gradni charged through the flames like the karkadan would have, and shot his sword out toward the grand neck of the rising beast.

Then, a pull from his back, a moment of disorientation, and he was several feet from the red drake.

Stunned, Gradni brought his sword up. Three inches of it were covered in blood. That was all, from a beast twenty times his size. Something had knocked him back before he had completed his attack. There was no time to ponder what happened. He stood up, still winded, and took frantic steps toward his target. But his steps slowed to a stop when he saw what was now between him and his prey. A man of some kind, whose skin was made up of dark dragon scales.

It just stood there, as if in denial of the abomination that it was. Delthurk had never spoken to him of this. It took a step forward. Gradni lifted the point of his sword. What was this thing? Why had Delthurk never told him of it? Was this the dragon's secret, the reason why Delthurk had never won a substantial victory against them? The creature raised its own sword that glinted green, and put itself into a perfect fighting form.

"What are you?" Gradni whispered.

It did not respond. It just returned his gaze. Only when their eyes met did Gradni realize that it, too, was studying him.

The dragons surrounding them did not attack—even the red drake that was bleeding from its neck was watching him from the ground instead of trying to fly. Gradni's death would be at the hands of their strange champion. Gradni changed the angle of his sword.

"I am not dying today," he declared, and attacked the

other man. Gradni faked a thrust twice and slashed toward the neck. Blocked. He tried to strike toward the stomach. Parried. Stepping back and then forward, Gradni swung his blade in a full circle toward the creature's chest. The monster beat it away, jarring Gradni to the bone. Gradni shuffled away to take four seconds to himself. The monster had strength that matched its grotesqueness, and skill that no beast had any right to. Whatever it was, it had to die. He recalled his training, reminded himself that this monster was somehow also a warrior, and attacked again.

Steel hit against steel every third of a second. The dragon man was stronger, so Gradni defended with his sword marginally loose while trying to sway the other's blade. Occasionally he would tighten his grip when he saw an opening, but the dragon man would either evade or hammer it aside. Gradni wind channeled to try and circle around his opponent, sometimes doubling and even tripling back, but the creature inexplicably kept up.

It spun around, back-fisting a spew of blood from Gradni's mouth. Gradni crawled back up and rushed his opponent again. Another short round of clanging metal and the beast sent him back toward the jagged ground with a solid kick against his chest.

All his training, all five years of it—for this? Where was the karkadan? Gradni rushed forward, holding his sword like a lance. His opponent sidestepped and grabbed Gradni's wrist. It was a foolhardy attack on Gradni's part. He had failed to maintain his serenity and now the thing was crushing his wrist.

Gradni withheld his scream within a grunt, but his jian fell heavy upon the ground. His sword of dev steel was meant to make other blades useless by now, but it was just an ordinary sword against this creature's. Pain erupted from his chest where the creature grabbed his tattered leather with its clawed hands. Gradni found himself limp from exhaustion while face-to-face with the monster.

"Fine," Gradni whispered as he held his head high "kill me then."

He heard a soft roar, saw turquoise lips uncovering teeth and fangs, and to end it all, a blur of green.

EPILOGUE

Within a clearing outside the Delthurk castle, a hundred wooden pillars mounted with torches were spiked into the ground. Ferklen stood among them with eight hundred other people of Delthurk. Mogurn stood forefront of the other senators on the recently built platform of the castle that jutted out. It had to be Mogurn, the senator who had brought the mighty Gradni from Scandar.

Ferklen raised his sword and chanted the senator's name. Whether he was the first to do so was unclear, for soon all of Delthurk was doing it. The senator respectfully accepted the worship for a minute before silencing them with a motion of his arm.

"Delthurk," he began, "yesterday was our greatest and most tragic day in the war against the dragons. Yesterday, Gradni the Dragon Slayer sacrificed his life to the war. I know that some of you believed that he was out for nothing more than glory. You believed he was arrogant, foolhardy, and not worthy of the title Dragon Slayer of Delthurk. I would fault you, except there were times I myself thought him this way. But yesterday, Gradni rode to the nest of the red dragons and began to slay them," Mogurn said boldly, "In our entire history, have we ever seen a single man slay more than three horned dragons?"

Ferklen yelled the answer with the rest of the crowd.

"Never!" Mogurn repeated loudly. "He started slaying them. We then sent the karkadan back to ride him to safety, but it returned without him. We thought our slayer had fallen. We thought our slayer had failed. How foolish of us to not have faith in his bravery. The karkadan trainer discovered from the beast that Gradni refused escape! That to escape then would mean that horned dragons would still live. How many of you have lost friends to the horned dragons?" The crowd banged their swords against their shields. Like Ferklen, they fully trusted their wise senator who was knowledgeable on both the amesha people and the strange karkadan. "Gradni has avenged them! How many of you do you think would have been killed by a horned dragon? Gradni the Dragon Slayer has saved you! He could have returned to us a hero who had slain a few red dragons, but in the end Gradni never cared to be seen as a hero. He stayed instead of escaping, so that he could slay at least twenty more red dragons. So I ask you, people of Delthurk, is he not still our hero?" The banging and jeers outdid the earlier cries. "Dragon Slayer Gradni has saved countless numbers of us. Not for honor, not for glory, but for you! For Delthurk, and to end the dragon threat, a quest that he single handedly made possible yesterday!" After another round of cries and cheering that rivalled the chaos of a battle field, Mogurn silenced the crowd with another wave of his arm.

"We will remember Gradni and his sacrifice always, by finishing what he started! To do so, we need the one who Gradni himself saw as his successor." Another joined Mogurn on the ledge. He was not an elf. He was an amesha—taller than Gradni. Like Gradni, Ferklen noted, this warrior was not intimidated by the crowd. "This is Erdūn. I found for you Gradni, and I have now found for you Erdūn. Tell me Delthurk; are you as loyal to Gradni as he was to you?" Ferklen shouted his praise while banging his sword, trying to outdo all those around him. "Then to honor our fallen Dragon Slayer, will you loyally serve Erdūn, in Gradni's name, so that we can slay the dragons that killed him?"

"Erdūn for Gradni!" Ferklen screamed, beginning a chain that within a minute linked all of Delthurk together. "Erdūn for Gradni! Erdūn for Gradni! Erdūn for Gradni!"

⸺◈⸺

Bamay stood with Minister Sheemu some steps behind the Fire Spirit Ta'ar on the Aristahl palace balcony. She wished that she could be with her son on this moment of his glory, but it was important for him to be seen without her or the Disciples for him to fully absorb Delthurk's praise. And besides, she wanted her people to see her with Ta'ar so that they knew it was she who had brought him back, even if it was only for a visit. She did not want to be hated by them anymore. This visit from Ta'ar was only the beginning in gaining their future support for Erdūn. Ta'ar had finally returned to the amesha nation he once ruled, and the people were bowing and cheering, feeling blessed that he remembered them in the midst of his sacred quest. They bathed in his wondrous warmth while Sheemu edged closer to Bamay.

"They will willingly work again because of this visit, Bamay. I cannot express enough gratitude to you for convincing him to come regularly."

"There is no need. You delivered handsomely on your end, and thus I have as well. The karkadan was of more use than I even expected. A pity that we will never again see the beast that changed our fortune. Who knows how far it ran in order to never again be tamed."

"I did warn you that this would happen; karkadans cannot be fully controlled."

Bamay turned to her.

"You did, but it is no longer relevant. Erdūn has been cemented as the king of the Dragon Slayers. He will lead the forces against them as he was destined to do."

Sheemu moved away from her when the cheering got louder. Bamay smiled proudly. Tales of karkadans were common in Aristahl. She had known from the beginning that the karkadan would not return, as did Yagura, Mogurn, and the rest of the senate of Delthurk. By his death, Erdūn's competitor was now also a servant to his destiny. Now that Delthurk was fully behind him, only good things would happen for Erdūn.

INTERLUDE

ARISTAHL, SEVEN AND A HALF YEARS AGO

Shah Zahk of Aristahl swung his wooden blade at his soldier's head twice. The soldier brought his weapon up to defend himself, and Zahk shoved his foot into the soldier's chest. Zahk loved to fight. Before becoming Shah he was Aristahl's beloved general. By all accounts, Zahk was a handsome man. His dark brown skin always seemed to glisten. His inset eyes balanced out his prominent nose, and his triangular goatee highlighted his sharp features and wide smile.

He called a second soldier to join the first one against him. After a long bout of clacking swords, Zahk knocked both their wooden swords away with his, shoulder rammed one of them, and kicked the other in the hip. They would not have been able to continue if not for them all wearing leather padding. As Zahk helped them back on their feet, a bright light entered the fight room. Zahk scowled. The Fire Spirit Ta'ar had come into his space.

"Wait for me until I call upon you." Zahk said to his soldiers before turning to Ta'ar. "I've told you not to interrupt me when I am in here, so I hope this is important."

"We have visitors. The Disciples of Gaorda are here to meet with us."

"The dev dragon killers? What reason could they have to come all the way here? Whatever it is, as it is unannounced they can wait till I am ready for them."

"It was not unannounced. I invited them."

Zahk's whole body tensed. "Of course you did. How foolish of me not to immediately know that. What are you hoping to gain from this, Ta'ar?"

"The same as always. To rid the lands of the wretched dragons, an evil that you refuse to combat."

"This was a foolish move Ta'ar. All the Disciples care about is killing dragons, no matter what damage they would do to Aristahl in the process. Even the dev nations want nothing more to do with them."

"Foolishness will be your rejection of their proposal before even hearing it."

Zahk grimaced. He knew better than to reason with the Fire Spirit. Ta'ar's manipulation of the previous shahs against dragons was precisely why his nation was so downtrodden when he assumed the title.

"Fine." Zahk said spitefully, "I will see them, but they can still wait till after I finish my training."

Zahk sat on his throne and waited for the Disciples of Gaorda with the rest of the Aristahl council. This included Ta'ar, who floated above his own pedestal several feet adjacent to Zahk, Zahk's two sturdy guards who stood with poleaxes on either side of him, Minister Sheemu, and Ambassador Bamay, who was also the head priestess in Ta'ar's temple. Zahk saw her as a trusted and fortuitous ally in the growing friction between himself and Ta'ar. Though she had been a life-long devotee to Ta'ar long before Zahk made her ambassador, the reason he did that ensured her loyalty to him over the Fire Spirit. He had had no motive to have an ally in Ta'ar's circles at the time, but suspected that Bamay's position in the temple was about to prove essential.

The throne room door opened. Fifteen dev Disciples of Gaorda stormed in as if the palace was theirs. Zahk instantly disliked them. They were dressed in traditional dev armor, though parts of their blue skin, including their faces, were exposed- all except for one of them furthest to the right. Every part of her skin that would be visible beneath her armor was wrapped in strips of cloth. Even the area around her eyes was concealed, though her eyes themselves were hypnotic. Zahk had to pull his attention away from her when the front most deva stepped forward from the rest of them. The deva put his palms together for less than a second before speaking.

"Shah Zahk of Aristahl. I am Kshatriya Yagura and we are the Disciples of Gaorda. Our founder of decades past, Gaorda, created our order to rid our world of the evil of dragons. It was us who annihilated the sesha dragons that terrorized the dev kingdoms. We-"

"I know already of the Disciples history, Kshatriya. What brings you to Aristahl?"

"Of course, Shah Zahk," Yagura replied with a bitter tone. "Though we are of different people, we have a common enemy. Both sobekian and wyvern dragons plague the lands around your kingdom. Allow us to operate from Aristahl, and with your nation's help and resources we will lead your people in exterminating all the dragons in this area."

Zahk nodded. "Perhaps I should not have interrupted your tale. As you have said, we are different people, so tell me, why come all the way here after your success against the sesha dragons? Wouldn't it make more sense to go east and destroy the longue dragons that live amidst your dev nations there?" Ta'ar's aura flared. Zahk ignored it and glared at the dumbfounded deva. "I have asked you a question in my court deva. You must answer."

"The timing is not right," said the devi covered in strips of cloth. She stepped ahead of Yagura. "After disposing of the seshas and the toll that war took on our people, they are not ready for another immediate war. We will return to deal with the longue when we can, after we have made an impact on ridding these lands of the other dragon species."

Zahk nodded. Her answer, sadly, made sense. He looked his new opponent over. She was harder to read, and he wasn't sure if it would be easier to do so if he could see her face. She carried two swords. One was in a sheath at her hip and had a rose shaped pommel. The other was on her back and also wrapped completely in cloth strips.

"You are a curious creature." Zahk said plainly to shake her nerve as he did Yagura's. "What is your story? What happened to you to make you choose this path?"

"I am Kshatriya Naviya. I have been with the Disciples of Gaorda for over ten years. In my last battle with the sesha dragons, their flames burnt my skin to nothing. I am in constant pain because of the dragons, and would have died, if not for my kshatriya husband whom the dragons mutilated right in front of me. This is his sword," she gestured the covered up sword on her back," I carry it in his honor. I have no husband, no skin, and no face because of the dragons. This is what awaits Aristahl if you take no action. Your people know this, so why don't you?"

"I am sorry for what happened to you, Kshatriya Naviya. But my people are happier than they have ever been."

"Are they? For generations, for the reign of the two shahs that came before you, Aristahl fought against the dragons. Now, all of a sudden you have changed that. Do you think your people will forget their history and the dragons' evil so quickly? All because you have made the grass a little greener?"

Zahk stood up. "Aristahl fought the dragons as long as it did, gave up lives, food, and well-being, all because of Ta'ar's mad quest against creatures that have shown no hostility against us, except in retaliation. I will not give in to the fear and war mongering that would bring Aristahl further into ruin. I reject your proposal, Disciples of Gaorda. You are banned from Aristahl. You will leave my nation immediately."

"No, rumbled Ta'ar. You insult me, the Spirit of Aristahl! Who are you to oppose my will? The Disciples of Gaorda are welcome in my ziggurat."

Zahk gritted his teeth and tightened his fist. He looked at Naviya and the rose pommel of her sword, willing her to pull it out so that he would have someone to fight with. By welcoming the Disciples in his ziggurat, the Disciples could stay in Aristahl for as long as the Fire Spirit wished. "Fine, but you are still unwelcome in my palace, and if you incite war with the dragons whilst here, I will hand your heads over to the dragons personally. Now get out of my court. The Disciples marched out. Yagura grinned snidely at Zahk as he left. Ta'ar also traded glares with Zahk before vanishing in a cloud of fire.

The devi woman's words haunted Zahk. Were his people truly turning against him, despite all the good he had done for them? He wiped the sweat from his brow. The rest of his court was overwhelmed and waiting for his response. "Ambassador Bamay, as head priestess in Ta'ar's ziggurat, I will need you to watch them closely and report to me any suspicious activity. The future of Aristahl might well be in your hands."

Book Two

CHAPTER 1

Blood. Gradni tasted the bitterness in his mouth as he woke up. He immediately tried to move, but pain paralyzed him. He couldn't even tell where it was coming from. After a minute's rest he pushed past it, but still couldn't separate his arms or legs from one other. Rope was biting into his ankles and wrists. He stopped struggling and took a moment to recall what had happened.

He had ridden the karkadan all the way to the top of the Zipacna Mountains; he had moved past all the dragons to get to the red drake that he had started to plunge his sword into... Then the monster, and the rest of it instantly came back to him. Gradni pulled himself up into a sitting position to see where he was.

He was in a cave where the only source of light was daylight swooping into the sloped entrance above him. Gradni stopped fidgeting for a moment and wondered if the dragons had ever captured anyone before. A soft hiss sounded at his right. Gradni jerked his head toward it and sprung back. A graying green head of a serpent was at his eye level less than two feet away. The head hovered toward Gradni and then twisted around to leave the cave. Its body slid like liquid over the uneven rocks. Gradni waited until the tail slipped around the bend.

The bonds were so tight around his wrists that they cut into him as he tried to pull them apart. It had to have been the monster who tied them. Gradni's armor had been stripped from him, leaving him no sharp edges that he could use to cut his binds. His remaining clothes were in tatters, and he saw that the leather strips that bound his feet were from his own armor.

Along the side of the cave was a rock that appeared jagged enough to saw through his binds. Gradni crawled toward it. The ground was warm. He placed an open palm against the floor. There was heat coming from it. It was the equivalent of having his palm inches away from a lit candle. There was no question now that he was on the evil mountain of Zipacna.

Up close, the rock was not as sharp as he hoped. Gradni placed the binds around his wrists against it anyway and vigorously tried to wear them out.

He heard the unmistakable sound of fluttering wings approaching the cave. He pushed himself from the rock and shuffled away. A wyvern came into view first. The karkadan had moved so quickly, that though Gradni saw many wyverns on his way up the mountain, this was the first time he could see the beast's detailed features. It flew into the cave and clung to the cave wall with its clawed feet. The serpent from before flowed back in around the rocks. Gradni was pulling himself up when a flash of red suddenly hopped into view over the bends of the serpent. The red salamander came closer to him than any of the others dared, eyeing him like a predator with its open mouth and hot breath. Gradni edged away from it. It had off-white seven-inch curved horns coming from its forehead, and its skin looked even thicker than the red drake's. It was no wonder that Yagura had given him the dev sword; anything less would have done little against these creatures.

More light was blocked out as the monster entered the cave. It did not seem real. Gradni looked toward its feet, hoping there would be a betrayal to its disguise. They were fairly large, and curved a little with the rocky floor. They reminded him of Erdūn's feet. The monster stepped past the serpent and horned salamander and looked right at Gradni.

"How old are you?"

Gradni stared. How could a thing like this talk?

"How old are you?" it said louder.

"Seventeen years," Gradni answered.

The lines of anger around its face inexplicably softened. It broke eye contact and looked Gradni over.

"What are you?" Gradni asked, so astonished that he barely knew that he had spoken.

The beast looked at him again. "What do you think I am, elf?"

Somehow the creature did not seem as monstrous now as it had before it spoke. Its hair, though unkempt, was simply coal-black, and besides the dark green scales of its skin, there was nothing off-putting about the creature's eyes or facial structure.

"I know you are not elven," Gradni said.

"And how do you know that?"

"Because in my entire life, only those who are not elven have called me 'elf'."

"How clever of you. When did they bring you into this war?"

"You have not answered my question. Why should I answer yours?"

It leaned forward. "You have not guessed by now?"

"Guess? How am I to know what you are? You are just a monstrosity."

"You have never heard of anything in your teachings that look like me? I know you have been taught by devs, by the Disciples. Your sword and style make that clear. Did they never teach you what I am?"

The way the creature had said 'devs'. They were as alien to him as elves were.

"You are amesha?"

The other straightened immediately. Gradni had guessed right.

"I am Zahk. I was amesha a long time ago. I am a naga dragon now."

"Then you are less than what you once were."

Zahk looked him over again. "You are only seventeen. Yet you hate us so much that you would give up your life to slay us."

"Gladly," Gradni spat. "Where is my steed? What did you do with it?"

"The karkadan? It fled as soon as you were off it. That it even brought you up here is a miracle. Did you think that it was going to carry you back? That was never going to happen. Never in history has a karkadan remained tame once put back in the wild."

"You are lying!" Gradni said. "What do you know about such things?"

The naga kneeled down toward him. Gradni backed away, but the clawed hand of Zahk reached toward Gradni's neck. Gradni tensed in anticipation of being choked as he looked directly at Zahk's eyes. "Whose is this?"

Gradni peered down. The naga was holding his father's pendant in his hand.

"Whose is this?" the naga asked again. Gradni did not answer, keeping his eyes on the pendant. "Whose?" the naga shouted.

"My father's!" Gradni yelled back. "It was my father's! He died here on Zipacna, killed by your dragons. I will avenge him. I will kill you all!"

Zahk stepped away and the other dragons followed suit.

"You are here for revenge, against us." It seemed that Zahk was talking to the cave instead of him. Gradni grew angrier. "Yes. Your dragons killed him!"

"Unlikely," Zahk stated. "If he was a dragon slayer, as your pendant implies, then it was probably me who killed him."

Gradni's heart sank. He didn't know what this creature was. It stopped him from killing the horned drake, and now, had also killed his father?

"You are the one who killed him?"

"I have killed numerous dragon slayers who have tried to invade us, so most likely it was me."

"You are not even a dragon. I don't know what you are. You came into a fight that is not yours, and you kill my father?"

"This is as much my fight as it is theirs. I am one of them."

"You are not!" Gradni yelled. "If you really killed him, why haven't you killed me? Why am I still alive?"

The naga replied plainly, "I do not kill children."

"I am not a child! I am a man! I am the Dragon Slayer of Delthurk!"

Zahk's head hung low. He abruptly turned to leave the cave.The other dragons followed suit. "I am sorry that my actions have brought you into this war. But I do not regret protecting my kind."

"I'll destroy you all!" Gradni screamed. "All of you! All of you!"

The dragons did not respond as they left the cave.

Tears were dripping down Gradni's face. With his hands bound he could not wipe them away. Gradni shook his head madly to get rid of them. He wanted them gone. More than anything right now, he wanted his tears gone.

CHAPTER 2

The soft growling and gentle barks from the twenty dragons stopped as Zahk came down from the cave. They twisted their necks toward him, but dispersed when they realized he had nothing to say to them. The serpent and wyvern beside Zahk separated as well. Only Zahk's close friend, the red salamander, didn't seem to understand his need for silence. He hopped from rock to rock beside Zahk while growling toward him.

Zahk turned and roared, "I do not know, Sirrush!" Sirrush hissed and bounded a couple meters away to take a drink from the river. Zahk didn't wait for him, salvaging the moment of peace.

When Zahk was brought here years ago, he picked up quickly that the differentiation in the dragons' barks, growls, and roars, was a sophisticated language. The meanings of each sound weaved into his understanding quickly. From the dragons' previous encounters with the races, they were able to understand Zahk from the beginning. Within months they could understand each other just as well as if they were using the same language.

The growling began again along with the sound of Sirrush's feet landing from curved rock to curved rock behind him. Zahk continued on. There was no answer he could give. The elf boy had seen him, and they could not release him now that he knew. But at least Zahk now knew that the

Disciples had not even mentioned nagas to their allies. For whatever reason that was, it meant that his own existence with the dragons was all the more a secret.

Zahk could not help thinking about the boy. He was only seventeen years. Seventeen, and one of the greatest warriors Zahk had ever seen, and he had seen many. The boy had been trained by the Disciples and was good enough to already be of their class himself, if not better due to his insane bravery. They must have brought him in when he was a child.

Sirrush barked at Zahk just as they were about to climb down a ledge toward the cave they had reached.

"I know," Zahk said. "I know he wants to kill us, that he would have killed Tiamat if I had not stopped him. What would you have me do about it?"

Sirrush hissed back, the answer eluding him as well. Zahk turned back and leapt down to enter the cave.

The life-size statues of Irath and Kallini were waiting for him. Irath had been the king of the sesha dragons, and Kallini the naga who fought beside him. Kallini was sitting on Irath's folded coils while his hood towered over her. The statue had not always been here. Zahk had given the order to retrieve it years ago. The decision was made reluctantly as he could not join in the retrieval, as it was decided even then that his existence be kept secret. But the dragons agreed so readily, as if waiting for the command. It was because of Irath and Kallini that the seshas lasted as long as they did in the war. All that was left of them was this statue that was further damaged by being brought here, when the drake who carried it was forced to pierce its hood with her talons to lift it.

Dragons died to bring it here, yet there was no regret in the action taken. The seshas were fellow dragons, and the statue of Irath and Kallini who served them was all they had to remember them and their history.

Zahk looked into Kallini's ruby eyes. Perhaps together they could come up with an answer. But even with Irath's might shielding him, the evil of his enemies shone through the cracks. He thought that Erdūn would be the only child brought into the war, and that due to the malicious Fire Spirit Ta'ar. But this elf child had no connection to Ta'ar. Was there no limit to the hatred the races had for dragons, that their own children were being sacrificed?

Something had to be done to stop them. Zahk's head lowered even farther beneath the gaze of Kallini, till his forehead was against the coiled stone body of Irath. Sirrush did not join him this time, and he was grateful. It would be better tomorrow, perhaps even in a couple hours, but he had just come from seeing another youth ruined; one who had both sorrow and hate within him, who might not have even joined the war if not for Zahk killing his father. Zahk raised his head to the statues.

"I have had enough. What they do to us, due to reasons we have never given them. I have had enough. I cannot bear the evil they put on us."

After night fell, Zahk left the cave for his own. He sank into his bed of leaves and animal skin, hopeful that his strength would return to him in the morning.

CHAPTER 3

"We will wait by the triumvirate of trees for you," Yagura had promised. Gradni was leaning out of the cave when he heard a fierce flutter. He swung himself back around the crooked wall and waited for the piasa's hot breath to finish echoing through the cave. It was the worst time to try to escape.

His wrists still hurt. It had taken him a couple days to wear down his binds with the flattened edge of his pendant. He had worked his fingers to the point of stiffness and he was frustrated, so despite the light of the sun and the sound of dragons everywhere, he would not wait any longer. In less than an hour the dragons would come again with meat and fruit in their claws. He had to leave before then.

Besides, the sooner he escaped, the better the chances that Yagura and the Disciples were still waiting for him. The naga beast's lies about the karkadan were still swirling in his head. He had to show them that they were not true. Gradni peered outside again. Nowhere around him was the land flat. There were slopes of different magnitudes going in different directions, and along them were flame shaped rock formations. Some were four times the size of him while others were not even as high as his ankle.

Through the gaps between the protrusions there were an infinite number of ways to find his way down, as long as he knew the general direction he was going. The karkadan had ridden up so quickly that Gradni was unable to remember any landmarks. Not that that would have helped. Each rock formation was so unique that none of them stood out on their own. He could not see the bottom from here. He had no choice but to run, and hope to see the cluster of trees once on the outer peaks.

Gradni darted out of the cave. Almost immediately he heard the roar of a drake from behind him. Without looking back he weaved between the crevices of the mountain. Behind him the drake's roar continued and changed, followed by growls and barks and the sounds of flapping wings of dragons giving chase.

A serpent curved past the boulder in front of him. Gradni wind channeled himself around the other side of the stone and continued to rush down at a pace so frantic that his legs felt disembodied. Ahead of him the slope he was running down ended in a steep cliff. With no other alternative, Gradni climbed up another incline to get to the outer mountains. Instinct was all he had to go on. Another roar sounded, this one different from any he heard before because of an underlying human sound. It was the naga, probably ordering to give him chase.

A gust from a pair of wings hit Gradni's back. Wyvern or piasa, he did not check before leaping over a rock into a crevice. He went right to break from always going left, hoping that any differentiation would throw them off the way the karkadan had. It was a lucky decision, for between two boulders he saw the forest, and almost sprained his ankle when stopping to dash between them. The forest was still far away but he ran anyway, all the while knowing that more and more dragons were accumulating behind him. On his left, light from the foaming mouth of a salamander caught his attention. Gradni ran right past it before the beast could attack. His throat burned for water and his lungs for relief. But he ignored the scorching along with the dying strength of his legs. The triumvirate of trees—he could see them now, he was almost there. Somehow he had made it this far.

Dragons were not just behind him. They were above and around him. His goal was directly in front of him, but around the borders of his view there was trampling, slithering, and flapping wings. There was no time to think of them as his feet touched level ground for the first time in days. With the flapping coming in closer from above, Gradni leapt into the forest toward the intertwined trees that were standing out like a pillar of hope through the foliage. The dragons followed him through it, each by their own way, but it no longer mattered when they would get to him. Soon he would know.

With the little energy he had left, Gradni swatted leaves and branches away to see the base of the knotted trees and the clearing around it.

His legs crumpled. He fell hard against the dirt. Vomit immediately spilled from his mouth. As the dragons surrounded him and perched above him, Gradni pulled his head up in the hope that his first sight had deceived him. It had not. There was not a single footprint of any kind in the soft base of the trees. Yagura, the Disciples, and Delthurk, had abandoned him just as the naga had said they had, as they had always intended to.

Zahk stepped less than a foot from his vomit. Gradni heaved himself onto his knees. Zahk's earlier roar had not been to recapture him. There was no possible way that Gradni could have gotten down the mountain unless the dragons had let him. The naga wanted to see where he was going.

"Kill me," Gradni said, his hands and head bowed down while Zahk further studied the area.

"You knew they would not still be here. You just needed to know if they were ever here at all."

"Kill me. Please just kill me."

Zahk came toward him, and for an instant a panic of true fear flashed through Gradni. But instead of grabbing the fearsome sword, Zahk took Gradni's hands and brought them around his back to tie them. Gradni would have resisted more if he were dead. His people had abandoned him. After everything he had become for them, they had left him to die.

Gradni was gently pulled up by his collar. His legs automatically aligned without thinking. Halfway up the mountain he fell again. He did not get back up, but cried and screamed in front of those he thought he hated.

Somehow they brought him back to his cave.

The bonds around his wrists had been removed. He had stopped screaming; but the crying went on. His entire face was covered in tears, yet still he continued, as if to make up for all the times in his past when he should have cried but never did.

CHAPTER 4

Gradni waited for the serpent to leave before taking his hands out from behind him. The piece of meat she had dropped was smoking in front of him. A gust of wind blew its flavor in his direction. His stomach growled for it, but he had other matters on his mind.

It seemed that for as long as Gradni could remember, he had been basing his life on one man. Yet after all of it, while that man's medal still hung down from his neck as he sat in the corner of his cave, he could not remember what that man looked like.

When his father was alive and off fighting dragons as he always was, Gradni's care had been entrusted to servant households of Scandar. With no warning, he was passed from one household to another like a gift that no one wanted. Each one came with its varying difficulties. Only one aspect of his life was constant, and that was that his father did occasionally return. Each time he did, Gradni ran out of whichever house he was in to see him. Sometimes his father would even welcome him.

"Did you kill any more?" Gradni would ask.

"Many, Gradni!" his father would reply. "And what of you? Will you also become a slayer of dragons?"

"Yes," Gradni replied each time, before sitting down to listen while his father told him how he had dutifully killed the dragons that kept him away from his son.

It got worse as the years went by. Gradni craved more freedom as he got older, but it was never permitted by the people in charge of him. Several times he vowed to tell his father that he was unhappy. He never did. Why shame his father, the great Dragon Slayer Yorn, by showing him what a whiny son he had—and that too during their few moments together. Instead he shook his father's hand every time he left, and waited for the next time he would return with new tales of the dragons he had killed.

Another whiff of the meat traveled up his nose. It was still smoking. He was about to reach for it when the naga started walking into the cave. Gradni shuffled back into the corner and once again put his hands behind him. He cursed himself for not wiping away any tears that might still be around his eyes.

Zahk came right up to him. He looked toward the part of the cave wall that had specks of blood upon it before turning back to Gradni.

"Stand up," Zahk said to him. Gradni rolled up on to his knees and stood. "Let me see your hands." Gradni replied by looking back at Zahk without moving. Zahk forcefully yet slowly pulled Gradni's hands into view, and turned them around to see his bleeding knuckles. Even the slight pressure that Zahk applied was hurting him. Gradni looked down at them.

"Are you mad?" Zahk said.

"Yes!"

Zahk let go. "Wash them in the spring left of this cave before you leave."

"Leave?"

Zahk stepped away and unstrapped a sheath which he placed against the cave wall. It was Gradni's own sword, the one Yagura gave him on the condition that he *'Stain it with dragon's blood.'*

"You are no longer our prisoner. This is a good weapon. It may still be useful to you."

"Where will I go?"

"I know you will not go back to them. I ask that wherever you go, that you do not tell anyone about me. Our survival here depends on Delthurk not knowing that I exist."

"I promise."

Zahk nodded. "Eat before you go."

Zahk left. Gradni looked down at the meat for several minutes. He ripped off a couple pieces and shoved it into his mouth as he looked at his sword. It was lying at an angle with light glinting off the blade. They had already washed away the stain of the horned drake's blood. He still remembered the shape of the stain, and his disappointment in not having thrust his entire blade in. Suddenly with no appetite, Gradni pushed himself up. His cracked knuckles stung. After a couple minutes he left the cave, leaving the sword where it was.

The river was mildly hot as Gradni rippled his fingers through it. What he assumed was mist over the water was actually a thin layer of steam against the cool winds. Everything on this mountain had an innate warmness to it. It was no wonder the dragons remained here despite all the attacks. This was their home, the site of their creation that was infused with the essence of their fire. The warm liquid washed away the blood without him even having to wipe it off.

The horned dragons' nest was in the highest of the peaks. Gradni shook the water off his hands and began to hike it. The peak was far away. Everything here was big and far away without the karkadan rushing him through it.

Almost twenty clustered curved spires of Zipacna were

scattered before him as he traveled from one to the other. He imagined what they would be like a couple years from now, knowing even as he did that there was no way to anticipate how they would reshape. His admiration of the mountain range increased as he traveled over it, the way it shifted like a leisurely fire, free from any discipline.

There were approximately four thousand dragons here on the mountains. It was strange walking right beside them and seeing them circling around the spires he passed. They didn't look any different than before, and yet everything else about them was. They were no longer cruel—if anything there was actually a gentleness to them as they chased each other around. He took his time as he climbed around the peaks, sometimes choosing to look at a group of dragons while his hand felt around for a rock to grip on.

The horned drake's head was already raised when Gradni curved around the bend of the nest. Its eyes rested on him as it opened its mouth, sending a stream of hot air that ruffled through Gradni's brown and green hair. Gradni bent his head and hiked closer.

Immediately, the dragon raised itself farther up, drawing its neck away from him. The movement agitated the scab at its neck. Gradni looked back up and raised his arms in surrender. His torn tunic showed no place to conceal any weapons. From beside and behind him, other dragons were scrutinizing him. A rumble started within the horned drake's throat. It could have been anger, or fire rippling beneath the thin layer of skin. Its mouth opened wider to reveal a line of thick razor teeth.

"I'm sorry!" Gradni yelled. The horned drake's growl subsided slightly, but it bent closer. Blood was trickling down the disturbed scab. Gradni looked back toward the eyes. He had to say it while looking at the eyes. With one jerk of the jaw, the teeth could tear into him without warning. Gradni's hands were now completely up. "I am sorry," he yelled again. "I am sorry!" A harsh puff of breath drew sweat from Gradni's skin. The dragon pulled back and settled itself down with its head between its wings. Gradni waited a couple minutes before lowering his hands. He backed away from the nest and turned to leave the mountain for good.

The descent down Zipacna was slow. Some of the dragons looked toward him and some did not. He had tried to kill them. He had even told them that he would after they spared him. And yet instead of anger, the only emotion he got from them now was pity. Pity, for he who was destined to become a great hero. Anger would have been preferable. Even Scandar's abuse was preferable. Gradni looked back more and more often the farther down he got. The Zipacna Mountains looked different each time as each angle presented a new way of seeing the range. The one thing that he had never been able to see from Delthurk was the number of caves that also rippled through the mountain. Like the variation in the rock formations, each cave promised something different to explore.

But it was getting dark, and he was too far away now to see inside any of them. Gradni turned away and walked into the woods that separated Zipacna from Delthurk.

Gradni no longer trusted if his actions were by his conscious will or not. He was on a high branch where he could see the fiery peaks of Zipacna on his left and the wall of Delthurk on his right.

A glimmer of light was rising from beyond the Delthurk wall, and though he could not hear the words even when straining his ears, there was the unmistakable sound of chanting. They were planning a new scheme. That much he knew. On that long ago day when he had joined Delthurk, Gradni remembered Mogurn's exact words: *Do you not want to honor your father?*

Gradni yanked the pendent from his neck to look at it. Apart from the dents it had sustained before he had left Scandar, there was no further damage to it. It was on that day due to what he had done to Ferklen when Mogurn decided to bring him to Delthurk. Gradni balanced himself on the branch, and hurled the pendant as far as he could. It glinted pleadingly before falling beneath the green.

Scandar mistreated him when his father was alive, and more so after he had died. But Delthurk had used him. For what purpose he did not know or care. He had worked to become everything they wanted, only to be betrayed for some greater purpose against the dragons.

Delthurk would never stop the war against the dragons, the creatures who had every right to kill him and yet gave him mercy instead. The cheering from Delthurk suddenly got louder. Gradni became worried.

In spite of Zahk, Gradni had come within inches of killing the horned drake. Whatever was starting in Delthurk now, it meant the end of the dragons. What would the dragons do against the other slayers that would come? Mogurn had probably lied to him about Erdūn as well, the slayer who would truly become their greatest dragon slayer. Even with his strength, Zahk would have trouble against Erdūn and the army that would come with him.

The dragons turned toward Gradni as he started hiking back up Zipacna. For every curved boulder that he climbed past, the soft growls, barking, and hissing became louder. Behind him, Gradni could hear serpents pushing up the pebbles he had passed. Up ahead, wyverns and longues were hovering in the air. When several drakes crowded round where the others were hovering, Gradni headed for the largest cluster of rock he could see, where he knew Zahk would come to as well.

There were an equal number of dragons, fifty or so, who were following Zahk from the peak. Gradni knelt before Zahk. The growls and barks settled into a soft rumbling. It was not just because of circumstances that Gradni knew they were communicating about him; it was something else. He was somehow able to detect the differentiation in their hissing to understand that they were more than just curious about his return.

"Speak," Zahk said.

"I should never have served with Delthurk against your kind. I need forgiveness."

"We have given it already."

"Not from you, my lord. Your forgiveness is too freely offered. Delthurk is planning something. I do not know what, but you will need my help. I beg you; let me redeem myself by joining you so that I may turn my blade against them."

The hissing turned to growls of excitement, and Gradni, despite himself, began to smile. But the growling was silenced by a roar from Zahk.

"Stand up. And do not call me lord. I cannot bring you into this war."

"I am already in it. I served against you my entire life. I need redemption."

"You do not want redemption. You want revenge."

Gradni grew angry. "What does it matter; you need me."

"Need you?" Zahk barked back.

"I served Delthurk. I do not know what they are planning, but you need my help."

"Boy! You are not half as valuable as you think you are. What Delthurk did to you should have proven that much."

"I can fight better than most and you know that. Why won't you let me fight with you?"

"We killed your father, boy! I killed your father! Leave. You do not want to be here."

Zahk turned around, but before he could take a single step Gradni reached out and grabbed him.

"I know. My father was not who I thought he was. My place is still here." Zahk rolled Gradni's arm off him. He was about to say something, when his face changed inexplicably. "What is—" Gradni could not finish, for Zahk's hand shot out to clutch Gradni's chin and cheeks. "What is it?" Gradni squelched, as his face was turned to the right while Zahk's gaze burned upon him. The naga grunted as he grabbed Gradni's hand. The surrounding dragons all crowded in closer. The horned salamander hopped closest, and bent so close to Gradni's hand that he could feel the heat upon it. Gradni peered down at it while his face was still held to the side. The pinch of skin between his thumb and forefinger had a hint of green to it. He remembered seeing a little of it while in the woods, but he had assumed that it was just a discoloration caused by climbing the tree. But it was something more, for he could see now that the green was actually his skin and not something exterior. Apart from the color, it seemed different in other ways. It was denser. His eyes narrowed as he studied it, till Zahk suddenly released his hand and looked up at him. Gradni looked back, despite being curious about this mild but odd change in him.

The naga's voice seemed almost regretful, but there was also the unmistakable sound of relief as he looked Gradni in the eye. "It is out of my hands. You are apparently already one of us. Your inner fire has been lit, Gradni. We will find a cave for you."

CHAPTER 5

Mogurn kept a safe distance from the black tusk tattoos that ran down Tikal's arms while standing beside him. Two Disciples of Gaorda shot arrows of burning cloth at the entrance of a cave in the grassy valley below. Mogurn did not like the weather here. During winter his hair was usually a powerful yet sleek icy blue. Here, however, where the temperature was much warmer, the blue was so weak that it was closer to grey.

Thick black smoke began to rise from the arrows. Tikal was more focused on Erdūn and Ta'ar who towered over them from behind.

"You seem troubled, Tikal," Mogurn said. Other qui-lahk from his elephant tribe were atop their armored elephants, and watching the developing smoke and fire from the other side of the valley. They were deliberately keeping their distance from Mogurn and his little group.

Tikal leaned toward Mogurn and away from the others. "I thought that your champion was an elf boy?"

"This here is his successor and better, Erdūn. At fifteen years he is even younger than Gradni was."

"Fifteen? With his stature he cannot be fifteen."

"He is, and has no more reached his full potential than you or I did at that age. You will see in a moment what he can already do."

It did not surprise Mogurn that Tikal had trouble

believing Erdun's age. The amesha boy was already taller than all of them by a head. Even Ta'ar had to float higher to remain above him. It wasn't possible to see Erdūn's youth by looking at his face either. The hardening of his skin through his time with Ta'ar and his magic had taken that away.

Mogurn continued watching the smoke blow into the cave as Tikal took another glimpse at Erdūn. "I do not know if this is a good idea. The piasa in that cave has not been a threat."

"Every dragon is a threat Tikal. Why continue to endure a creature of sin that is living right outside your borders? Consider this act a gift on our behalf, no matter what you decide."

The piasa launched out of the cave, roaring madly. Before Tikal could complain to Mogurn again, Erdūn leapt over both of them and raced toward the dragon. His feet had grown to twice their regular size since arriving here, allowing him to travel down the soft valley with ease.

"He carries no weapons!" Tikal shouted. Mogurn and the Disciples said nothing. Erdun was able to sell himself.

Erdūn leapt from the steep of the valley toward the fireball that the piasa shot at him. With a wave of his hand, he wiped the flames away before throwing his other fist against the side of the dragon's head. The dragon stumbled back on its four legs and jumped into the air. Erdūn leapt and brought the beast back down by its flapping wing. The dragon screeched as Erdūn ripped the wing down the middle as if it were paper. A frantic claw swiped at Erdūn's throat. Mogurn heard Tikal gasp as Erdūn effortlessly caught hold of the claw. With the dragon in his vice grip, Erdūn pummeled the dragon continuously. Between strokes, the piasa tried to use its fire, but the flames never got passed its teeth.

Mogurn turned toward Tikal as Erdūn dragged the dead

beast back up the valley. He tossed it toward their feet and stepped back.

"Forgive him," Mogurn said, as Tikal backed away from the corpse. "He can be a little abrasive."

Tikal swallowed a lump as he turned from looking at the stout Erdūn to Mogurn.

"Are you sure he is only fifteen years of age?"

"Yes. He will lead the Delthurk army that will slaughter all the dragons of Zipacna, as assuredly as the Disciples of Gaorda led the army that killed the seshas. Do you not want to be a part of that?"

Tikal stepped farther away from the others to whisper to Mogurn. "This is not what we were expecting."

"No. It is much better, isn't it?"

"Yes. The other qui-lahk tribes might disavow us at first, but we will be there for the final battle."

"Excellent," Mogurn said. "We shall keep in contact, Tikal. We must continue to visit other nations, but the last time we met, you promised me a solution to one of our main adversaries on Zipacna."

"Here," Tikal said. In his open hand was a red stone that had been carved into the shape of an elephant's head. "When you see the rukh rider, give him this so that he knows that you have our support."

Mogurn took it from his hand. "Thank you, Tikal. It will be good to have the qui-lahk with us in this war."

Tikal nodded before climbing the rope ladder of his elephant.

Mogurn followed the Disciples and Erdūn into the large and many horse drawn carriage. Ta'ar rose to float above them. Erdūn had the entire opposite seat to himself while Mogurn sat beside the Disciples. He smiled toward Erdūn to catch his attention.

"You did well, Erdūn," Mogurn said. Erdūn nodded and looked away. Mogurn looked away in turn. Erdūn was not at all like Gradni. Whenever Gradni accomplished something, whether it was by Mogurn's will or against it, you could see his pleasure. Erdūn never showed happiness or any other emotion. He was the perfect product of what he was being trained for.

CHAPTER 6

Whilst wind channeling, Gradni slashed his sword right, revolved it left by circling around himself, and thrust it forward. He had found an area of Zipacna that was secluded and flat enough for him to practice. He wrenched his sword back with a grunt and swung it in angled arcs all around him, as if defending himself from multiple opponents.

Alongside the gradual change from elf to naga came newfound strength that made it easier to handle his sword. The scales had not yet fully formed, but all his skin was now faintly green. He often stroked his teeth with his tongue to measure his developing canines. Not everything about him was changing though. He became excited when he noticed that there were thicker strands of green hair within his brown, but then realized that it was because spring had arrived and had nothing to do with becoming a naga. Perhaps when the transformation was complete his hair would no longer be dependent on the weather. But it seemed more than likely that some traces of being elven would always remain. It was already clear that he would be a much lighter green instead of the dark green of Zahk. Zahk still also had his amesha liquid-like hair, and his broad fingers and bendy feet were his amesha adaptations to living on the mountain. Gradni could still feel the weather's energy within him, and was able to wind channel. Thus, even when he would fully become a naga, he would still be an elf.

He raised his blade and swung it against a crooked rock. The impact shuddered through him, and he dropped his sword as he halfway collapsed. He looked up. Zahk was staring at him from a spire three meters away. Gradni stared back until Zahk came to him.

Gradni straightened up. It was so easy for Zahk to get around on these mountains—more proof that he was still amesha, and Gradni would always be an elf.

"You think you are ready to fight your own kind?" Zahk asked.

Gradni grumbled. "They are not my own kind!"

Zahk nodded. He handed Gradni one of the two items in his hands. They were wooden jian swords. Gradni took it reluctantly. He remembered his time in the arena at Delthurk when Yagura gave him one. It was insulting to be holding one again at his skill level.

"Where did you get these from?" Gradni asked. "Why do you even have them?"

"Longues brought them from a dev city," was all Zahk said. He raised the other wooden jian as he spread his feet into a stance.

Gradni huffed. "Zahk, I do not wish to insult you, but your strength aside, I am better with a sword than you are. I am ready for battle."

Zahk smiled. Gradni could not tell if he was being snide or angry, nor did he have time to figure it out as Zahk's blade swung toward his chest. Gradni barely managed to block it, but the blow knocked him off his feet. Gradni got back up and readied his weapon. Zahk swung his sword again. Gradni defended himself, but was once again unable to hold his ground. His sword was knocked aside by a third attack

---

176

before Zahk's open palm struck Gradni in the chest. Gradni went limp as the blow was made, minimizing its impact so that he was able to land on his feet.

"This is not fair; you are not holding back your strength!"

"There will always be an opponent who is stronger than you."

"Not when I become a naga!"

Zahk charged. Blocking having failed twice, Gradni jumped to the side instead and whirled around to strike, but Zahk had already leapt away despite balancing on a rock with half a foot. His amesha connection with the earth combined with his dragon strength made it an even more uneven fight.

Zahk leapt over Gradni, twisted in the air, and landed facing him. "There will be an opponent who is stronger than you. And there will be many who are weaker. Those who are weaker will face you all at once. You must not underestimate how vital your strength will be when using your skill!"

Yagura. Zahk was acting like Yagura. Gradni kept his blade in constant motion to channel wind into his attacks as he ran ahead. Clacks sounded in sets of two and three as Zahk switched between engaging and hopping away. Gradni chased him, determined to strike a blow to show him he was the better fighter. Zahk moved in close. Gradni's sword was in a downward swing when it struck.

Zahk had raised his arm up against the wooden jian. Gradni froze, trapped in Zahk's gaze. Zahk grabbed the sword with one hand, removed Gradni from it with his other, and pushed him away. Gradni stumbled back. Their eyes were still locked on to each other.

"Why are you so angry?" Zahk asked. Gradni was panting. He turned to avoid Zahk. Zahk gripped Gradni's face and turned it back to him. "Why?" He was genuinely concerned. Gradni pulled himself out of the grip.

"I will never wholly be one of them. I will never belong here."

"What are you talking about?"

"I will always be an elf. Even when the change is complete, I will always be one of the elves that tried to kill the dragons. I thought I would not be, but I will. Even now, I am elven enough to still sense strong winds coming." Gradni sat with his knees tucked in. "It was a mistake to come back here. I had nowhere else to go."

Zahk's steps got quieter as he started walking away.

"Come here," he said.

"Where?"

"Just here." He was standing on a small spire three meters away. It was high enough to look out over much of Zipacna. "Come!" Gradni got up and went over. "Look."

The view was unremarkable. Gradni saw dragons that were either lying on the rocks, circling each other in the air, eating together, or wrestling playfully. It was nothing he had not seen before.

"What about them?"

"Are you blind? Wyverns, piasas, longues—all together. They do not segregate themselves the way the races do. They might all be dragons, but they share less amongst their physical selves than the races do. They do not care who you once were."

It was true. A longue was circling around a wyvern while both were flying upward. It was as if they did not see any difference between them.

"But they are still all dragon?"

"So are we. That is how the magic of dragons work. The reason you are changing is not simply because you are here with them. It is because in your heart, you are a dragon. You would not be transforming if you were not one of us. That is why I did not send you away when you came back. I still do not want you here. You are young, stupid, and arrogant. But I cannot deny the workings of dragon magic. You were one of us even then."

Gradni backed away from the ledge. It was true and comforting to hear, but it almost seemed too easy.

"Are you sure?"

"They have come across many people over the ages, and only those who share their values have ever undergone the change. It is a certainty."

Gradni looked toward the drakes that were circling around with longues right beside them. He did care more for the dragons than he ever had his own people. There was some sort of connection between them, a true source of real inspiration. It was so unlike the connection he thought he had with a father he barely saw. What he felt here was alien to him, possibly because it was real. But that just made him guilty for what he had tried to do, and for what his race was still doing. Zahk placed his hand on Gradni's shoulder.

"It will take time," he said.

Gradni nodded and started walking away.

"Wait!" Zahk's tone was suddenly immediate.

"What is it?"

"The weather, you can sense it?"

"Yes."

"You must tell us when it is about to empower you."

"Why?"

"Because that is when Delthurk attacks."

Gradni nodded. He should have remembered that himself. Delthurk always attacked when they were able to channel the weather's energy through them to make them swifter and stronger. Gradni did not like being an elf, but he would now be able to get his revenge by using his elf traits against them. Like Zahk, whose amesha adaptations to the mountain were further enhanced by his dragon strength, so too was Gradni's bond with the weather.

Gradni buried his fangs into meat as he sat beside Zahk. The horned salamander, Sirrush, leapt down from a higher ledge and rested beside Zahk.

"What about them? Are they born red like that?" Gradni blurted, spitting out meat as he pointed to a horned piasa. Zahk followed the finger. The piasa, as if attracted by the action, suddenly flew behind where the nagas were sitting. Gradni's hand was prevented from flopping down when the piasa propped her head under it so that his hand was between the horns.

Zahk in that time swallowed the chunk in his mouth and ripped off another. "Yes. But they are green when born. They transform later, whenever."

Gradni stroked the red piasa's neck as she rested her head on his thigh and folded her wings. She purred as she looked up at him, sending a tingle up Gradni's spine. This was the most affection he had received from any of them so far.

"I don't understand." Gradni said.

Zahk tossed his last piece of meat upward, and Sirrush clasped it viciously between his jaws. "It is very rarely a surprise when a dragon transforms. It is always the bravest or wisest of us, and such qualities in these times are difficult to hide. Every dragon who transforms was destined to."

The dragon growled affectionately as Gradni lightly stroked the area between her eyes and horns. Every piasa reminded him of the one he had seen so many years ago in the forest, the first dragon he had seen up close. He wondered if that piasa was somewhere around, or had died in battle since.

"She was one that surprised us," Zahk said toward the piasa. "Her transformation began days after you joined. Their transformation is not like ours. It takes only hours and it is excruciatingly painful and exhausting. Her name is—"

"Chimera," Gradni said with confidence. He was still unable to figure out most of their language, but was quickly figuring out the unique combination of grunts and growls that translated into names.

"Yes. She came to Zipacna despite living within qui-lahk land."

"What difference does it make where she lived before?"

"She was never in danger with them. She came here to help us."

Chimera grunted and drew away in embarrassment. Gradni leaned back with her.

"Can't we approach them, the qui-lahk?" Gradni asked.

"The qui-lahk will not get involved." The statement from Zahk was decisive- too decisive. He was an amesha before he was a naga. How could he know how the qui-lahk would react?

"I have looked through the library at Delthurk. They have always refused to help the races against us. There is no record of them ever attacking dragons except for having slain Zipacna in the previous age. Even that may not be true."

"Nor is there a record of them ever aiding dragons."

Gradni was silent for a moment. Zahk seemed to have all the answers, and Gradni still did not know where he was getting them from. "That is true. Why is that?"

"You have been sheltered, haven't you? The qui-lahk worship animals. They are affected by them the way ameshas are by the land, elves by the weather, and devs by the sun and moon. To them, dragons are abominations, monsters that have stolen elements from all the different beasts."

"Then why have they not joined the others against us?"

"I just told you. They are afraid."

"There must be some who are courageous." Zahk stopped chewing. Sirrush growled softly. Gradni realized what he had said. "I don't mean that those who fight us are any less wrong. There just has to be a better reason why they have not joined the others, especially if they think dragons are corrupted beasts. In Delthurk there are many who are afraid of dragons. Yet they come anyway."

Sirrush grunted and continued chomping his meat.

"Publicly, the qui-lahk think dragons to be abominations. Privately, they wonder if dragons are actually superior animals, and so are caught between their deductions," Zahk continued, in between bites, "They believe in the story of the creation of these mountains, but do not know if their ancestors acted correctly or not. They will not take a side."

The silence continued for a while as the four of them ate. Gradni could no longer bear not asking.

"When will you tell me who you used to be, before you became a naga?"

Zahk tossed his bone away and stood up. "What I was no longer matters. Did you not say that you were happy to lose what made you look like an elf?"

"Yes."

"Then you agree. My past before I became a naga is not who I am now."

Zahk walked away. Sirrush scampered after him, growling. Though he could not decipher what exactly was being said, Gradni detected anger from Sirrush. They could still hide things from him in conversation for now. Once his transformation was complete, there would be nothing that would escape his understanding.

Chimera lifted her head and stared at him sympathetically, a facial expression he was glad he was able to identify. He showed his own appreciation with a smile... which dropped into an open mouth as he recognized her face.

"It was you!" he squealed. "You were the one I saw in the forest!"

She puffed a ball of smoke at him, marginally annoyed that he had not known all along.

CHAPTER 7

Bamay stood on the ledge of the Delthurk castle and looked to see if her son was returning. She knew it was fruitless. He had only been gone for six weeks, but there was little else to do. With Ta'ar gone with them, the little respect she got from the Disciples was gone as well. They trusted her even less than before. Despite how things turned out for the better, they resented her scheming behind their backs for the karkadan. Either that, or they were afraid of what else she would do without their knowing. For whatever reason, she was banned from accompanying them to Aristahl. She no longer served a purpose to the Disciples, and it would only be a matter of time before they found a way to get rid of her.

The sun was setting. Bamay turned to go back inside the castle. This was her home now, the rival mountain base to the Zipacna Mountains. For some reason, she never imagined being here for the great battle, where she would be able to see her son destroy the dragons. It was a moment to look forward to, one that provided her with needed strength. In Delthurk, among not one but two races that were not her own, she felt even more alone. Her feet were large and bended like rubber here, and the elves she passed in the corridors never failed to stare at them when she stepped along the uneven ridges of Delthurk's castle. She would never get used to it. Perhaps they looked to learn how Erdūn would travel up Zipacna, as they only saw him occasionally since being introduced to him. It was mainly still Gradni who inspired them. Mogurn had arranged for a statue of the elf boy to be built at the entrance of Delthurk. It was made of a reflective steel and depicted Gradni looking toward Zipacna with his sword in hand. The sculptor even included that pendant that he always wore.

Bamay hated the statue. It was her idea to sacrifice Gradni for Erdūn, but she did not like being reminded of it. Mogurn had agreed to the plan reluctantly, so the last thing she expected was for him to capitalize further on her scheme, by building a larger than life figure that was the first thing every newcomer saw. Still, she respected how calculating the senator was. The more they were made to love Gradni, the more they would follow Erdūn into battle.

Her room in the Delthurk castle was a small one. It was next to the hall that still served as the soldiers' dorm, as the recently built barracks was not big enough to contain all the men that were now flooding into Delthurk. Bamay was only able to get peace and quiet after they went to sleep, something soldiers did not always feel they needed to do.

She sat by the window of her small room and looked out. From here, she could see almost nothing.

She missed her son. Sacrificing him to his destiny was more painful now that her usefulness to him was over. Though it was the devs who brushed her aside, she knew it was Mogurn who was instrumental in making sure that she did not accompany them on their tour. It was his way of getting back at her for sacrificing his prodigy. By touring with Erdūn and Ta'ar, Mogurn's fame was growing. He had purposely replaced her. Besides his cunning, he was as cruel as all the other rulers she had come across, all except for the kind Shah Zahk. She still remembered vividly how he saved her from men who were at their worst. He was not like any of the others. He was good to her.

Bamay shook her head. It did no good to have thoughts of the good Shah Zahk, yet it was difficult to not remember him while everyone else saw her as a nuisance. It was probably best for her to sleep early tonight. She was blowing out her candles when someone knocked on her door.

She did not react. It would make no difference, as the Disciples never waited for a response before entering. It was rare that they even knocked.

But whoever it was who knocked, did so again.

"Come in," she said idly, and he entered. Surprised, she stood up. It was not a dev, but a short elf man carrying a book that looked to weigh as much as he did. She recognized him as the one who always followed the senator Mogurn; the one who greeted her on Delthurk's behalf on that very first day she came here so many years ago.

"Lady Bamay, I hope I am not disturbing you."

"No. What is your name again?"

"Lays, assistant to Senator Mogurn. While he is away, he has left me with instructions to be carried out on his behalf." Bamay nodded, hiding as best she could her intrigue from his visit. "We are putting together a plan to attack Zipacna, one that utilizes the strength of ameshas. We wish to send a group of emissaries to Aristahl to recruit for the cause. We are hoping that as you are their ambassador, that you could accompany them. I must add that on your return to Delthurk, we will have ready for you a large room near the top of the castle. It is just below the senators' floor and has a view of Zipacna. Everything that is here will be ready for you there on your return."

Bamay stepped unsurely toward him. She attempted to

create an illusion of having composure. "Why did you not go to the Disciples for this?"

"We are giving them the rest they need, rewarding them for all that they have done for the cause already. There is no need to involve them." Bamay waited for a more acceptable answer. Lays complied. "The senator has deduced, from the way you hid the karkadan from the Disciples, that you have much more influence on your home nation than they do. For our last three visits to Aristahl, only elves have gone. The Disciples do not see a need to go themselves, as they prefer to remain here at Delthurk, where we are honoring them for their past achievements."

Bamay's interest peaked. It was all Mogurn's scheme. The spoiling of the Disciples, keeping her here all this time where the devs would never see her. Mogurn despised being their dog as much as she did. She sat down. "The senator presumes too much. Aristahl does what it does for the cause, not because of me, or even Erdūn, but because of the Fire Spirit Ta'ar."

Lays smiled. "The senator considered your amesha culture before leaving. He plans to address this issue during his time with the Fire Spirit, while you and I address the ruler Sheemu."

Bamay was in awe. "When do the emissaries leave?"

"Tomorrow at this time, that way not bothering the devs. Can you join them?"

"As Aristahl's representative, I will certainly join them in our war with the dragons. You will not regret this, Lays."

"The senator Mogurn rarely does, Lady Bamay."

Lays closed the door as he left. Bamay sat up on her bed. She had purpose again.

CHAPTER 8

Gradni inhaled as the harsh winds blew all around him. Delthurk would attack soon. He stepped into the river to get a closer look at his new face in the waterfall reflection. His skin was now completely made of green scales. As expected, he was a lighter green than Zahk. He cocked his head to the right and felt his pointy ears. Even they were made of scales that were tougher than his old skin. He grinned at himself to see his fully developed canines. Despite all the green, his facial structure was still the same. They would recognize him today. If his physical changes threw them off, then they would recognize the armor they had dressed him in, even though he had scratched Delthurk's insignia off all the metal plates. He glared at his sword, the flawless weapon that had been designed by the treacherous devs themselves. If only Yagura could know what the weapon would be used for now.

Gradni heard the dragons roar. Shadows crossed over his back as wyverns flew towards the elves that were mounting an attack at Zipacna's base.

Gradni let the end of his sword drop, glancing at the tip that had almost gone right through Tiamat's throat. "You are here for them," Gradni reminded himself, and he took up their roar as he leapt from the river to join them.

There were a couple hundred elves at the base of the

mountain. The dragons flew down and obscured Gradni's vision. He let out another roar and jumped, but before clearing the stone in front of him, his foot was grabbed by Zahk who pulled him back down. Gradni was mildly disoriented.

"Stay!" Zahk commanded

"Stay? They are fighting down there!" Gradni yelled back, as Chimera flew over the both of them and toward the chaos. Sirrush was probably already there.

"We will stay here, and only enter the fight if they come far enough to guarantee that they will not escape."

Gradni looked toward the battlefield. The elven force was not going to come up much higher. It was a guerilla tactic, and the longer he and Zahk remained up here, the more dragons would die.

"You stay if you like. I'm going down to help my kind," Gradni said as he tore the other's hand away. But Zahk brought him down again with more force than Gradni knew he had.

"Listen to me. Our survival has been dependent on that they never know I exist. Whenever they try something new against us, or succeed in bringing a force up the mountain, it is because they do not know of me—or you now—that we are able to defeat them. You and I are the dragons' secret weapon that they must never know about!"

Gradni pushed back, but Zahk held him firm. "They are dying down there. We can save them!"

"If we do, we damn them in the future! Think about that before your need to prove yourself."

"They are dying!" Gradni repeated.

"They are dragons! They will fight for their survival more than any other being that exists."

Zahk took his hand away. Gradni stood up, paralyzed from doing anything else while under his gaze. He knew he had to obey. Placing his hands on a boulder, Gradni looked down toward the battle.

The elves were shooting arrows at the longue dragons. The longues watched the missiles come toward them before weaving at the last second to avoid them. The elves continued to fire at the hovering longues that kept their distance, and only a few arrows did more than scar their targets. As the volleys of arrows continued, serpents and salamanders raced on the ground toward the elves. Gradni watched as on either side of the elf guerrilla phalanx, wyverns dashed ahead to surround the enemy. It was a good strategy, for though the wyverns could not weave in the air as successfully as the longues, they travelled faster. The longues were merely the distraction while the other species moved into prime positions.

The piasas in the meantime, being slower than their land and air siblings in either regard, hovered above the land dragons and used their powerful flames and claws to fend off arrows.

The elves turned their arrows against the coming onslaught of land dragons, and in that instant the longues and wyverns shot toward them. The elves retaliated with their weapons, only some of them successfully blocking the fire with their shields and slashing flesh with their swords, while they were in turn raked by wyvern claws and longue bladed tails.

Leading the Delthurk force was an elf dressed so royally and fighting so proficiently that Gradni wanted to face him most of all. But as he leaned forward, Zahk's one hand gripped his shoulder while his other directed Gradni to Python, the horned serpent who was slithering between the dragon ranks so smoothly, that it seemed like she knew exactly where they would be before passing them. She whipped her tail an inch from the commander and back again, effectively leading the commander's sword away from its defensive position before she snapped forward and snatched his throat in her jaws.

Elves began to surround her as she slammed him against a sharp ledge, but other serpents moved in to protect her. They shot their fire toward the front line of elves, while salamanders leapt over to attack the second and third lines. The piasas beat their wings and flew over to attack the fourth and fifth. All the while the wyverns and longues surrounded the army as well, breathing their fire, raking with their claws, and whipping with their sharp tails.

A faction of elves broke free from the wall of wyverns. A serpent immediately snaked toward them and breathed fire to keep them detained, but an elf held a shield to the fire while another threw a spear into the serpent's belly. There were no dragons behind these elves, allowing the elves to focus on one less direction. The dragons tried to surround them again, but doing so thinned the wall and weakened the barricade around the rest of the Delthurk force.

"Come on," Zahk roared, as he bounded toward the opening. Gradni leapt after him.

Zahk had gotten a head start, but Gradni was able to keep pace. Though he was not bounding with as much efficiency as Zahk, he moved swiftly in the air with strong winds cycling around and through him.

Zahk slashed his burning blade through three elves. For a moment, while in the air from a leap, Gradni froze. These were his people. They were wearing the same steel that he was wearing. Their swords and shields were the weapons he had seen in the barracks and in the arena. Falling beneath their helmets was hair colored green, blue, orange, and white. Gradni landed on his haunches and took a breath.

An axe came at his head. Instinctively, Gradni blocked it with his sword, the strong winds giving him swiftness to move with more speed than usual. His naga strength stopped the axe immediately. The elf attacker's eyes stared fearfully at Gradni through the helmet. Gradni front kicked him out of his sight. His breathing became heavier. An animalistic scream came from behind him. A longue had been gashed around the midriff, but was still breathing fire at an elf. The elf dodged the fire and was swinging his sword at the longue.

There was no time to think. Gradni dashed forward and drove his jian into the elf's stomach. He pulled it out and swung his blade around defensively. Movement kept him alive and from thinking about what he was doing. Around him, dragons were wounded, dying, or fighting. Zahk was covering his own area, so Gradni moved away to another. He parried two separate blades, and in a downward swing slashed both of his attackers' sides. He dived into another three elves while the roaring around him got louder. He was stronger, more skilled, and had a superior blade. Gradni hacked his way into the heart of the Delthurk force.

"Gradni!" Gradni drove his sword in and out of the elf he was fighting and turned to look behind him. Zahk was the source of the roars. He was coated in blood, much like Gradni imagined he himself was. "Come on," Zahk roared again. Gradni stared him in the eye, aware that he was being consumed by fury. "Now!"Zahk commanded.

Gradni roared and charged back up. Zahk turned as soon as Gradni was by his side, and together they climbed up the mountain. Hot painful breath was pouring out of Gradni's mouth. Zahk did not notice as he was looking down toward the battle. Dumbfounded, Gradni followed his sight.

It was too much for the elves. They were backing away and focusing more on defending themselves and escaping instead of pushing forward. Zahk roared a particular roar, and the shadow of low flying drakes surrounded and passed over the two nagas.

The land dragons stopped pursuing the elves, while the smaller air dragons rose up so that the drakes could fly freely. Gradni feared that the elves would bring the drakes down with their arrows, but few of them even turned around, as Tiamat and the ten other drakes let loose flames that washed over the remaining elves.

Gradni watched the drakes return while Zahk and he crouched behind rocks like cowards. He was unable to decipher the expression on Zahk's dark-green face.

Chimera came and settled herself next to Gradni, and Sirrush hopped over the rocks safely a minute later. Bodies of dragons and dead elves were littered over the mountain. Wyverns and salamanders were on their backs with the arrows that killed them still in their hearts. Serpents and longues were curved around the rocks, their blood smearing the stone as they slipped down to lower ledges. Gradni turned away. The strength he gained by becoming a naga failed him. He leaned against a boulder.

A hand touched upon his shoulder.

"You did well, Gradni. I know that this was not easy, to fight against those you once fought for."

Gradni swatted Zahk's hand aside.

"We could have saved them!"

"I already explained it to you."

"You stay up here, too cowardly to fight for them, and you make me do the same!"

Zahk grabbed him suddenly and swung him against the mountain. Gradni growled back, his fist aching to strike. "You let them all die," Gradni continued. "What kind of a king are you?"

"Silence, boy!" Zahk's yellow teeth showed as if he was going plunge them into Gradni. "How dare you! You think I do not want to? You think that for each of us who dies, that I do not wish that it were I? I am their shah; they are my responsibility. I know I could have saved them, but then what? Tell me that, Gradni, what happens then? What will they bring against us when they know of us?" He pushed Gradni away. Other dragons stepped between them. Gradni grabbed the hilt of his sword but he did not remove it. Zahk's words swirled in his head. "You know the lies that they believe, that dragons curse others by infecting them with their will. That is how the Disciples see us, as those who have been cursed instead of blessed."

"It is not the truth!"

"Don't be naïve. What difference does it make what the truth is to them? Whatever faith they had in my character, that they had in yours, it no longer matters. They will think us overrun by evil, by sin, and they will not only fight us with more ferocity, but they will find others as well. That is the truth."

"So we do nothing? I have the strength of a naga and have been trained by the Disciples themselves. You expect me to just stand here with you and hope that they will come to the inner mountains each time?"

Dragons tried to stop him, but Zahk once again seized Gradni by his collar. Gradni grabbed the hand with his left hand while his right pulled on his sword. It was out by an inch when Sirrush roared for them both to separate. Finger by finger, Zahk's hand released Gradni.

"We cannot afford your lust for vengeance here," he said with finality before leaving.

Gradni's mouth opened to speak, but no words came out. He circled around to look back at the mountain. Dragons that were still alive were picking up those that were dead. Blood poured from a dead longue's neck as a piasa pulled the body onto his back. Gradni hiked back to his cave. He went right to the end of it and sat against a corner.

It was Sirrush who came for Gradni. He ignored him, but Sirrush growled demandingly. It was not an option to refuse. Outside the cave, other dragons were making their way across Zipacna, all of them going to a specific place. Gradni took off his armor and blindly followed Sirrush and the others, looking only at his feet as he hiked from mountain to mountain.

Sirrush barked toward him once they got to a peak. Gradni lifted his head and looked toward Sirrush who was looking back from a higher ledge. In the sky behind Sirrush was smoke so thick and red that it looked like it was taking fire up with it. Gradni could hear the fierce crackling of the flames giving birth to the smoke. The smell, though faint where he was, was pungent. He followed Sirrush toward it anyway. He had never been to this area of Zipacna where three of the innermost mountains met. Gradni pulled himself over rock that was claimed by two of the three mountains and looked at the spectacle.

The three mountains created a deep pit between them. How deep the pit went could not be known at this time, for it was filled with a conflagration so huge, that even from here it was hard to see anything else.

Surrounding it were sobekians that were fueling the fire with the unequalled force of their breath. High above, bark was being dropped into the pyre by winged dragons. Wood was only an aid to the burning. It was the purpose of the fire itself that fueled it and gave birth to the fumes and red smoke. Drakes and other winged dragons were flying to and from the fire and were bringing the bodies of dead dragons from the battle. Each dragon dropped into the inferno intensified the thick red smoke that rose and disseminated into the air.

Dragons not flying above were formed into lines according to their species. They were making their way toward the heart of the fire and then away from it. Sirrush left to join other salamanders. Gradni hiked down the mountain and stood in a line of sobekians. In spite of all the movement around him, there was little noise. Even the crackling of the fire seemed unreasonably soft now. He passed by other sobekians that were fueling the fire. The dragon in front of him came out of the thick of the smoke. Gradni waited for him to pass before walking forward. He walked so deep into it that he could not see where he was going. It was far enough. He inhaled the red smoke that was his onetime fellow dragons through his nose and mouth. His nostrils and throat burned as the smoke seeped in past his scales and stung his eyes. Then, all his own feelings stopped, as the spirited remains of the fallen dragons absorbed his senses and consciousness.

He smelled the clouds high above the southern amesha nations while gazing at the bronze domes of their palaces. Sounds of a waterfall crept in as his four feet felt damp within the cave that the falling water hid. Blue flowers the size of his head had a sweet-scented aura about them as he slithered over the crooked roots of jungle trees. Snow and ice of a harsh winter blew against him as he beat his wings fiercely to move closer to the ice fortress ahead, an effort made easier when a large-winged white beast with black spots shielded him from above.

Zipacna then came in, its peaks shifting furiously like the fire that it was. From the constant combustion came the dragons that were floating away, all made of soft bright fire. They were leaving trails of dim fire as they weaved through villages and cities of the four people. When the people came across the trails left by the dragons, their hearts started to glow. The people moved on, illuminating those they came across, who in turn did the same for the ones that they passed, until it was evident that the nurturing warmth within everyone would inevitably be lit.

The light separated into mist and turned red, Gradni was back within the haze of red smoke. He took one more short breath and walked out.

While on the same rock that was part of two of the three mountains, Gradni watched the ritual continue. Every living dragon had partaken in the ceremony. The pyre was left alone to burn out so that the smoke could disperse into the air. Though not as thick, it remained red as it kept going through the night. Gradni did not leave until it was completely burnt out.

CHAPTER 9

With Erdun, Ta'ar, Yagura, and three other Disciples behind him, Mogurn handed the item to the lone qui-lahk. The image of an eagle's claw coated the entire right side of the qui-lahk's bare chest.. Mogurn waited impatiently as the rukh rider examined the carved red stone. Satisfied, the qui-lahk tucked it away. "So they'll be there for the last battle as well?" The qui-lahk's voice was rough, as if the words had to battle through his throat to come out. It was disconcerting to Mogurn, that though the qui-lahk was lean, he was still skinny and only marginally taller than Lays.

"Yes," Mogurn replied. "Will you join them?"

"Long as you give me the promised pay, yes, we'll be there. Just don't expect us to come down to the rest of you. We'll remain at that horned drake's level where your arrows can't reach him—any lower and we won't have a chance against the rest of that drake's ilk."

"Agreed," Mogurn stated. He had expected exactly as much from this character.

The qui-lahk cocked his chin to the side and started to rub his bristles. "Anything else I can do you for?"

Mogurn exhaled a short breath. "We were hoping to see the beast."

The qui-lahk continued to stroke his cheek with his open palm. "Beast? You mean my partner?"

"Yes, your partner."

The qui-lahk put his hand down. "Sure."

They stood saying nothing for almost a minute. The qui-lahk just smiled while looking at them all, particularly Erdūn and Ta'ar. Mogurn grew impatient. "We were hoping to see your partner before leaving," Mogurn repeated.

"Can't your long ears hear the disruption in the wind behind you?"

Mogurn turned around along with the others. An eagle was coming toward them. At first it didn't seem so spectacular, until he realized that the bird was much farther away than he thought. The rukh came rapidly toward them, its wingspan growing at an unnatural speed. This monster was larger than any drake. It flew over them before circling back around. It slowed down, though its size made it hard to see that. It landed right by the qui-lahk, ruffling the clothes of everyone who stood before it. Its muscles were surrounded by gray feathers that were as big as shields and looked just as tough. Even fire from the horned drake would have trouble burning through them.

"Satisfied?" The qui-lahk grinned.

Mogurn's mouth opened with glee. "Yes. We shall see you before the battle. I will make arrangements for the both of you as soon as we return."

The qui-lahk nodded as the rukh bent low so that he could pull himself up onto its back. The great bird leapt into the air and rode away with the rider on top of it.

Mogurn and the others watched it leave before returning to the carriages. They would remain here for the night before visiting the next kingdom.

The Fire Spirit and Erdūn were facing each other, oblivious to Mogurn who was watching them from a distance.

The Fire Spirit, six feet himself, now hovered a foot to keep eye contact with Erdūn. Mogurn stared as Ta'ar raised his right hand and placed the top of his fingers against Erdūn's chest.

Erdūn's mouth pried open as if pulled by the air that rushed in and out of it. Yagura came to stand beside Mogurn. The ritual used to be performed in private, but while moving from nation to nation there were no doors to hide behind, and Mogurn took advantage of being privy to the daily spectacle that further bonded Erdūn to Ta'ar.

Ta'ar pushed his hand farther, and his fingers- instead of pushing Erdūn away, sank into him, as if the skin, flesh, and bone that protected Erdūn's heart were all the consistency of oil. Erdūn's next immediate breath was a gasp, before a wheezing cough followed. His hands began to move wildly yet stiffly, as if he were trying to restrain himself. But he was as able to do so as he was able to control the energy forcing itself out of every uncomfortable breath. It had never been this violent a reaction before. Unwilling tears clouded Erdūn's vision, and his wide legs, which were always steady before, trembled. Erdūn stared into the burning eyes of Ta'ar. It was too much energy. Erdūn was not yet able to handle so much, but he did not break away from Ta'ar. Mogurn could tell that every muscle in Erdun's body was telling him to do so. Ta'ar did not pull back either, though clearly aware of Erdūn's discomfort, as Ta'ar's aura was behaving as erratically as Erdūn's breathing.

Once the shock passed, Erdūn's arms straightened beside his legs, though his muscles were still twitching. The gasps of air slowed as well. Now that the connection was accomplished, Ta'ar's aura pulsated dimly as Erdūn's heart steadily pumped the fire through his body.

"He will not live long, will he?" Mogurn said to Yagura.

"All this energy being forced into a body that is not ready for it. He is strong now, but at a cost."

"He has a destiny. It is all he lives for. He is fortunate that his destiny will happen soon, and that all of us are readying him for it."

"At the expense of his longevity."

Yagura turned to Mogurn. "What we do not tell him is so he can remain true to the purpose that he has accepted willingly. Can you say the same for the one you sacrificed?"

Erdūn's twitching was replaced with a constant jittering.

"I am not aghast to the methods. I am simply pointing out the facts. Gradni could have been a fine asset to our cause. My participation in his upbringing and his sacrifice should be enough to show you that I know enough about the power of a martyr."

Yagura realigned himself beside Mogurn. "Yes. This is true." he said. It surprised Mogurn. It was the closest to an apology he could ever expect from the deva. Two more minutes passed before Mogurn decided that now was the prime time to take advantage.

"We are going to the elven nation of Darona next. I am not on good personal terms with their senate, though they are supportive of Delthurk. Their history with spirits has also left them distrustful of them. It is best if you go with Erdūn to see them without the Fire Spirit and myself."

"Darona has no ill history with spirits."

"It does, and we cannot risk not getting their support."

Yagura said nothing in compliance. Ta'ar removed his hand from Erdūn's chest. After a couple minutes of soft breathing, Erdūn was ready to go. They entered the carriage and continued their journey to Darona with Ta'ar floating above them. The Fire Spirit was not as bright as he was on that first day he arrived at Delthurk. The ritual between him and Erdūn was going on even then, but with Erdūn having so much of the Fire Spirit's energy, the lack of brightness was visible, especially with so few people around to fuel Ta'ar with their convictions in his cause.

The Disciples predicted that when Erdūn went to battle on Zipacna, no matter what his fate, Ta'ar's aura would burn brighter than ever. The world would hear about Erdūn and the great battle, which would lend to Ta'ar's fame and thus his aura. Ta'ar burning brighter would in turn fuel the races into finishing off all the remaining dragons that were scattered across Adijari.

It was a viable theory, for no one could think of Erdūn without thinking of Ta'ar. The bond between them was stronger than the bond people assumed existed between Mogurn and Gradni. But Ta'ar was still a spirit in need of worship. He was once the spirit of an amesha nation, and now that Erdūn was reaching his pinnacle, the Fire Spirit would need new ways to pursue the cause.

Yagura and the other Disciples rode ahead to Darona with Erdūn running between them. Mogurn waited for them to disappear into the sloping valley of the nation before approaching Ta'ar with his head lowered.

"I am sorry, great Fire Spirit, that you could not accompany them. It was I who suggested they go without us. The nation of Darona does not have much respect for spirits."

"I have come across disbelievers before," Ta'ar boomed.

"Yes. I have witnessed as such. Fortunate for us all that at least the Disciples' cause is common to ours." The crackling of Ta'ar's aura changed. Mogurn lifted his head. Ta'ar was staring down at him.

"I was not speaking of the Disciples of Gaorda."

Mogurn's shoulders sank, and his fingers tapped nervously on his chest like the legs of a spider.

"I am sorry. Fire Spirit," Mogurn uttered, "I meant no disrespect to them or you."

Ta'ar lowered himself till he was eye to eye with Mogurn. "You see that the Disciples of Gaorda are not respectful toward me?"

Mogurn felt the heat of Ta'ar's anger with every word. He hid his inner smile with a frown. "It is their own folly, great spirit. Delthurk was pleased at your arrival, for we have always known of your pursuit to end the dragon threat. We follow Erdūn not because of him or even the Disciples, but because of you, Lord Ta'ar. I am sorry to make such insinuations. They are based only on what I see, which is that that they do not offer you as much as we at Delthurk would, if given the chance."

Ta'ar's fire crackled a different tone, this one less intense but with odd bursts. Without another word, he floated away to be alone. Mogurn did not see where he went, but the lack of heat told him he was far enough.

Mogurn allowed himself a smile as he wiped the sweat from his forehead. He did not know if he would have been able to manage it. For the journey home he would need to nurture the thoughts he planted today.

When the others returned, along with telling Mogurn that they had met with success, Yagura took pride in telling the Delthurk senator that he was wrong about Darona having a grudge against spirits.

"Really?" Mogurn said, his eyes squinting with his forefinger above his upper lip. "Well, in any case. We got what we needed."

CHAPTER 10

W hich cave is he in?"

Python's tail turned and twisted in the air to mimic a path along the mountain. Gradni followed it with his eyes, seeing tens of different caves on the way. He wondered if it was possible to explore every cave of Zipacna. He had not even seen all the caves within the central mountain. That was where Zahk's cave was, and not along this path that Python guided him on.

Gradni hiked along the path till he got to the specified cave. It had a large circular opening and spiraled downwards at a steep slope. It was a deep cave, and for a second Gradni thought he would wait for Zahk to come out. But the sudden idea that he was fearful of going in angered him, so he started to climb down it. It was like climbing down the mountain, but more difficult with less room to maneuver. Several feet down and finally below the roof of the cave, Gradni looked over his shoulder while still clinging to the wall. Zahk was on both knees with his back toward Gradni. His head was lowered, and before him was the statue of a magnificent upright sesha. Under the dragon was a jade statue of a woman.

Gradni slipped off the rock under his right foot and fell a good two feet. He scrambled to stop himself from creating any more noise, but the effort only made it worse as he released more pebbles and gravel in his struggle to grip something. His own back toward Zahk's now, he glanced at Zahk once again. Zahk's posture hadn't changed. Gradni silently climbed back out of the cave.

Fifteen minutes later, Zahk came out. "Come inside," he said.

Gradni stood before the statue of the sesha he instantly knew to be Irath, the king of the seshas who was slain by Gaorda. For a moment he remembered the beautiful stand that held the sword he now wielded. This was much more stunning. The hood of the Irath statue was wider than him when he stretched his arms out, and even the hollowed eyes and broken fang did not detract from its beauty. Irath's mouth was open and the forked tongue was pulled back. The stone that the statue was chipped out of was a darker brown than the mountains here. The body of Irath was layered beneath it, where the jade statue of the woman sat comfortably. Her eyes were sculpted out of piercing rubies. He could not make out the expression of her face, but she sat very proud.

"Why have you been looking for me?"

Gradni remained looking at the statue. "I want to know why we have never taken the fight to Delthurk."

"It is not an option."

"Why? Why do we wait here for them to attack each time, on their terms? It is why we are losing numbers."

"For the same reasons that they cannot know of us. If we fight them, the elves of Delthurk will inform their brethren and get more support from the elf nations. Most nations, though they are afraid of us, see no need to get involved because they do not see us as a threat to them. That will change if we attack them. I have told you before that we must consider the consequences of our actions."

Gradni turned toward Zahk. "Then at least let us wage war upon the devs? They already hate us."

"I said no."

"The devs want us all dead. They have already killed all the seshas. We cannot let them get away with that!"

"We cannot afford for vengeance here."

"This is not about vengeance, Zahk. It is about justice. It is about survival. The devs must all die for us to be safe."

Zahk did not answer immediately. "The Disciples of Gaorda—you have heard the dev stories from one of them?"

"Yes, he made me believe that their deeds were heroic, which I know now were not. We must do this, Zahk. It could make all the difference!"

"He lied to you," Zahk growled.

"I already said I know that, we—"

"No, you do not!" Zahk interrupted. "Even if we could, we will not punish the entire dev race for the actions of the Disciples."

"How can you defend them in front of this homage to the one they killed? The Disciples led them, but the rest of the devs followed without question. They must pay."

Zahk drew his sword and placed its edge vertically between the two of them.

"Look at the blade!" Zahk instructed.

"I have seen it."

"Look at it"—he pushed it into Gradni's hands—"and compare it to your own."

Gradni did. He had always wondered about its origin. Even the statue before them paled in comparison to the beauty of the blade. The handle was dark green, and made of pieces that perfectly mimicked the scales of longue dragons. The crossguard was fashioned after dragon wings, and the base of the hilt was a fashioned three-pronged claw, similar to the fore claws of salamanders. A serpent was wrapped around the handle, and then once around each side of the crossguard. The head of the serpent opened up at the top of the hilt and out of its mouth emerged the blade. The steel blade was as good as the steel of his own, though it had a greenish hue to it and was not as clean a finish since it mimicked an actual flame. Its edges were curved and even had curved prongs unevenly jutting in the same direction as the point. There were also some small gaps within the steel itself—each like a tiny hole of flame dancing within the sword.

Gradni held it away and brought his own sword out to confirm what Zahk wanted him to notice. The steel was not just similar, but was in fact the same dev steel. The entire sword's design was similar to his own, which was unlike any other sword he had come across in Delthurk. "This sword, it was made by the devs?"

"By dev nagas; they came together with their knowledge of magic, smiting, and forbidden dragon lore to create this weapon. See the hilt."

Some of the scales that made the hilt glistened a brighter green. "What is it?" Gradni asked.

"Jade. Alchemist dev nagas melted the jade with their magic. It was spread from the hilt to meld with the steel of the blade. It was made at the end of the Dev-Sesha War. The steel and jade combination was softened by the fire of the last five red sesha dragons, before naga smiths folded and hardened it with their tools.

Ash from fallen dragons and clay from the caves of these mountains were used to temper the steel."

Zahk put his hand out. Gradni gave him back his sword. Instantly it became alight. Gradni stared first at the sword, and then at the intensity reflected in Zahk's eyes.

"The fire comes from you," Gradni said, half questioning, half exclaiming. Zahk lessened the flames to a soft ripple along the blade.

"Fire is part of the dragon's being. It is the main reason they are feared. The races think that because fire is their natural gift that they are dangerous. They are correct, for there is nothing as potent as fire, but dragons do not misuse fire as the races so readily believe they do. It is their birthright. In the case of nagas, like you and I, we were not born to it, but being dragons as well, with the sword as a conduit we too can summon fire from within. It is a dev weapon, but also a dragon weapon. Not every dev was out to kill the dragons. Some understood that dragons were in fact virtuous. They honored them with weapons like these and with statues like this one of Irath and Kallini.

"The Disciples of Gaorda believe that devs who become nagas are infected rather than blessed. There were many devs who fought for the dragons, knowing that their fire, like all fire, is divine. There were dev nagas of all skills who created weapons such as these, but under the misguidance of the Disciples, all these talismans were destroyed. This sword and the statue might be the only legacies of the onetime union between devs and dragons." The flame of the sword died. Zahk handed the blade back to Gradni. "Will its flame to life, knowing that it comes from you," Zahk said. Gradni tried. He looked to Zahk when nothing happened. Zahk took no action. He tried again, repeatedly trying to bring fire from his core. A few minutes later, a couple flickers danced upon the sword. Gradni took a breath. He felt the spark travel from his center and through his arms to be revealed upon the blade. "Only nagas can bring out the flame. The magic is not within the sword, but within ourselves."

The feeling of Gradni's core burning through the sword was enriching, but still foreign. Gradni handed the weapon back to Zahk. He turned to the statue. Somehow it had not occurred to him that the green jade signified that she was a naga.

"Was she one of them who created the blade?" Gradni asked.

"No, she was here generations before the Dev-Sesha War. Her name was Kallini; we know her as the first who embraced the dragons. She is the first naga. You have never heard her name?" Gradni shook his head as he moved closer to her. The jade of her skin was finely carved to form scales. "She was Gaorda's cousin." Gradni immediately turned from the statue back to Zahk. "Gaorda was always wary of dragons. It wasn't until Kallini became a naga that Gaorda began to act against us. As cousins they were very close, despite their disagreement regarding dragons. Gaorda convinced himself that she had been poisoned to their will, which was confirmed to him when she changed. Kallini was also a kshatriya like Gaorda. She rallied the seshas to defend themselves and fought valiantly for them. She blamed herself for Gaorda's war, and became the greatest leader we have ever had. When Irath was killed in a battle with Gaorda, Kallini took charge. She decimated enemies with her superior tactics. She targeted only the Disciples, restricting the fight to them so that other devs would leave the war. The Disciples of Gaorda breed hate, Gradni. That is all they do. By slaying them alone she contained the Dev-Sesha War from becoming a war against all dragons."

"Prevented, or delayed till now?" Gradni said. Zahk did not answer. Gradni regretted his remark. "I was told that Gaorda died in battle against Irath?"

"No, he died against Kallini. Their fight was short. They were equally skilled, but Kallini was faster and stronger because she was naga. In previous encounters she was merciful, but not after he killed Irath. Too many of her kind had died due to him. She herself was overrun later."

"Why did I not hear of any of this when I was at Delthurk?

There are shelves of books of dragon history in their library, but there is no mention of nagas, even within the chronologies of the entire war."

"I know. I know that the Disciples believe nagas no longer exist, so I knew there would not be much written about us. It was only after meeting you that I learned how far they went to hide our existence. It is because of her. They do not want the name of their founder to be tarnished by his blood relation to the first naga. Gaorda's secret shame is what has protected us from discovery.

"I do not contest that the Disciples are our enemy," Zahk continued. "They are fanatical. We have been looking for them for many years, before they came to live in Delthurk. But the dev race is not our adversary."

"You don't think they are to blame?"

"They could have done something. There were many who did nothing, and if they had acted then perhaps the seshas would still be alive. They were already afraid of dragons before Gaorda instigated war using guile and subterfuge. By the time the nations understood that the Disciples were inciting the seshas to attack, they were already too deep in the war with them. This is why the Disciples of Gaorda are banned in many dev nations. They no longer trust the Disciples. They want nothing more to do with them, or with dragons."

"So they are not seen as the great heroes they profess to be?"

"Not by dev nations. But these same nations are unwilling to accept the shame of being manipulated, and so do not contest the Disciples' self-proclaimed heroic standing. I know you want a simple solution, Gradni. There is none. All we can do is defend ourselves from our enemies." Gradni stared idly at Irath's coils. "Was there something else?" Zahk asked after a while.

Gradni shook his head at first, but then remembered. "The bodies of our enemies, the ones the dragons take so that their wounds by our swords are not discovered.

Where are they taken?"

Gradni could not see how deep the pit was because of all the bodies dumped there over the years. His own father, slain by Zahk, could be somewhere in the rotting pile before him. He turned away from it and started walking away. It was too much death to accept.

CHAPTER 11

B amay turned away from the carriage window. Every
time she came to Aristahl it was in a worse state. For
the brief period that Ta'ar returned for after Gradni's
death, there was a boost in morale, but Ta'ar soon left again
to join the Disciples at Delthurk. He visited periodically after that which helped, but that too stopped once he started
touring with Erdūn. It had been more than two years now
since Ta'ar had visited Aristahl, and yet her people still
worked themselves to the bone to provide for Delthurk and
the cause.

Sacrifice, Bamay reminded herself. She sacrificed being
a mother to Erdūn; Aristahl needed to sacrifice as well. It
had paid off after all, for they could finally step out from the
background and accompany their fellow amesha and savior
Erdūn, and thus lead all the other amesha nations in the
final glorious war against the dragons.

Bamay got out of the carriage alongside the two elven
delegates that accompanied her. She felt her people glaring
at her. There was a time when she served the shah when
they looked at her with gratitude. No matter how much
she did now, no matter that she was Erdūn's mother, she
sensed only resentment from them. Even the steadfast
guards showed no goodwill toward her. She wished there
was a way she could hide the rich brown of her skin from
the grayness of theirs.

She turned to the elves. "It would be best if I see Minister Sheemu alone."

The elves nodded without hesitation. Working with them was already much easier than working through the Disciples. She walked past the guards. They did not even nod in her direction.

Bamay waited a while in the palace room. It was not like Sheemu to be late. When she finally came, Bamay stopped herself from looking away. Sheemu was grayer than ever. There was so little brown in her exposed skin that it seemed that she would never recover. She was no longer trying to hide it either. Her royal clothes had been discarded for simple ones that were well below her status.

"Lady Bamay!" she said excitedly; a semblance of a smile formed on her face. "It has been some time. I did not think I would see you again."

"There have been some changes, Sheemu. Good changes. I come with great news."

Sheemu's smile widened a little more. "Sit, please," Sheemu insisted. She pulled out a chair and directed Bamay toward it like a servant would. This was not the woman Bamay remembered. Bamay sat. Sheemu looked at her intently as if attempting to pull the words out of her.

"Sheemu, I am here directly on the elves' behalf and not the Disciples of Gaorda's. The elves see things rightfully and know that we can be of help on the fields of battle. I come as an emissary for soldiers. Finally, as we planned, Erdūn will fight alongside his people." Sheemu sat back in response to this. It gave Bamay a better view of her face, and she saw that the smile was gone. "What is wrong?" Bamay asked.

"Forgive me, Bamay. But when you said you had great news, I was expecting something else."

"Something else? This is what we hoped for. This is what

we wanted, for Aristahl to regain its honor! What else could we ask for?"

Sheemu looked at her for a while without saying anything. "I was hoping, foolishly, that you were going to relieve us of our responsibility. Certainly not ask for more. We have done so much already. Can't you see that it is destroying us? Aristahl barely survives. It is a shroud of what it once was. And now you ask for our soldiers as well?"

"Your spirit demands it!"

Sheemu's hand smacked the table. "It is because of him that we do all this, in the hope that he will forgive us for the transgression that one amesha committed against him!"

"He will return once the dragons are destroyed, once the ameshas join the battle against them."

"After everything we have already done, Bamay, after getting nothing for it, for a threat that does not even concern us anymore- I do not wish to send more of our people to die needlessly."

"But you must! You were chosen to rule so that you could rectify the mistakes committed by Zahk, not repeat them!"

"Do you remember what Aristahl was like when Shah Zahk ruled, Bamay? It was a happier place. I could say I was an advisor in the court of Aristahl, and ameshas of other nations would applaud me. Now, I tell them I am its temporary ruler, and there is shame in their polite words. I am starting to think they are correct to feel this way."

Desperate, Bamay took hold of Sheemu's arm. "Slayers and warriors are coming from all over to fight the dragons. To finally end them so that our spirit can return to Aristahl! Imagine how they will react when they find that Erdūn's own nation is no longer willing to sacrifice for the cause? If you do not send ameshas from Aristahl, then you stop everyone else from joining Erdūn as well. And you will prevent the dragons' end more than Zahk ever did. We have done so much, as you have said. If you stop now, then it will all be for nothing." The words were cold and her stare colder. Sheemu felt none of it. She removed Bamay's hands and turned toward the faded marble wall.

"I wish for many things, Bamay, but I am powerless to grant them. There are many who are still desperate for Ta'ar's attention, and will gladly go to war for him. But I warn you, there are many ameshas now who have not been influenced by the Fire Spirit, and our love for him is dying as his has died for us. I will not force my soldiers to go to war with you, but I will tell them that they are being asked for, if they so wish to join you. Do not worry. Though I do not understand why, Ta'ar and Erdūn still have great influence here. There are many who will die for them. You should be ashamed of the loyalty you have gained."

Sheemu stood up and walked out of the room without even closing the door. Alone again, Bamay drifted to wait by the window in case she returned.

The once swift horses that once raced on the paved roads were now struggling without muscle or fat. They could not even bear the weight of their masters who walked beside them. Shah Zahk would never have allowed it to get this far. His warrior eyes, hero's smile, and perfectly shaped slightly arrogant goatee came to her before she realized it. Things could have been different if she had not betrayed him. Zahk was a good man. But Ta'ar had offered to make her son a hero. As a mother, she had to do what was best for him.

Realizing that Sheemu would not return, Bamay quietly returned to the carriage.

CHAPTER 12

The respite that Mogurn had hoped for after returning to Delthurk was for naught. He was grateful that most of the nations had promised to send soldiers days before they were needed for the great battle instead of months, as that was easier on Delthurk's limited resources. The problem; however, was that nations could break their promise at any time. This meant that Delthurk could only rely on the eight thousand already here instead of the fifteen thousand they were meant to have.

The only one nation that they could rely on unconditionally was Aristahl. Lays had done his part as instructed. Bamay was now the link, and she was being treated more royally than Yagura had ever been. The Disciples of Gaorda were no longer the complication between them. The Fire Spirit Ta'ar had also agreed to sit with the elven council a mere two hours ago, and thus again, Delthurk had the hold on Aristahl that the Disciples once did.

Mogurn was sitting at his desk going over Lays's logbook when he heard first arguing outside his office, then what he knew was his guard being pushed aside. The double doors of his office swung open against the walls. Yagura stepped inside and searched, his head jerking from side to side before coming toward Mogurn at his desk. The guard chased in after him, but Mogurn motioned for him to leave.

Yagura's shadow covered the logbook as Mogurn fought the urge to stand up.

"Disciple Yagura, do not blame the guard. I told him not to let anyone disturb me. I would have told him that you were an exception, but this is the first time you have come to see me in the entire time you've been here." It was day time, and Yagura's bitter pale blue face matched the stream of light coming in from the window.

"I know that this is all because of you. You have been trying to become prestigious no matter the cost since the moment I arrived here. First when you brought the Gradni boy here, and now by working against us. Delthurk would have died long ago without us bringing you the riches of Aristahl. Now you have made enemies with us."

"Our only enemies are the dragons, Disciple Yagura. What I have done, I have done to stop them. You brought Aristahl to us, but that is not why we allied ourselves with you. We did so because we expected you to fight beside us. But you do not, so I had to find others who would. I could not do that when working through those who refuse to fight."

"Refuse to fight! We are the ones who train Erdūn still! I trained your Gradni. The horned dragons he killed before dying are because of me!"

"No, Yagura," Mogurn said calmly, "that is not how it is seen. Your clan's reputation has fallen. We ourselves were seen as weak for having to work through you. The Dev-Sesha War was decades ago. Now it is elves and ame-shas who fight the dragons. Not devs, and certainly not the Disciples of Gaorda. People have been asking for years why the once brave followers of Gaorda now cower in fear from the dragons."

"We will not be insulted like this. We killed the sesha!"

"Decades ago!" Mogurn yelled back, as he gave in to the urge to stand up. "The sesha have been forgotten. Most nations that are not dev have not ever seen them. What they know about them comes from you, and they have lost trust in you because you do nothing. You were slowing us down, Yagura. I had no choice."

Yagura backed away. He straightened himself to try to recall his composure. "I expect you to bow and beg for forgiveness once you see otherwise." The Disciple stormed out of Mogurn's office.

Mogurn sank back into his chair. He watched as the guard's hand crept inside and pulled the door closed. As soon as the lock clicked, Mogurn smiled. He laid back in his chair and smirked.

The next few days went on without additional visits from Yagura. Lays had seen him in talks with the other Disciples, but Mogurn instructed him to keep away. Mogurn had played to the deva's pride, and all would be lost if Yagura even suspected that that was the case. The best thing to figure out now, was how to use the Aristahl ameshas in the upcoming skirmish against the dragons. Their strength due to their connection with the land had come back to them since their arrival at Delthurk. The skirmish was to be a test more than anything. The way ameshas' adapted to the earth was going to be useful on the jagged mountains of Zipacna. This battle would show to what extent.

It was custom for a while now for the leaders of battle to meet with a senator beforehand. Initially it was with any senator, but as of late, with Mogurn's ever-growing popularity, it was decided that he was the most inspirational senator to visit. Mogurn accepted reluctantly. It was becoming increasingly difficult to put on his show of positivity. However, he read the logbook entry about the commander of the next attack with keen interest. "He is young, only twenty-three years," Mogurn said toward Lays who stood before him. "Why has he been chosen to lead this battle?"

"His connection to Gradni makes him inspiring. And this is mainly a battle to test the capabilities of the ameshas on the mountain. They will not be taking such heavy chances. It will be good for him to have some practice before we position him in the final battle. He is certainly a highly accomplished warrior as well."

Mogurn huffed as he closed the logbook. "How heavy a battle this will become depends on Yagura. Show the boy in as you leave."

"There is one other matter, sir, one that I did not dare write down."

Mogurn stretched his eyes as he looked up from his desk; it had been a long day already. Lays removed a large pouch from his tunic. He fished inside it and placed the item on Mogurn's desk. It was several moments before Mogurn recognized the pendant as the one that belonged to Gradni. He dragged it toward him to validate once more whose it was. The unmistakable unique flat dent was embedded across the sword. There was no room for error. It was the same object he had held many years ago.

"Where did you get this?"

"It was found by one of our soldiers patrolling the forest. I told him it was lost by an earlier slayer from ages past and to forget about it. He will obey."

Mogurn had never seen Gradni without the pendant. He was wearing it when he rode the karkadan. "You have no idea how it became lost in the forest?"

"None, sir. The solider said it had been there for a while. That is why I thought it prudent to bring it to you and have no written record of it."

Mogurn placed the pendant back on the desk. He clasped one hand over it and rubbed his head with the other.

"Thank you, Lays. Tell the boy to come in after twenty minutes."

"Not now, sir?"

Mogurn scowled at him. Lays nodded quickly and heaved up his logbook before exiting the office.

Mogurn fixated on the glimmer of gold shining between his fingers. Gradni. The boy he had martyred for the cause. It had not been his idea; it had been Bamay's. But he went along with it and was wise to do so. Gradni's martyrdom had secured Erdūn's popularity, leading countless others to join the ranks against the dragons. He had opposed it at first. He thought it was due to pride, as Gradni was his personal project. It was only when he found ways to make it work for him that he agreed to assist in it. Gradni's sacrifice had pushed forth a plan that allowed him to cut Delthurk from the dependency of the Disciples. The boy did much more for the cause in death than he ever would have managed in life. Mogurn placed the pendant in his drawer when he heard a knock.

"Enter," Mogurn said as he stood up and straightened his robes. The young commander bowed as he entered. Mogurn initiated his false persona by bowing back. "Sir Ferklen, it is an honor to meet one who has made commander so young."

"It is I who am honored," Ferklen replied.

"Sit," Mogurn said, taking his own seat again. "I remember you, Ferklen. You were a friend of Gradni's."

Ferklen reeled a little. "I do not know how true that is, sir. We did not always get along. I am also from Scandar. I knew him then."

"You were the one seen with him most frequently here in Delthurk. From what I know of Gradni, and few knew him as well as I did, it was not easy for him to make friends. I know from my time with him that he found a friend in you."

Ferklen looked away, unable to accept the prospect. "I am here because of him, sir." Ferklen went on, saying how he remembered Mogurn's visits to Scandar—first to get Gradni, and second to recruit himself for the fight against the dragons. Mogurn nodded automatically as experience had taught him to do.

"Gradni has indeed inspired many of us, Ferklen. But to allow such inspiration to drive us, as you have, is in itself inspirational. You will be a very effective leader for this fight. I am confident in your ability to lead others into battle." Mogurn's smile widened. He held it until Ferklen realized that the meeting was over.

"Thank you, Senator Mogurn, for your confidence and for seeing me. I hope to meet your expectations." Ferklen stood up and bowed once again as he prepared to leave.

"Wait!" Mogurn said, as Ferklen was at the door. Mogurn opened his drawer. "I almost forgot. Gradni did believe in you. He asked me to give you this when you made commander." He went up to Ferklen and handed him Gradni's pendant.

Ferklen's jaw dropped as he weighed the pendant in his hand. He held it for a while before saying anything. "Then, he knew that he was not going to come back? He wanted me to have this, sir? Not you? Are you certain?"

"Yes. It was meant for you. I am sorry, but there is much I need to do before the battle. Good day to you Ferklen, and good luck once again."

Ferklen left, not once looking up from the pendent. Before Lays could come to him with other concerns, Mogurn quickly put his documents in order and left for his quarters.

CHAPTER 13

With Chimera flying beside him, Gradni pivoted over a boulder on his hand and landed next to Zahk. Zahk put his arm out to stop Chimera from joining the battle.

"Where is Sirrush?" Gradni asked.

"He is down there already," Zahk replied. Chimera roared at Zahk and dove down the mountain. Gradni watched as she half soared and half jumped from boulder to boulder.

"There is something more going on," Zahk stated. "This part of the mountain is too jagged for the elves to climb up."

"And why now, at this time? They've always attacked during the day. I can understand them trying something new at night, by why during dusk?"

Zahk looked toward the sinking sun and rising moon. "I do not know."

Gradni leapt behind a boulder closer to the battle as the dragons clashed with the elves far below. There was something different in Zahk's voice, a wavering authority. He did not know the answer to the question, but he had a theory that he was not sharing.

There were perhaps two hundred elves of Delthurk that were divided into two phalanxes and dividing the dragons into two forces as well. Zahk was right. The land was so jagged that the elves would have to concentrate more on balancing than they would on fighting. There was no reason for them to have chosen this ground for the battle. The wind was not even strong enough to truly empower them. Nothing about this attack made sense.

Gradni squinted as he looked between the divided elf factions. Another group of fifty was coming up within the gap. With the waning light, it was only when they came closer up that Gradni could tell that their armor was different.

It was not the sepia colored steel, but a dark reddish bronze that was breaking past the sepia and coming up the jagged slope. They moved from stone to stone in a less effective way, but similar fashion to Zahk. In their hands were all manner of weapons from this different metal.

"Ameshas!" Zahk spat from behind. "Let them climb to us." Zahk's impatient sword crackled to life.

But the ameshas stopped not far from the mountain base, deciding to fight where their backs were guarded by the elves. Gradni and Zahk growled in unison. Unless the ameshas climbed far enough away from the elves, the two nagas could not fight them without risking discovery.

Aware that Zahk would be focused on the ameshas, Gradni slid to the next closest ledge to keep a closer watch on the elves. A wyvern above the chaos stopped suddenly and fell dead. Gradni let out a sorrowful growl. He did not see what killed the wyvern, and an arrow would have still been visible in spite of the waning light. He hopped into a lower cranny. Zahk hissed behind him for getting too close, but Gradni ignored him. It was not just ameshas that were new in this battle. Something else was happening, and if it was brighter he would be able to see what it was. Gradni leapt even closer. Zahk made a noise between a growl and a whisper, but it did not matter anymore, for Gradni saw slivers of clandestine blue within the farthest elven phalanx.

"Disciples!" Gradni leapt over the jagged stone and ran over and between the rocks of the mountain. "Disciples of Gaorda, Zahk. They are here!"

Gradni raced straight into the battalion of ameshas— through them was the quickest way to the Disciples. He swept under a spear attack and attacked with both his arms, sending one amesha into his fellow man and another against jagged stone. He caught an axe aimed for his head with his hand. He pulled the amesha toward him and threw his palm against the metal mask which spat out blood. More ameshas surrounded him. With his right leg Gradni swept half the assailants behind him and stood up again. The ones in front paused upon seeing him clearly. Gradni rammed through three of them shoulder first.

"*Your Dragon strength is something they will never have. Use it,*" Zahk had always told him. Gradni ran forward, pushed another amesha off a cliff and leapt from it. Now past the ameshas, Gradni took out his sword and ran toward the elves and devs.

There were no further interruptions as he made his way down. Ameshas were fighting the dragons behind him. Those ahead of him did not see him coming. Gradni ran quickly, suddenly annoyed at the shape of Zipacna's rocks that slowed him down as he moved either around or above the protrusions. Between the curved rocks he saw flashes of elves and dragons falling in battle.

Finally at the border of the battle, Gradni steadied his sword at an angle as he ran at the elves. They had brought the Disciples into battle. They would get no mercy from him. In a single arc, his gold and silver blade stabbed into one elf's armor and ribs, and sliced out of them to slash through the stomachs of two others. Some more slashes and parries, and the elves backed away from him after bearing witness to the monstrosity of his form. The other dragons immediately took advantage of their enemies' hesitation. Wyverns swooped their claws and teeth against the enemies' armor and leather, and blew fire into the slivers of their helmets. Other dragons were still coming from all around the mountain, taking the risk of leaving other areas unprotected to face the Disciples. Gradni broke past the elves to fight them himself. To the able Disciples of Gaorda, his fellow dragons were just lines to their slaughter, and they would escape back into the woods long before allowing themselves to be overwhelmed.

Gradni commanded the dragons battling them to turn their attention toward the elves that were chasing him. They obeyed reluctantly—all except Sirrush, who was fighting a single Disciple. Still seconds away, Gradni shouted toward him, but Sirrush was focused only on his chosen enemy.

Sirrush had not yet drawn blood from the deva, but neither had the deva done so from Sirrush. The Deva swiftly swept his blade toward Sirrush's right. Sirrush leapt over it and swung his left front claw out while in the air, missing by an inch the deva's throat. Fire erupted from Sirrush's mouth before he even landed, but the deva put out his shield in time for the flames to crash against it. The impact of the heavy fire against the deva's shield hid the deva from view as he dashed toward Sirrush.

"Sirrush!" Gradni screamed as a blade shot out from the fire toward Sirrush's heart. But Sirrush was prepared, and hopped back away in time for the sword to jar against stone. Gradni grinned sadistically. On those occasions when he was able to fight, it was always on the inner mountains, whereas Sirrush was always one of the first to meet the enemy at Zipacna's edge. He had never fought at his side before.

Sirrush backed away from the deva till he was beside Gradni. Gradni did not make the mistake of again commanding him to leave. Ten devs formed a semicircle around Gradni and Sirrush while other dragons and elves fought close by. The deva that was fighting Sirrush placed himself in a different stance. He did so in a specific way, swinging his sword across twice before drawing it back alongside his head as he bent his legs. It was a pattern Gradni recognized. Yagura glared intensely at Gradni. Gradni huffed back at him. He did not know how to react. Gradni had imagined enjoying this inevitable encounter. He thought he would laugh maniacally at his onetime master. Yet he felt only estranged. He kept his wrist relaxed slightly so that it would move with more ease. The shock of them seeing him would soon be at its height. It would soon be time to attack.

Suddenly, from Yagura came a flash of gold. Gradni shifted away, but the attack was so swift and sudden that though it missed his heart, it still grazed his arm. Twilight. The sun enabled the Disciples to move with more power while the moon blurred their movement. Gradni bared rumbling teeth toward Yagura and his fellow Disciples. But he could not clearly see his foe. It was not just because of the moon. His head swirled and he fell to his knees. Poison. The image of Yagura was quickly coming toward him. Gradni lifted up his sword but could not grip it, could not even swing it or keep it upright as the blurry blue and gold image completely clouded his sight. A sudden heat from Gradni's left shot toward the deva in a beam of yellow and orange, followed by a cloud of red. Sirrush had resumed his battle with Yagura. Yet other images of blue were still coming closer.

Gradni looked away from the overwhelming blur of

colors, trying to focus on a spire of stone that was swirling ahead of him to steady himself. He raised his sword up again, knowing that it would not be enough to ward off the devs that were coming toward him. It was a fatal mistake to depend on his appearance stunning them like it had the others.

A roar he would recognize no matter his state echoed around him. Zahk pounded against the ground as he landed beside Gradni. "Get up!" Gradni heard, as he felt the flaming sword press against his wound.

Gradni let it burn. He felt the strengthening heat of the fire coarse through his veins and eradicate the poison that was running through him.

Gradni stood up without difficulty. It was as if Yagura's disc had never touched him. His sword in his hand, Gradni crossed it in the opposite direction to Zahk's just as Sirrush hopped back to stand with them. Chimera landed beside Gradni. There were splotches of blood all over her. Whether any of it was her own she did not show it. She was ready to continue fighting alongside them.

Zahk's throat rumbled a command. As deadly as the Disciples were, there were only ten of them in this battle, and this would be the dragons' best chance to decimate their numbers. Somehow, perhaps from the way the dragons readied themselves after the command, Yagura understood what was said.

"You may try, naga," Yagura yelled, "you have the strength, but you do not have the skill of the Disciples of Gaorda."

Gradni readjusted himself as Zahk's turquoise lips opened into a grin. "Maybe not me, Yagura. But my ally does."

Yagura's confident eyes sank into shock. It was more

than just the mention of his name. Yagura recognized Zahk's guttural voice.

Disciples closed in on the four dragons on either side. Sirrush and Chimera shot toward those at the edge while a devi moved closer to Yagura.

"Gradni," Zahk yelled, "fend off the others while I deal with him!" He launched himself toward Yagura. Yagura was more skilled, as he had threatened, but he could not match the speed and power of Zahk.

Zahk, however, was battling two Disciples, and each time he created an opening by knocking one of their weapons aside, he had to instead deal with the other's weapon coming toward him. Three other Disciples ran toward Zahk's back; he had made his move so quickly that Gradni was barely able to move in between them in time.

Three blades came at Gradni at various angles; from the front, left, and right. The techniques they used were ones that Yagura himself had taught him. Gradni slid to his left, and smacked the left sword away with his own. He then swung his sword in a low arc, parrying both other blades away. The deva in front of him hopped away, while speedily trying to bring his sword back in front of him. Gradni's weapon was too far away to take advantage of the opportunity, so instead, he pushed himself forward and hammered his elbow against the deva, knocking him several feet back.

The devi on the right took a swipe then; Gradni ducked under it while simultaneously swinging his blade to defend himself from the deva on his left. The front deva had still not recovered from the elbow attack, and his third opponent had backed away after his sword had been jarred to a stop. Gradni turned his attention back to the devi.

She had disappeared. The discrepancy in the wind above tipped him off. Gradni leapt up and swung his free arm over his shoulder, knocking the Disciple away before the sword could come down on his neck. Whether she landed on her feet or not, Gradni could not look to see, for both other Disciples were coming for him. He needed to remember not just his training and wind channeling, but his strength to survive against them.

In one swift motion with his sword, Gradni parried the left deva's weapon away before bringing his sword back to rest inches from his eyes. He pounced like a cougar toward the deva in front. His sword clashed against his foe's sword and shield. It did nothing but send his adversary flying backwards, who somersaulted and landed on his feet unharmed. However, Gradni had successfully distanced himself from them.

The first Disciple was racing hurriedly toward Gradni from the front, and the second was in the process of standing up behind him. For the next few seconds, Gradni had only one enemy to deal with.

He parried the next two attacks from the first deva as he backed away. On the third, Gradni sprung forward and swung his fist into the deva's face, sending a spew of blood from his broken jaw to splash upon the stone. Gradni booted him away with a kick to the stomach and prepared himself for the remaining two.

A shriek from Chimera directed Gradni to look toward Zahk, who had taken his fight farther from Zipacna. The devi that had been fighting Zahk alongside Yagura was dead several feet from him, but another deva had taken her place. Chimera shrieked again as she leapt away from a spear. It was not Zahk whom she wanted Gradni to see, but the elf commander who had broken from the battle and was silently heading toward Zahk's unguarded back. Gradni raced to defend his ally with the two devs he was fighting chasing after him.

"Zahk!" Gradni screamed, when he realized the elf would get to him first. Zahk uttered a terrifying roar as he pivoted and knocked the elf's blade out of his hand. Startled but not paralyzed, the elf commander bounded towards his airborne sword. Two Disciples were now behind Zahk, as he had turned to face the elf, and two were still running behind Gradni. This new elf had tipped the battle so badly against them that neither Zahk nor Gradni had time to turn back around.

Gradni's eyes met in that instant with Zahk's, and they understood what to do as Gradni ran right at him. Gradni leapt forward with his feet curled halfway into him while Zahk dived underneath. Gradni twisted and swung his sword in a low arc against Yagura's blade that was inches from Zahk back, while he felt a wave of heat behind him as Zahk's sword defended his own.

Gradni's sword clanged against the weapons of his new opponents while Zahk fought his old ones behind him. Suddenly, Yagura broke away and commanded his partner to do the same. Gradni did not pursue the attack, but kept his sword ready in front of him, the same sword that Yagura was staring at. All this action, and Yagura did not yet know whom he was fighting, not until he recognized the sword that once rested on the golden stand in his room.

"Gradni?" Yagura said.

Gradni breathed deeply in response. There was nothing he wished to say to his former master. Yagura turned his attention back to the sword. "Not again," Yagura whispered before yelling. "Not again!" Yagura came at Gradni in an inexplicable bloodlust.

Gradni met his blade against his former master's. Yagura attacked erratically and skillfully. He had never fought Yagura like this. Gradni loosened his wrist to keep up while also dealing with the other deva. This was not the first time Yagura had fought a naga of his dexterity. After a continuous run of parrying both blades, Gradni managed to interlock both of his opponent's blades above him. Heat sliced unexpectedly beside Gradni's stomach, as Zahk's sword slipped past him and sliced through Yagura's chest armor.

It slid out as easily as it had slid in. Yagura fell upon his knees. There was no bleeding, for Zahk's sword cauterized the fatal wound it created. Yagura uttered something inaudible and fell onto his back, the suppleness of his body allowing both his thighs and shins to be side by side upon the ground.

The other Disciple that Gradni was fighting circled around to get to Zahk. Gradni pivoted. He and Zahk now fought side by side against the three Disciples. Surprisingly, the Delthurk elf commander had reclaimed his sword and was fighting alongside the three Disciples, but only for the next few moments. Zahk was about to run his sword through him as he had done to Yagura.

But from the fire of Zahk's blade, Gradni saw the elf's face. Gradni's heart dropped so far from him that it felt like it had fallen from his body. He hammered Zahk's sword down before the fatal lunge was made, and shoulder rammed Zahk away. The elf commander, confused after thinking himself dead, looked toward his savior.

"Gradni?" he said.

Gradni grabbed Ferklen by the leather under his neck, and hurled him with all his strength into the bordering forest. Ferklen flew into the foliage and out of sight. Gradni moved quickly back to Zahk in time to defend him from being stabbed. Together they slew the three remaining Disciples that were still fighting.

The Delthurk forces had retreated from the mountains.

Gradni turned toward the forest in time to see two of the remaining Disciples slip in with the elves and ameshas. He could still hear them all, racing through the forest toward their base. The battle was over. Fighting in the forest was something that neither side was willing to risk. He turned back around. Zahk was standing in front of him, dressed in layers of blood. His dark-green face was more vicious than ever. Gradni did not challenge him. Zahk turned around and plodded up the mountain alongside the other dragons. Several deep breaths later, Gradni followed.

Outside his cave, Gradni heard his fellow dragons carrying the dead to the pyre while he stared idly at his sword. He had not washed the blood off yet. A shadow entered his cave. Gradni stood up and faced Zahk.

"I am sorry," Gradni declared.

"Tell me why you did it."

"I knew him."

"You knew others. You knew Yagura, yet you fought him."

"Ferklen is different. He was my friend."

"He was the elven commander! By saving him you have killed every dragon that he will slay!"

"I was not thinking. I am sorry."

"I want the truth! It was not just because of friendship. Why did you save him?"

Gradni's gaze wandered. He was suddenly aware that his eyes were damp. He had never seen so many dead. Ferklen could have been one of them. This was the second time Ferklen had returned to his life. "He is here because of me. He is fighting the dragons to honor me."

There was a minute of silence.

"That cannot stop you from acting. Ameshas and

Gaorda's Disciples have now joined the war as well. They know about us now, and we have lost the best advantage we have always had. We cannot afford to give them any mercy."

"You would rather I did not engage Gaorda's Disciples? Didn't you see how many they killed before I got there?"

"I saw them all!" Zahk yelled. He regretted it, and lowered his voice. "I saw them all. I understand why you went. The Disciples are too much for most dragons to handle. That they have decided to once again battle instead of working behind the scenes is bad for us. It was right of you to engage them, but we cannot afford to give them any mercy now that they know of us. We have lost our advantage against whoever will come at us next."

"Erdūn," Gradni stated.

"Yes. Erdūn."

"Zahk, tell me who you were? You knew Yagura; you know Erdūn. Who were you?"

Zahk sat down. He did not look up. "I recognized your sword the first time I saw it in your hands. It was wielded by the same devi naga who gave me my sword. For years, she masqueraded as one of the Disciples of Gaorda, but gave up her secret and her life so that I could live. I was the Shah of Aristahl, Gradni, and before she died, she told me all she knew of our enemies machinations, and that the dragons would need my leadership to survive."

CHAPTER 14

Mogurn paced in his office while Ferklen sat. Ferklen had not touched the bread and meat that was set out for him, but fortunately he was having the wine. Something had happened at the battle. A devi had come to tell Mogurn that Yagura had died, and that there would be a meeting shortly. She left before Morgurn could discover any more details. He had Lays fetch Ferklen right away; he would not attend this meeting unprepared. Ferklen's state of shock was affirmation that there was information that Mogurn needed to know before stepping into a meeting with the Disciples. Mogurn waited for Ferklen to take another swig as he looked out the window. The dragon's celebratory billowing red smoke was rising up from the inner Zipacna Mountains.

"What happened, Ferklen?"

Ferklen tapped the mug upon the wooden desk after guzzling down the wine. He was looking idly at the other edge of the table. "The Disciples called them nagas. Men like you and me, but covered in green scales like the dragons. Their eyes, teeth, feet, hands, all like dragons, but they are men that carry swords, and have monstrous strength. There were two of them. One was a very dark green. I went to attack him first. He was strong, I think maybe even stronger than the other one, though he was not as swift with his blade as the other. Yagura called it Zahk before it killed him. The other Disciples of Gaorda confirmed it."

"Zahk, the old Aristahl shah? I thought the Disciples killed him years ago."

Ferklen nodded. "The other, my Lord . . . the other I recognized. He killed many of us, and more Disciples than the other one, but he saved me. It was Gradni."

Silence followed for many minutes.

"Gradni is dead; killed by the dragons." Mogurn declared.

"I saw him, sir. It was him."

"He is dead!" Mogurn slammed his palm against the table. Ferklen looked toward the edge. Mogurn raised his reddened palm to his closing eyes. "He is dead. How do you know it was him? You said his skin was made of green scales. How dare you state it was Gradni, the one who fought so nobly for us, the one who is the reason we fight."

"The Disciples of Gaorda say it as well, that Yagura recognized him before being slain. He was right next to me—his face, even his hot breath upon mine. It was him. It was Gradni."

Mogurn lowered himself into his seat. "We are done. You can go."

Mogurn turned back to the red smoke that was spreading out beyond the mountains. Gradni was alive, yet had become a monster. He should never have betrayed him. It was the Disciples fault. They knew all along about these nagas and said nothing to any of them. Mogurn headed to the conference room.

He arrived late and they had not waited. Without even pausing to show respect, Mogurn took his seat. Ta'ar was floating behind the senators. The surviving devs from the battle were huddled on chairs in a corner behind the Disciple who had the floor.

"They are called nagas, once men and women like us who have fallen under the dragons' sway. Some become nagas willingly. Others are infected by the spell so completely that they might as well also be willing allies. The evil magic empowers them. The horned dragons should no longer be our concern, not even the drake. It is because of these nagas that we have failed thus far to conquer them."

"How gracious of you to tell us this," Mogurn said. His eyes had fallen from the Disciple midway through the speech. He was grinning cynically. "Now what can you tell us that we have not already just discovered. Something of more use perhaps?" A slight arousal emerged from the senate. They too wanted the answer that only Mogurn dared to ask. The deva broadened his shoulders as he came toward Mogurn. Mogurn met the glare.

"We killed all the nagas that existed during the Dev-Sesha War. We saw no need to bring in old information."

"Fools," Mogurn spat. "For years we have been wondering why our soldiers who make it to the inner mountains never come back!"

"And you think that if you'd had known about nagas that you would be able to discover the truth?"

"If we had known, we would not have sent warriors alone into battle!" Mogurn shouted. "All the support that we have gotten recently has been because of Gradni. How do you think that will change when they discover what has happened to him? We stand to lose everything because of what you withheld from us!"

The deva slammed his fist on Mogurn's table, but Mogurn stood immediately to meet the challenge.

"Say what you will," the deva said, "but the truth remains that it was not devs this time who surrendered to the will of the dragon. It is because of the amesha Shah Zahk, and your elven boy Gradni that we have been losing so many."

"The same Zahk that you said you killed many years ago? How is this not borne of your deceit?"

"We are not to blame for this! We did not know that all the races could be consumed by their magic!"

A scream echoed through the room before Mogurn could retaliate. It was so shrill and loud that when it stopped there was only silence. The lady Bamay, who had come in after Mogurn, was trembling in her chair from the opposite side of the room.

"Who did you say these nagas were?" she uttered meekly.

"Your old Shah Zahk, and Gradni the elf," the deva repeated, emphasizing the words 'your' and 'elf'. He didn't see that it was the names themselves that struck her.

Bamay shook her head so strangely that it seemed that each part of it was shaking at a different speed. She murmured almost inaudibly, "No. No. They are both dead. I killed them. I had them both..."

Her words were no longer comprehensible. The entire room was flashing looks to one another, all except Mogurn who did not look away. She screamed again. Mogurn turned from her to a guard and commanded him to escort her out. She was mumbling even as they took her away.

Mogurn turned back to the devs. The break in flared tempers had given him time to think. "You did not know that all the races could be consumed by their magic? That is why you stopped engaging them; you thought that you alone were at risk of becoming nagas?"

The deva nodded. "It has happened to our most dedicated Disciples. The one who wielded the sword that Yagura gave to Gradni became one."

"We must move on," Mogurn said stoically. "This knowledge will be damaging as it spreads. Gradni is the reason they fight. Once they hear of him, I do not know what will happen." He turned to the Disciples. "You said that when someone becomes a naga unwillingly, that he is as much under their spell as those who joined them. Yet Gradni saved his old friend from Zahk? Have you ever tried to revert a naga back into what they were before? He could be a valuable ally if it could be done."

The Disciples said nothing at first. The existence of Zahk and Gradni as nagas, and Gradni saving Ferklen, was causing them to reevaluate everything they thought they knew about nagas. "We have never tried. It is the dragons' presence that is poisonous to him. But to attempt to remove him from them—we would lose too many. He is as good a warrior as any of us, but stronger."

"But he is once again the key, as he always has been, to ending this war in victory. The information that he would share with us would be vital," Mogurn stated. "We must continue planning our ultimate battle. Erdūn will be our focus. The qui-lahk will join us for that battle along with their elephants and a rukh. Until we know what the discovery of Gradni and Zahk will have on Delthurk, we cannot presume to know what will be the best course of action."

Mogurn pressed his fingers together over his mouth as he sat down. He was consumed by one thought. His Gradni was still alive, and still able to bring him glory.

CHAPTER 15

The high-flying drakes called out to the nagas when they saw the rider coming toward Zipacna. The single horse was coming from the west, across grassy land that few ever traveled. Zahk followed Gradni as they moved to the outer mountains. After years of having to hide within the inner mountains, it was a strange experience to Zahk to be so plainly in the open. He leapt off a ledge to land beside Gradni. The rider was covered in a cloak despite the heat.

"It is an amesha," he told Gradni, recognizing the material of the cloak as it flapped in the wind.

The amesha stopped her horse and dismounted at the base of the mountain. Two wyverns glided toward the stranger. They flew right back up and cawed at Zahk and Gradni.

"What is she doing here?" Gradni asked.

"I do not know. I will handle this."

"No. I'm coming with you."

Zahk grimaced. "Fine. Then stay some distance back."

Zahk leapt from rock to rock down the mountain toward the visitor. He noticed Sheemu's age before anything else. It had been some years since he had last seen his onetime advisor, but not so many to explain the grayness of her face. A sudden streak of ancient anger welled inside Zahk. When he had first arrived at Zipacna, he suspected that Sheemu might become Aristahl's temporary ruler. After himself, Ta'ar wanted someone who could not challenge him, and as a woman, Sheemu could never become Aristahl's true shah. The cost of Ta'ar's machinations was painfully evident in the lack of life in Sheemu. He did not even want to imagine how downtrodden Aristahl must be.

Zahk jumped off the last ledge and landed in front of Sheemu. His old friend did not seem intimidated by him being a naga.

"Shah Zahk."

"Sheemu. Why are you here?"

"I had to know if it really was you," she said, while stroking her horse's mane, "Aristahl is dying. It would normally be foolish for me to leave it even for this long, but I am desperate. I do not know what to do, Zahk."

It was not what he expected to hear. But what other reason would bring her here, hopeless and defeated as she was. Being Ta'ar's pawn had taken its toll on her. Zahk sat upon a boulder.

"What is Ta'ar doing now?"

"He is here, Zahk. He stays at Delthurk now. He is part of them more than he is us. He has not returned, and yet still Aristahl caters to his quest. That is until we discovered that you were alive, and here fighting for the dragons. Now there is only chaos. Infighting has started over issues that are too many to count. Some want revenge on you, some question Ta'ar, some remember the better times when you were our ruler, some see those times as the illusion Ta'ar told us it was. You killed ameshas during the last attack, your own people who once would have followed you into battle."

"I had no choice. They abandoned me for Ta'ar's will. After all the suffering they have endured, they follow him still. The dragons are my people now, Sheemu."

"Indeed. They always were though, weren't they?"

"Do not dare question the love I had for Aristahl. They betrayed me. I served Aristahl loyally as its shah. I risked everything to repair the damage that Ta'ar did, and was cast out and almost killed for it. Whether you can believe me now more than you did then, I don't care. I'm telling you again anyway. The dragons were never a threat. The opportunity for them to attack us was always there and they never did, except in retalliation. You know this."

"I don't know about the dragons, Zahk. Ta'ar and you are what is tearing Aristahl apart."

"So you blame me for Aristahl's state?"

"No," Sheemu said honestly. She sat crosslegged on the ground. "I do not know what to do, Zahk. Aristahl is falling; our people are dying. What should I do?"

"You know who I serve now. How can you trust that what I say is not purely for the benefit of my kind?"

She shrugged. "I saw you turn Aristahl into a better place. You did so despite all the lies working against you, lies that I do not know how to fight."

He sat beside her. It was a while before he thought of something to say. "Give whatever reason you need to. Lie if you must, but let Aristahl benefit more from their own work, and give less of them to Ta'ar's whims. Do it slowly, though. Tell them that Ta'ar wishes it if you need to, or that you do this so that Aristahl can serve Ta'ar better in the future. That way his supporters and those who question him will not oppose you too much. Start weaving him out, to gain loyalty to you instead of allowing it to remain with him. Take advantage of any gratitude they will have for you for making their lives easier by building upon it. Ta'ar abandoned Aristahl a long time ago to his mad quest. He has no intention to ever return unless it is to drain it as he always has. He cares nothing for Aristahl. Ultimately you will need to find another spirit who will."

"So you want me to do what you did? To adopt your strategy that failed?"

"Isn't that why you came to me? You have to go farther than I ever did, and be better at it. He will not be there to stop you, so at least you have that advantage. Still, I do not envy you."

They sat for several minutes in silence.

"You would not come back if I asked you to, would you?"

"What good would that do? I am a dragon now."

She stood up and got back onto her horse. She cleared her throat as she straightened herself. "Aristahl has been making armor for our champion. It is thick and heavy armor that would be impractical for anyone except him. It is so that even your sword and strength cannot carve easily into him. Delthurk asked for it to be delivered immediately instead of later as planned."

"Why?"

"I can only assume. Many of the soldiers loyal to Ta'ar have been summoned earlier than expected as well." She tugged at the reins and started riding off the way she had come. Zahk growled some seconds later and climbed up the mountain, passing Gradni on the way.

"Why was she here?" Gradni asked after catching up to him.

"To warn us; the ultimate battle will happen soon. We must send word to all the dragons. I hope you are ready."

CHAPTER 16

News of the last good shah of Aristahl and the savior against the dragons being nagas traveled quickly. Nations that had agreed to support Delthurk were either disillusioned to find that Gradni was now warring against them, or were confused by the return of Shah Zahk. The doubts grew every month, and every time one nation went back on their commitment, it gave others the excuse to do the same.

Mogurn stood at the threshold of the blacksmiths as four workers dressed Erdūn in the armor from Aristahl. The boy was now at his pinnacle height of nine feet. A worker heaved up a shin guard. With the help of another it was latched around Erdūn's leg. Each piece was more than an inch thick, and too heavy for anyone who did not have Erdūn's strength. Apart from his great height, Erdūn's skin was already as tough as most metals due to his sessions with Ta'ar. From what he had heard of the nagas' strength, Mogurn believed Erdūn to still be a match for both the shah and Gradni. The blacksmith placed a piece of armor on Erdūn's foot to measure how much it needed to be modified. Though there had been some communication with Aristahl as they made this armor, there was still a lot of adjustments that needed to be done because of how Erdūn adapted to the mountains.

The blacksmith wiped his brow with his forearm before

hitting the metal again. He was not accustomed to working with metal this thick.

"Let me see him with the helmet." Mogurn said.

With the helmet in both his hands, a worker struggled up the ladder and placed it on Erdūn's large head. Erdūn turned and looked at Mogurn through the slivers. The helmet sloped down to his neck and left a gap for his chin and lower lip.

Mogurn nodded at the giant. "Remove more from the space so that his entire mouth and jaw are free," he said to the blacksmith.

"That will take some doing, Senator."

"How does that matter? I want it done and I want it looking right."

"Yes, sire."

Mogurn nodded once more toward Erdūn before leaving the heat of the forge. It was important for others to hear Erdun's battle cry during the final battle. The more immediate problem was ensuring that enough people would follow him. Mogurn struggled to keep the support that had come from Gradni's martyrdom. There were some whom Gradni inspired more than Erdūn, for Gradni was an orphan who did not have the power of a spirit behind him. In that respect, Gradni was more like the hero Gaorda than Erdūn could ever hope to be. Still, in order to regain some of the support that they were steadily losing, he had to focus on Erdūn. And for that, Mogurn needed the participation of Aristahl. Since the discovery of Zahk, there had not been any response from Aristahl. The amesha nation even refused entrance to the last envoy that was sent. It was as if the armor they made for Erdūn was their way of absolving themselves from doing anything more.

Lays had been to see Bamay twice now, but failed to overcome the sudden madness that had consumed her. He tried to excuse himself by saying that it was as if she had lost her senses, as she appeared to neither see nor hear him. Mogurn cursed him and sent him out. He was angry. With Delthurk's walls suffocating him with responsibility, his aide had failed to lift any of the burden from his shoulders. They needed Bamay to connect them to Aristahl; the Fire Spirit was simply not enough anymore.

There was no answer when Mogurn knocked at her door. After three sets of three, Mogurn turned the unlocked knob and walked in. The furniture was arranged differently from when Gradni was here. Bamay was sitting with her back to the window with no table in front of her. The bright sunlight that revealed her thin frame seemed to also be weakening her hair into a stringy brown.

It had been only a couple months since her outburst in the hall, but she was deteriorating quickly. Mogurn called her name softly, and then more harshly. First saying, "Bamay" and then reverting to, "Lady Bamay." Her eyes twitched. She was listening; Lays had just been too much a fool to detect it. "We know that you are distressed over the reappearance of the Shah Zahk. I know him by reputation, but not his relationship with you. You must know his capability more than any other to be this fearful of his return as a naga. You have also deduced that he is the reason we have lost so many to the dragons over the years." Her head turned. Mogurn smiled inside. "But that can end. Whatever threat Zahk poses, has posed for all these years, it can end. Naga or not"—Mogurn bent on one knee, resting his hand on hers, and looked into her eyes as she stared above his—"he is no match for Erdūn, no match for your son." He said it so softly, and saw her chest move ever so slightly. He had known for years that she was Erdūn's mother, even when she alone seemed to be the only one still aware of it. Some things were simply too obvious. "Your son is mightier than any being I have ever seen. Born of amesha, empowered by the Fire Spirit, and trained by Gaorda's Disciples. Zahk is no match for him."

She said nothing. Nothing for whole minutes until Mogurn's hand slipped off her knee. "Zahk is amesha as well," she whispered. "Gradni was also trained by the Disciples of Gaorda. They are both nagas who have come back from being killed by my hand, and are stronger than ever. There is power behind them, power that I saw but did not submit to when I witnessed it. It will end us all."

"No, Lady Bamay, no, it can be resolved. Bring Aristahl into this war as you did before, and we will win. You and Erdūn will be our champions."

"No, I will do no more."

"Then all is lost; you, and you alone—"

Bamay screamed. Mogurn fell back from the dual attack of her flailing arms and piercing shriek. Embarrassed, he tried to stand up. But she screamed again, paralyzing him with her eyes as much as her voice. He looked up at her. There were no words on the tip of his tongue as there always were, no actions he could think to perform to soothe her, just the mind-numbing realization of her madness as he watched her fingernails dig into her forehead. She twirled and looked to the window. Nothing else was said from either of them. Mogurn crawled away on his back before standing up. He took a deep breath and realigned himself before leaving her quarters. "Beware the dragons," he heard her say as he left.

There was no other alternative left to them. Allies were

lost every day, and it was unknown how much time Erdūn even had left before the fire in him burned him out. Mogurn stood up in the council meeting he had called. The eyes of the senators, Disciples of Gaorda, the Fire Spirit Ta'ar, and Erdūn burned against him. "We must attack them now. Mobilize everything we have."

"What about the nagas?" a senator asked. "Our elves form the bulk of the battle, and none of them want to move against Gradni."

"How many do we have in total, including all our allies?"

"Almost twelve thousand."

Mogurn straightened himself. "It will do; we stand to lose more the longer we wait. Get everything ready for this battle. I will deal with Gradni personally."

CHAPTER 17

When Gradni was twelve and looked upon the Zipacna Mountains from the carriage taking him to Delthurk, the dragons were just specs hovering around the mountains. He wondered how it looked now, after dragons had come from all over Adijari. Word spread fast due to the quick-flying wyverns, and there were now five thousand dragons inhabiting the mountain.

Gradni hiked up toward Zahk, but paused to scratch his leg.

"What is wrong?" Zahk said, before Gradni had a chance to ask him the same question.

"Just an itch," Gradni said. With the pressure mounting, his skin had begun to irritate him.

"And the scowl you are making? Is that from the pain that was already there, or your nails tearing at your leg?" Gradni stood straight in defiance. "You have been feeling head pain and body ache for some days now. If you are going to fall sick, then do so now. We will need you later."

Gradni leapt up and swung himself around a rock to be beside Zahk. "Why do you scowl?" Gradni grabbed Zahk by the arm when he did not answer. "Why?"

"Our swords are both made of dev steel, and we are stronger than any other. They were our best chance of defeating Erdūn. But now, he will be wearing armor so thick that even with my fire coursing through my blade, it will still be difficult to cut cleanly into his body."

"I am sorry I revealed myself to them. When the Disciples—"

Zahk cut him off with a wave. "You should not be. You were right to challenge the Disciples. Countless others would have died if we had not intervened. We must simply be prepared for what is to come."

A longue floated toward them and hissed.

Gradni leaned over the ledge. A lone figure had climbed less than a quarter way up the outer mountains. The dragons were keeping their distance from this visitor by several feet. He was wearing no armor of any kind, and his clothes were not thick enough to conceal any weapon. Gradni noticed his curly brown hair. He roared for the dragons to leave him alone. He was about to leap down when Zahk grabbed him.

"I am coming!"

"No," Gradni replied. "He is here for me. You already tried to kill him."

"I should not have done so?" Gradni knew better than to reply. "Why is he here?"

"I shall find out. Watch if you must, but give us privacy. He has reason to fear you."

"I do not trust him."

"And I did not trust Sheemu weeks ago."

Zahk let go. "Be careful."

Dangling from his old friend's neck, was the pendant that Gradni had never expected to see again. He didn't even want to know why the person who had dented it years ago was now wearing it.

"Ferklen," Gradni said as he came before him. His old friend was shaking. His feet looked as if they were ready to leap back down the quarter of the mountain he had climbed. The nervousness was strange, for the dragons had left the area, and Zahk was still a long way up. "You have nothing to be afraid of, Ferklen. You are unarmed, so they will not hurt you."

Ferklen looked up. Gradni's eyes softened. Dried tears were lined down his old friend's face. "Gradni, it is you! I was hoping that I was wrong, that we were all wrong. But it is you."

Gradni did not reply. Ferklen looked beyond Gradni's shoulder toward the distant figure of Zahk.

"Why have you come, Ferklen?"

"Gradni, come with me quickly. Come back with me, while he and no dragons can stop you. Now!"

Gradni cocked his head. "I am not leaving, Ferklen. My home is here."

"No, Gradni. Remember what you are? You are an elf of Delthurk; of Scandar. They have poisoned you. I came to bring you back, to save you from what they have done to you."

Gradni pressed his hand against his skull. His headache seemed to be getting worse with each word Ferklen uttered. "Ferklen, it is all lies. Dragons are not evil. I belong here, where I can protect them, and myself. There is no difference between us."

"No, Gradni, they made you this way, made you mad. But I know that they have not completely taken you."

Gradni jumped over to stand right before Ferklen. Ferklen backed away, but Gradni grabbed him and pulled him closer. "Look at me, Ferklen," Gradni said softly. "Do I look mad? You have known me since Scandar. Tell me, do I look mad?"

"But there is no other explanation."

"Yes there is, Ferklen. What point is there in me going through it all again? You need to know the history." He let Ferklen go. "Everyone knows that dragons never tried to kill us until we started killing them."

"No. Gradni. They did this to you, after you sacrificed yourself for us. They turned you against us."

"Sacrificed?" He came in closer. "Sacrificed? Is that why you fight as hard as you do? I did not sacrifice myself when I came to kill horned dragons, Ferklen. I was abandoned, purposely. The karkadan never came back to get me. They left me to die. But the dragons did not kill me; they sheltered me."

"No. No, Gradni, this is simply what they have—"

"Enough! Stop saying that. I am not mad, Ferklen. You would be dead if I were. If I was truly under their control, they would not have allowed me to be alone with you after I saved you. Why can't you see that?"

"I do not understand."

"Go back, Ferklen. Go back and look—"

Zahk roared from above. Gradni looked toward him and saw him bounding down toward the two of them.

"I am sorry," Ferklen whispered from behind Gradni. Gradni turned back and saw over Ferklen's shoulder. A large man, a man larger than any Gradni had ever seen was coming toward them, bounding off the mountain crevices with an unreal amount of speed, faster even than Zahk, despite being nearly twice his size. The man was covered in maroon armor, a hard thing to see as he was traveling so quickly. He would be at Gradni in seconds. Zahk and the other dragons were still far away. "I wanted to save you, after you saved me." Ferklen uttered.

"Leave. Now!" Gradni said, as he took out his sword. He knew it was Erdūn. He had seen him more than half a decade ago. Even then he was tall. Now he was a giant. He was wearing a flat maroon helmet that allowed only his eyes and lower jaw to be seen. Erdūn, Delthurk's great hero, was making an appearance at last, in bold inch-thick plates of armor and a weapon in each hand. One was a heavy sword that Erdūn carried with ease, and the other a poleaxe that matched Erdūn's height. Gradni gripped his sword and arched his legs as the axe head got closer. He needed to strike quickly, surely, and with surprise. He had to do the unexpected. Suppressing a roar, Gradni ran and leapt toward Erdūn as Erdūn leapt toward him.

Midair, Gradni drove his sword toward Erdūn's neck, a daring and thus hopefully unexpected move. Erdūn raised his poleaxe against the blade and directed his elbow straight. It thrust into Gradni's chest with the full force of Erdūn's massive frame behind it. The attack carried Gradni to a jagged wall of the mountain, the impact opening skin and flesh of Gradni's back. Stunned by the pain, Gradni's sword tilted out of his grip. But the very sensation of it falling awakened him. He tightened his fist around the handle. He turned the blade toward Erdūn and thrust it forward. Erdūn sprang back so quickly that it seemed that he flew, his face a good four inches from the sword at its closest. Erdūn's giant feet landed against the unreliable curved stone, and yet still he kept his balance.

Gradni gripped his sword in both hands. He would need all his strength to match Erdūn. He commanded the air around him to add more power and speed to his movements. Gradni skipped between rocks till he was a meter away from Erdun, and swiped false attacks in the midst of real ones, but Erdūn, using only the poleaxe, did the same. Despite his size, Erdun was still an amesha, and could balance upon the curvaceous rock far more effectively. Gradni saw an opening and slashed toward Erdun's chest, but Erdun's poleaxe pinned his sword, as the ball of Erdūn's heel crushed into Gradni's stomach. Gradni fell, winded. Erdūn's thumb and forefinger clamped around Gradni's throat. Finally, Gradni heard the roar of Zahk.

Finally, yet also surprisingly. He did not think Zahk would come in time against this monster, but he saw the fiery sword dent the poleaxe above him. Zahk landed on his feet behind Erdūn and attacked the giant. But Erdūn released Gradni and moved away before the blade made contact. Erdūn went for Zahk immediately after, hacking away and forcing him back with his strength. Gradni took a moment to gasp for needed air, but a moment was too much, for after hearing a strange *klang* he looked up. Zahk's sword was spinning free in the air.

Gradni sped forward and leapt at Erdūn. But Erdūn pulled the poleaxe back and knocked Gradni's sword away. Gradni, still in the air, felt the familiar thumb and forefinger under his throat, and then his body swinging. He saw stone right before he crashed into it.

Zahk scrambled to his sword; there was no defeating Erdūn without it. He saw Gradni go limp- his forehead covered in blood. Erdūn took up his sword, and turned his gaze squarely against Zahk. Everything was happening so quickly. Erdūn bent his legs to leap at Zahk, when a voice called him back. It was the elven commander, the betrayer who had acted as bait. Erdūn huffed at Zahk, and put away both his weapons.

Before Zahk could understand, Erdūn grabbed Gradni's still body and sped down the mountain. Zahk followed. The dragons were closing in, but Erdūn was fast, even with Gradni under his arm. Erdun grabbed the elven commander by his collar and leapt into the forest.

Zahk did not care that it was hopeless to catch up with Erdun. He continued to run down alongside the wyverns that had caught up to him, until he realized the magnitude of what the kidnapping meant.

He stopped running, the forest not even ten meters ahead of him. His mouth stretched wide open. From it came a scream of anguish so loud that even the dragons that raced past him turned back. The scream ended, and Zahk commanded them all to return up the mountain. Chimera and Sirrush roared back at him, louder than all the others that joined them.

"Get back!" Zahk repeated stridently, suffocating the opposition. There was no choice. Whatever plans Delthurk had for Gradni, it would have to wait. The ultimate assault against them would happen within hours. The final battle was upon them.

CHAPTER 18

Immediately after coming out of unconsciousness, Gradni scrambled to his feet. His right hand kept reaching for a sword that wasn't there. His sudden motion caught up to him, and he paused long enough for his dizziness to wear off. He wiped his forehead. It was damp with blood, and rougher than he expected, as if fragments of the stone Erdūn forced him against were embedded in his skull.

"Hello, Gradni."

He did not recognize the voice for its sound, but he knew its tone to be Mogurn's. No other would have dared to pull off a scheme like this. Mogurn was sitting two arm lengths away from the bars that trapped Gradni in his cell. He looked just as deceitful as he did the first time Gradni had spoken to him. Gradni inspected his prison. He was surrounded by stone walls. Three stones were missing from a spot in the wall behind him- a gap large enough for him to see the Zipacna Mountains. His jail was a high one. He did not remember the Delthurk castle ever having a jail this high.

"By Zipacna, what are you up to now?" Gradni turned to Mogurn when he received no reply. Mogurn's head was bent low beside the dim torch attached to the wall. He was smiling under the white of his hair. It was small, but it was still there. Gradni struck the bars with his open palm. "Why am I alive?" His voice echoed in the tiny room.

Mogurn's smile slowly disappeared. "It was never my desire to have you dead, Gradni."

"Really, after you sent me to Zipacna to die?"

"That was not my decision. Had I known that this happening to you was even a possibility, I would never have allowed it. Gradni, what we did to you we did for the cause, a cause you believed in, and will again once this curse leaves you."

Gradni snickered cruelly. "Curse? I don't know which is worse. How much you have poisoned others, or how much you have poisoned yourself. There is no curse. This is who I am now, a naga dragon. They are my kind more than any elf has ever been."

Mogurn's grin returned.

"Why do you smile?" Gradni demanded. "What are you up to? Let me out of here!" Gradni rammed the bars again. Three specs of blood flew off of him and landed inches from Mogurn. They landed with taps against the floor.

The specs had not come from his forehead, or any other part of him that was bleeding. Gradni raised his arm. Three scales were missing. Seven to eight spots of missing scales were missing from his other arm.

"You see, Gradni? Everything you have said is simply part of the convincing nature of the curse. Look where you lay down."

There was a large print of blood from his back from the wound that Erdūn inflicted. It felt as if the poleaxe was still cutting into him. Imbedded in the blood were too many fallen scales for Gradni to count.

"The curse is dying now that you are no longer with them," Mogurn said. "I know Delthurk left you for dead. But I make it up to you by bringing you away from the dragons. When you are better—which we can see will happen soon—you will return to a world where there will be no more dragons of Zipacna."

Gradni was about to pound the prison walls again, when he heard a rumbling outside. He rushed toward the hole in the wall. A great beast was flying toward Zipacna, a giant eagle with a wingspan as large as Tiamat's whole body. Below the beast was the largest army that Gradni had ever seen. There were thousands of them, and they were dividing up to attack Zipacna from all sides.

Gradni pulled away, and shoulder rammed the wall. The pain brought him to his knees. He strained his head upwards. Blood and scales were all along the wall.

The rising red sun was intensified within the eyes of Kallini. The last time Zahk saw the statue out in the day was when they retrieved it years ago. It had been kept in the cave to protect it from further harm. That was no longer a concern, so they brought it to the horned dragon's nest.

Zahk knelt before Irath and Kallini. Above him, longues danced in the air while wyverns and drakes circled around them. All other dragons rested unevenly upon the rocks in prayer.

He looked toward Kallini. "You were the first of us to ever listen to the wisdom of the dragons. What I do today, I do in your name."

Zahk stood up. It was time to act.

He saw the rukh as it came over the mountains of Delthurk. It would not stand a chance if it flew any lower. The multitude of dragons would tear it apart like ravens upon a carcass. But the beast maintained its high place in the sky where only one other dominated. Zahk and his dragons heard the roar that signaled acceptance of the challenge. His hair ruffled when Tiamat launched into the air from behind him toward the rukh.

First Gradni, now Tiamat. Their enemies had now removed two of their champions from the fray. No matter. The rukh was strong, but it did not have Tiamat's fire.

A united force was coming at them from all sides, though there were more ameshas coming up on the rougher terrain, and more elves on the flatter lands. Among them were qui-lahk as well, who were riding armored elephants. Zahk heaved a breath of anger. Though the lumbering elephants would not be able to travel high up the mountain, they formed a wall that gave the enemy control over the terrain.

Wyverns constantly whipped past Zahk to report the enemy's movement. Zahk turned to his left to face the main force. Erdūn was dressed in rust-colored plates as before, and a helmet that left his mouth exposed. Behind the amesha giant, were thirty gold-armored Disciples of Gaorda. Behind them, were Delthurk's finest elven warriors, dressed in their armor that proudly displayed the dying drake insignia.

There was a light above this main force. Zahk's hatred flushed through him when he saw Ta'ar. The Fire Spirit had come to see his final work. He was burning brightly above his blind loyal supporters. Zahk commanded his sword alight. The sound of fire, steel, and claws clashing against each other grew louder from the other parts of the Zipacna Mountains. With his finest fighting dragons around him, Zahk bounded toward Erdūn's legion.

Gradni reeled his arm back again and forced it against the wall.

"Please, Gradni, enough of that. I have met only one person who could probably break that wall, and he is out there now securing your salvation." Gradni rested his bleeding skull. He felt again its strange roughness. "I did not think I would be here either at this moment in history. The other senators are watching from the roof. But I know my place is here. I need to be here when you come back to us."

"Enough!" Gradni roared as he moved in one motion back to the bars. Blood from his forehead was trickling down his face. A few remaining scales were dotting it as well. He could feel the sting for each one that had fallen. "I will never return to that madness!" Gradni was about to yell again, when the sting in his back grew and cracked all the way down his spine. He fell to his knees. It was as if someone were slicing both sides of him with rusty knives. He thought he could feel his flesh unfolding from the wounds. "Even if I lose what makes me look like a naga, I am still one. I will always be one. Even if this spell your ignorance tells you I am under is real, do you think that I would fall under your spell again? After you schemed to leave me for dead? The first act I will commit once I get out of here will be to kill you."

Mogurn's grin vanished. "I have redeemed myself to you now!"

"You did nothing! You sent Ferklen to do it!" Gradni pulled himself off the floor, his own words swirling in his head. Mogurn did believe him under a spell. Yet he was not the only one. Ferklen did too.

The way Ferklen had reacted upon seeing him—he had been tense for the entire conversation on Zipacna. Gradni thought it was because he was afraid that Erdūn's presence would be discovered before the trap was sprung, but that was not it.

"You did not know your plan to capture me would work. You doubted it. You thought you were most probably sending Ferklen to his death. He truly thought that the other dragons, or even I, would kill him."

Mogurn edged closer. "That is what you are worth to us Gradni, for all your zeal."

"He was my friend, and yet you sent him on a suicide mission, just like you sent me." Gradni lifted his head, his words muddled with tears and blood as scales popped off his throat. "How many Mogurn? How many people out there are killing and dying in my name?"

Mogurn clutched the bars with both hands. He was smiling happily, "All of them, Gradni; they are all waiting for you."

Gradni peered out the gap. The entire mountain was now a blur of chaos. Beside it was the turmoil of red and gray where Tiamat battled the rukh. Gradni's palms slid down. He looked at his open, bleeding hands. "Zahk. I am sorry."

With both hands on his sword Zahk brandished it at Erdūn. Sirrush leapt at Erdūn's head, but Erdūn ducked under Sirrush and blocked Zahk's sword as well. Chimera attacked then, using the force of her back paws and wings to rush Erdūn's stomach. But Erdūn's thick armor protected him while his strength prevented him from falling. He spun Chimera off him. Knowing that only his blade could cut the armor, Zahk dashed toward Erdūn's back.

Erdūn leapt upward before Zahk could thrust his blade forward. Zahk leapt after him, but Erdūn turned in the air and swatted Zahk sword away with his own. Zahk was vulnerable in the air; there was no way he could move away from Erdūn's poleaxe now.

A blur of red rammed into Zahk's side as Chimera grabbed him. Zahk heard the poleaxe tear into her back leg. She released him in the air, allowing him to swing his feet underneath him to land. Erdūn was already charging at him. Zahk ran to meet him. He thrust his sword forward, but Erdūn once again locked it between his poleaxe and the stone ground. Zahk ducked under Erdūn's sword and let go of his own to leap at Erdūn. Erdūn was strong, and his skin had to be strong as well to maintain the weight of the armor, but perhaps Zahk could still tear into the giant's exposed jaw with his claws. A thud hit Zahk's chest. Erdūn's knee was so fast and strong that it cracked Zahk's ribs. Zahk fell on his back.

From high above, Ta'ar descended to be closer to the action. Chimera and Sirrush were both swatted aside by Erdūn. It was Python who brought Erdūn down. Her jaw, aimed at his throat, settled instead on his arm that got in the way. Her tail wrapped around one of Erdūn's legs and with every muscle in her body she brough the mighty amesha to the ground. Sirrush pounced on the other hand, pinning it and the poleaxe to the ground while Python kept the rest of him confined. But Erdūn managed to struggle his arm free and struck her head away with the bottom of his fist. He swung Sirrush off him and was back on his feet. Zahk grabbed his sword and ran again toward Erdūn, hoping to take advantage of the distraction that the others had created, but Erdūn kicked him away, and readied himself instead of following up the attack on Zahk. Python lunged at Erdūn. Zahk, too broken, was unable to warn her that it was expected. Erdūn evaded, and twisted round to catch one of her horns with his hand. He pulled her toward him, and wrapped his other arm around her neck. Her tail immediately circled around his right leg, but Erdūn went down on his right knee, trapping her tail between his thigh and calf. His hands on her horns, her body pinned, and her neck trapped, Erdūn twisted her head in a full circular motion.

He stood up and turned his gaze back to Zahk as she rolled off his body. Zahk attacked without waiting, without mourning, hoping to strike Erdūn while he was unarmed. But Erdūn managed to pick up his poleaxe, block the sword, and whirl his weapon around to strike the blunt end against Zahk's face.

Zahk fell down in a haze. He turned onto his stomach, pushed himself back up, and leapt away from Erdūn. Erdūn was about to follow, when Ta'ar blocked his path.

"Wait. Let him get higher," Zahk heard from Ta'ar as he climbed higher and higher, aching with every jump and pull. "Now," Ta'ar said. Erdūn broke forward like water from a dam. Zahk turned around and let his body go limp as Erdūn crashed him against the mountain. He forced himself to ignore it, focusing instead on the view. He could see so much of his home from up here. It was ruined by the bodies of his enemies and his brethren, and Python, but it was still his home, still under his protection. Delthurk was visible as well. Gradni was there in that castle.

The rusty red of Erdūn shadowed into view, illuminated by Ta'ar who came in behind the giant.

"I did not think that I would ever see you run, Shah Zahk," Ta'ar boomed. Zahk was pinned between the cross section of Erdūn's poleaxe and the rock. There was such fury in Erdūn's eyes. No depth, no reasoning, just fury. Zahk lowered his vision to Erdūn's other hand. It was shaking, as if a chain was holding it back. Ta'ar wanted to savor his victory. "I am glad you came up here, Zahk, where all your minions can see you die. They will fall quickly once they witness your death." Zahk merely continued to breathe. Ta'ar scorned him. "Kill him."

Erdūn's blade swiped towards Zahk's head, but Zahk brought his sword up in time to prevent himself from being decapitated.

"Ta'ar," Zahk wheezed, "you have never known anything about dragons. You are about to bring about your own end."

Erdūn screamed. He pulled his sword back and shoved it into Zahk's chest to the hilt.

All around them, dragons roared. Every dragon could feel him. Their united roar was mighty. Zahk dropped his own sword. He wrapped his fingers around the sword in his heart. The dragons' roar was angry, upset, driven, but not complete without him. While gripping the sword he opened his mouth, and past the blood that was dripping from it he roared alongside his brethren. He held nothing back. Like a constant eruption it came from him, so that even Delthurk could hear his death cry.

The sound was visceral. Gradni fell to his hands and knees. His scales dotted the floor beneath him. He could barely see them through the blur of tears. Spit dripped down from his open mouth as he howled. Zahk was dead.

The two cracks in his back tore wider apart. Any scales that were still on him were clinging only due to blood and sweat. Gradni tried to control his breathing through gritted teeth. The roar of the dragons was still going. Gradni uncurled so that he was on just his knees and could see out the window. He would not avoid his responsibility. The war was not yet over. Both sides were still willing to die . . . to kill.

Victims, that was all war led to—victims on both sides. As the thought was freed from him, his head exploded with pain as his skull began to reshape where it was bleeding. It was not just his skull. His entire body was now burning liberally as if he were a pyre, as if something within him had been trapped and was now coming out.

He screamed. His arms shot out to his sides, spotting the stone walls with the rest of the green scales as red pushed to the forefront.

Words came from behind him.

"You see, Gradni! Do not fight it! With Shah Zahk dead, you are reverting!"

As his muscles and bones realigned, Gradni revolved his neck to Mogurn. The pain in his skull amplified. Gradni reared his head back, his closed fists shaking furiously on either side of him as he let out a roar. Terrifying to start with, it grew deeper, louder, and primitive. It was beyond anything he was capable of before. Gradni welcomed the burning pain, accepting readily what was happening. He could hear his insides transmuting and it sounded good.

From the twin, equal sized tears on his back, red sheets flushed out on either side of him and flapped. He turned to the bars and coughed up a flavorless gray syrup. He hacked and spit the last of it out as he stood up straight. His body was still on fire, his organs thumping against his flesh while still molding into something new. Mogurn was off his stool, hypnotized by what he could not comprehend.

Overwhelmed and desperate to be outside with his wings flapping every which way, Gradni ran toward the back wall. With his knees up and his arms crossing his head in front of him, he leapt forward, and with a savage flap of his new wings, Gradni broke through the stones of his prison.

CHAPTER 19

G radni's strength came to him in sparks as he tried to flap the new appendages on his back. He moved erratically in the air, away from the hail of falling stone before landing with a 'thud' on the ground.

He probably needed rest, but he had to know what happened- he had to get to Zipacna. A wooden tank of water was a couple meters ahead of him. Spasmodically Gradni ran towards it and lifted it over himself to wash off the blood. He tossed the tank aside, and it shattered against a building. He shouldn't have had the strength for that to happen. He stood up to his full height. Ahead of him was the reflective steel statue of himself. Gradni stared at his reflection. Blood-red scales had replaced the green ones. The fine size of the new scales brought back the jawline that he lost when he first become a naga. What he saw coming out of his forehead required verification, so he traced with his fingers the two horns that had sprouted. They curved around his forehead and under his hair before rising from it, coming to points a half foot above his head. Gradni turned his head to the side to study the curve. His darkened yet still brown and green hair fell neatly around the base of the horns and behind his still pointy, now red, elf ears. He outstretched his bat-like wings to their full span. They too were red, and had curved spikes on the ends, just like the other winged dragons had on theirs.

The sounds of war from Zipacna beckoned his attention. The bones and other parts of his body were no longer cracking and shifting within him. His new self had fully transformed. His strength was no longer in flux. Gradni jumped up and flapped his wings furiously to go where he was needed.

He rose up into the clouds. The wind was full of energy up here, and each flap of his wings beat faster as his body sucked in the power of the weather. He might have denied it before, but by becoming a naga, he was not less of an elf- but more of one. The transformation, first into a naga and now into a horned naga, had not only increased his strength in itself, but made him more able to absorb energy from the atmosphere.

Zahk had said to him that it was always possible to tell which dragons would ascend to becoming horned dragons, but there were still occasional surprises, like Chimera. They thought that it was a matter of destiny, that the horned dragon spark was only in some of them. But if that were true, then it should never have happened to Gradni. He was born an elf, and there was no possible way for the horned dragon spark to have been born within him.

Gradni angled his body as he began his descent from the clouds. He was intuitively accustomed to his new wings. As he passed the mist of the clouds, he saw Zipacna from an angle he never had before, and it was a nightmare. The sounds he heard when above the clouds became real again when he saw the chaos and death that was splattering all over his home. Thousands of dragons and people were dead, dying, or fighting, and Gradni pushed down his anger and sadness to not be overwhelmed. He searched through the chaos for Chimera and Sirrush and found them. They were on either side of Erdūn, and were surrounded by dead dragons that had been cut by the amesha giant's massive weapons. Not far below them Python was dead, with her head twisted all the way around. Less than ten feet above, Zahk was sitting with his teeth showing past his open mouth, as if he was still in the midst of his death cry. There was fire everywhere, except around the half-mile radius of Erdūn. Gradni changed his trajectory toward him. The giant was charging toward Chimera, who was stumbling away after being struck across the face.

Gradni swooped and grabbed Erdūn's forearm with his clawed hand as he rammed him off the ledge and down a cliff. Erdūn lashed out immediately with his other arm, uppercutting Gradni across the chest before gripping him by the shoulder with his monstrous hand.

Gradni beat his wings viciously, succeeding only in slowing down their descent as they fought the way down. Hanging below, Erdūn began attacking with his knees. Gradni evaded the knee attacks and brought in his own knees against them to parry or divert them. Erdūn's armor was slowing him down; otherwise, Gradni would not have been able to keep up while fighting the pain of Erdūn's grip digging into his shoulder. Gradni pulled in both his knees for a final attack as they got close to the land below. But Erdūn suddenly removed his hand and struck with it. Gradni kicked out with both his feet just as he felt the fist whip across his face.

CHAPTER 20

G radni felt his kneecap break through stone as he skidded to a stop in the middle of six ameshas. He pushed his wings all the way out to shove the ameshas away while he remained kneeling. Coppery saliva swirled around in his mouth. Gradni looked up. Everyone around him was hypnotized by his appearance. The flying dragons were beating their wings only by instinct as they looked down at him. Even far beyond on the other sides of the mountains, the fighting had quelled. Right above, Ta'ar was floating. He had never seen the Fire Spirit, but in all of Zahk's descriptions of him, Gradni never expected to see him look concerned.

A rock the size of a sobekian flew up. Gradni flapped his wings forward and flew back from where it fell. Erdūn stood up from where the rock had come from. The sounds of war started to begin anew. Erdūn leapt closer to Gradni, cracking the stone that he landed on.

"Enough, Erdūn," Gradni roared, his voice carrying throughout Zipacna. "This battle is over. Go back, and take your army with you!"

Erdūn brought his massive hands up and removed his helmet. His teeth were grinding so hard against each other that it was if he were trying to shatter them. He proceeded to remove the plates around his arms. His skin looked like stone. Even his face seemed like it was frozen in place. It made sense now why the armor left his mouth exposed. Erdūn's commanding voice inspired the army, and though his skin was not nearly as thick as the armor he wore, it was possibly just as hardened. The armor was only slowing the giant down, something that was not an issue against the other dragons.

Gradni had only been a shade faster when Erdūn was wearing the armor, and each piece that Erdūn tossed aside was so heavy that it seemed to fracture the rocks they fell against.

"Do not do this, Erdūn!" Gradni yelled. "Do not!" Erdūn removed the plates strapped around his shins and picked up both his poleaxe and sword. He walked toward Gradni with intent reflected in the brandishing of his weapons. Both dragons and men distanced themselves as the gap between the two closed. The sounds of war and death were already loud again. Ta'ar sank into view. An arrogant smirk revealed him to indeed be the Ta'ar that Zahk had told him about.

Sirrush jumped between Gradni and Erdūn with Zahk's sword in his mouth. Gradni took it from him.

He looked at Erdūn. He did not see the boy he had once met. Even then, Erdūn was less a boy than Gradni was. What Gradni once perceived in Erdūn as his ability to control his emotions, Gradni now understood was a complete lack of feeling—except perhaps for unreasonable hatred.

"Get back," Gradni said calmly to Sirrush as Erdūn shifted his weapons. "You will only distract me from fighting him. Protect me from being attacked by others. All my focus must be on this fight if I am to stop him."

Sirrush barked at Erdūn and ran to help a serpent against a Disciple. Gradni arched a foot back and bent his knee. He lifted Zahk's sword up before him as he spread his wings to their full length. He called upon his inner fire as Erdūn stood less than three feet from him. A sheath of pure blue fire enveloped his sword.

Gradni beat his wings and rushed to Erdūn with his blaze held out in front of him. He swung his sword in an arc upon Erdūn. Erdūn met it with his poleaxe and drove his own sword out, slashing with it twice after it was parried the first time- each follow-up missing as Gradni curved around it with the aid of his wings. Gradni flew to the right, then up, then down, and again right, clashing his weapon with Erdūn's as he flew around like a rabid bat. A Disciple of Gaorda managed to break away from Sirrush. He took out his discus as he barged into Gradni and Erdūn's area. Gradni flew from Erdūn so that he could defend himself from the interfering Disciple, but as the deva arched his arm to throw, Chimera caught it in her teeth as she pounced on top of him. She mauled her new foe till he was helpless. Gradni felt the sting of a slash across his armpit from the pole axe. The other dragons were protecting him so that he could fight Erdūn. He had to trust completely that they would do so.

Erdūn's weapons were damaged due to Zahk's sword. They wouldn't last long against it, but Gradni wasn't sure if he would outlast them himself. They were as thick as Erdun's armor was, and the giant was skillful enough to minimize the damage done against them.

Erdūn suddenly charged forward and brought his knee into Gradni's chest. Before being crushed between the mountain and Erdūn, Gradni slid his red skin to the side, slipping away just before Erdūn's knee cracked through stone. Though winded, Gradni rammed his elbow into Erdūn's face. Erdūn fell off the ledge they were on and Gradni followed with a tight grip on his blade.

The three weapons clashed again, and those battling around them moved away.

Erdūn locked his sword with Gradni's and swung his poleaxe back and then forward into Gradni's left wing. Gradni beat his wings free and tore off skin from Erdūn's chest with a savage kick.

But the beating of his wings brought Gradni pain that he was not familiar with, shocking Gradni into flying upward instead of following the attack. Each flutter of his wings adjusted him to the sting. He relaxed them once safe in the high air, beating them enough only to remain aloft. As long as Erdūn was waiting, Gradni could as well.

From here he could hear it all. Screams, shouts, and yelps - the sounds of warfare rising like smoke from a burning village. Gradni could not tell from where each sound came from. The singular attacks of blades, claws, and teeth penetrating flesh were suffocated by the chaos around. It had to end. This needless war burning from hatred had to end.

Erdūn began to look for other dragons to kill to goad Gradni into coming back down.

"How are you doing this?" Gradni looked behind him to see whose voice was breaking through the chaos. "How do you have fire when in our presence?"

Gradni growled at Ta'ar and turned his back to him. Erdūn was racing toward a cluster of dragons. Gradni snarled and rose higher. "Erdūn!" he roared.

Erdūn stopped and faced Gradni. His weapons ready in his hands, his gritted teeth vibrated apart and from between them erupted a bellowing that pierced through the chaos.

Gradni roared back. He drew more fire from his inner core into his sword to give it an extra sheath of lightning blue flames, and shot toward Erdūn.

His wings fluttered so viciously while fiercely wind channeling, that they disrupted a longue's flight- his sword leaving a trail of brilliant blue light. Erdūn was stronger and was trained by the same people who trained Gradni. He anticipated moves as well as Gradni did. Speed was Gradni's only prospect. The power of his naga wings, coupled with his ability to wind channel was his only chance.

Erdūn hung his poleaxe back and his sword up, but that was not all Gradni saw as the gap closed. He saw the blood. He saw the dead on both sides, the victims of hatred born out of a fear of difference: the death of Yagura, the misguided sins of Ferklen, the body of Python, and Zahk. Gradni gave his wings a final flutter as he came crashing into Erdūn.

Gradni swung his feet below him and kicked Erdūn's defending sword with one of them. As Erdun's sword sliced into his heel, Gradni drove his azure blade down. The axe head swung toward Gradni's eyes. Gradni knocked it off course with his horns; it sank into the base of his neck beside his collarbone. The long edge of the poleaxe cut against Gradni's cheek as the weapon shifted. Gradni pulled on his own weapon to confirm what he hoped had happened. His sword was halfway into Erdūn by the shoulder. It was probably an inch from Erdūn's heart- his massive size preventing it from being reached. It was visible where the sword struck, for the fire surrounding the blade had gone out when the poleaxe hit Gradni—its own edge also hooked deep.

"Erdūn . . . Erdūn . . ." Gradni stuttered.

Erdūn swung his poleaxe and Gradni onto a wall of stone to prevent Gradni from using his wings. Gradni felt the poleaxe sawing through the bones that were protecting his heart. Gradni opened his mouth and roared. He focused on the pain so as not to be defeated by it. His sword lit up again. Erdūn yelled, but the poleaxe continued to cut at Gradni's bone. Gradni called upon Zahk with his roar, and infused everything into his blade as he forced it down through

Erdūn's flesh. The flame that came from it was so bright, that even Gradni could not see what happened before falling into dizziness.

Gradni was flat on the ground. He arched his head up and again felt the poleaxe edge. The head of it was still partially in him. He looked toward his feet and saw the mop of hair of his opponent. Erdūn's skin had lost its density. The empowering fire of Ta'ar had been purged from him by the flames of Gradni's naga sword. The giant shuffled. He was still alive. Gradni pulled the axe out from his own body before sliding his sword out of the defeated Erdūn. Silence surrounded them. The fighting had stopped. Chimera landed at his side. Gradni was about to rest his hands on her for support, when Erdūn started to rise. His massive hands plodded against the ground. They pushed hard and blood oozed from his wounds, including the partially cauterized wound beside his neck. He rested on his knees and looked at Gradni. Somehow, after everything, there was still true hatred in Erdūn's eyes. Gradni pushed down on Chimera and stood up. "Erdūn, it is over."

"Not until you are all dead."

It took such an effort even to say that. Gradni turned away. There was nothing more to be said. He turned suddenly back after realizing that Sirrush was skulking behind Erdūn. "No!" Gradni yelled, as Sirrush leapt forward and sank his teeth into Erdūn's neck. The giant man was no longer able to suppress the dragons' fire. Flames rose up from the gaps in Sirrush's closed mouth as he tore into Erdūn's throat. Gradni lunged, but Chimera held him back with her paws. It was already too late. Sirrush released the lifeless body of Erdūn and challenged Gradni with a look. Gradni did not meet it. "Fine. Fine. That was the last one." Gradni stood up. All eyes were upon him. "Leave our home." An elf suddenly ran at Gradni, but Gradni whipped his sword to life quickly as he pointed it at the elf. "I said enough, Ferklen. How many times must I offer you mercy before you will learn?" Ferklen backed away. Gradni turned to look at Delthurk. "Leave our mountains." Gradni stressed each of the three words. The elves turned away first. With one great hero dead, and the other against them, they descended down Zipacna. The remaining elephants trumpeted as their qui-lahk riders turned them around. The five remaining Disciples of Gaorda backed away as well. They kept their eyes on Gradni the whole way down the mountain, not once turning their backs to him as they struggled around the rocks.

Gradni's head fell back. Ta'ar had also left. He turned back to Delthurk. He tried looking away but couldn't. The dragons cloistered around him. "Start the pyre without me. I'll be back. I have to end this now." Gradni leapt into the air.

He beat his wings a couple times to reassess the pain, then flew toward Delthurk.

CHAPTER 21

G radni outraced the retreating army as he crossed high over the Delthurk walls. The archers on the wall tried futilely to fire arrows at him that had no hope of reaching him. Only the ballista arrows had a chance, but were inaccurate against anything smaller than a drake. Few missiles even came close to Gradni. He flew higher anyway. There were twice as many archers than usual on the roof of the castle. Mogurn and Ta'ar were expecting him. *Good*, Gradni thought. It meant that they were all together.

A ballista arrow was on course toward him. Gradni sank down so that it flew over him. Before they could refit another one, he flew toward the ballista and with his sword ablaze sliced it down the middle. He then flew toward the statue of himself. He landed before the pedestal. The statue was twice his size. The Delthurk insignia, the sword, himself—all of it was twice his size. Gripping his sword with both hands, Gradni jumped to the top of the statue and brought his sword down to split it in two. Both sides were still standing. He flew up and down and around the statue with his sword swinging through it. The pieces fell against the ground and rolled down the mountain toward the gate. Gradni turned back to the castle and bolted up toward it.

He evaded the arrows without difficulty and made his way toward what was once the window of his room. He swooped against it, breaking the small opening into one the size of a door. From here he knew best the way to the council room.

Soldiers met him in the corridor with their weapons drawn. Gradni swatted them aside.

When they piled toward him he spread out his wings to shove them all away. He flew toward the stairs and up them. He arrived with a skid outside the senate council room. Several guards stood with their backs against the heavy olive door. Their weapons were pulled in close to their chests, as if they were shields instead of swords.

"Move," Gradni said, as soldiers stopped several feet from him after coming at him from both sides. These elves had never seen Gradni with his horns. They began to slide away from him, but Gradni was out of patience. Gradni flew up and then across, splintering a hole through the top of the door.

Screams pierced his ears from his left as he landed. Gradni followed the banshee-like scream to an amesha woman. She was pressing herself against a corner and looking at him with a face that was drained of blood.

"Silence her!" a voice crackled.

A senator obeyed Ta'ar and went beside her. She turned from Gradni to the senator and whimpered. She could barely take her eyes off of him for a second.

The door had indeed been barricaded from the inside. It beat softly as Gradni heard the commotion through the hole he created. The guards could easily have climbed through if they really wanted too. The senate was alone with Gradni. A faint light at his right attracted Gradni to Ta'ar as he walked toward the senators. He was much dimmer than he was less than an hour ago. Gradni turned from him and found Mogurn. The senator was not in his regular position. He remained still as Gradni approached him. Those around

Mogurn moved away. Mogurn's face was straight, but he was trembling beneath the sweat on his brow.

"I can come here at any time and kill all of you," Gradni declared. None of them dared reply. He felt an angry tang of flame dance off Ta'ar, but remained focused on Mogurn. "You cannot stop me. We can kill you all, but we are not you." Gradni grabbed Mogurn's collar and pulled him to his face. The screech of the amesha woman pierced the hall again. Whoever she was, something had happened to her. Delthurk and hatred most likely. Mogurn's face still maintained a look of calm, but sweat was now lining his forehead with strands of his white hair. The promise Gradni made to kill him was running through his head. "I have seen enough blood," Gradni said. "You will disassemble Delthurk. You will send everyone away from our home. You will tear down these walls. The other dragons and I will be watching you closely. In three day we will come and destroy everyone and everything that remains." Mogurn did not move, but the other senators nodded their heads rapidly until Ta'ar suddenly bellowed.

"Never. Not until all of you—"

Gradni tossed Mogurn away and roared back at Ta'ar. "What can you do to stop me?" Ta'ar's flames danced furiously. That was all they did. "You should all die for what you've done! But I've seen enough."

Gradni looked to where he had discarded Mogurn.

"Three days," Mogurn murmured. "We will send everyone away."

Gradni lifted himself into the air. There was no longer any noise on the other side of the door. He beat his wings and flew from the castle.

The funeral pyre was just beginning as Gradni returned.

The flying dragons were hovering around it to fan it with their wings, while the ground dragons arranged themselves in spiral lines to the center. Gradni flew above the fire and toward the tallest peak where the dragons had left the body of Zahk. He floated down to it. Zahk's mouth was still open from his final roar. Gradni closed it. He delicately ran his hand under Zahk's hair and gently massaged his head. He remained with him for a while. "I will protect them now. I don't want to let you pass yet, but it is what you want." Gradni lifted Zahk into the air.

The fire was roaring. With Zahk in his arms, Gradni flew to the peak of the pyre. "I will miss you," Gradni said. He floated so close to the pyre that the flames almost touched him. Gradni lowered his arms to his sides. Zahk plummeted into the flames. A bright blue flame burst to life in the pyre's center.

EPILOGUE

The statue of Irath and Kallini stood proudly on the highest peak of Zipacna. As Delthurk was no more, there was no fear of the statue being destroyed. Gradni and the other dragons had hovered overhead during the evacuation, making sure that people were only leaving and that no scheme was afoot. His friends demanded that he rest during the three days. He reluctantly agreed. Hatred did not die so quickly, and he was not comfortable until Delthurk was gone. He knew firsthand of the schemes and madness that hatred could inspire, but he trusted his dragons who were as suspicious as he was.

They told him of an amesha carriage that came to Delthurk from Aristahl. Gradni was curious, but the carriage had left as quickly as it had arrived once the amesha woman was lifted into it. For her to have been in the senators' meeting room, she must have been important, though Gradni could not figure out what her role was.

There was still hatred against dragons. The Disciples of Gaorda—wherever the remaining ones were—would never surrender their ways after dedicating their existence to their order. But without Delthurk, the hatred had no focal point. And of course, Gradni had given them mercy. Delthurk had been lied to by their senate since its conception. Some lies they believed and some they did not, but the mercy the dragons had given them was an undeniable truth that they would always carry with them.

Gradni checked the commander's quarters first when they were making sure the castle was empty. Ferklen was not there, but Gradni's old pendant was lying on the floor next to the door. He looked at it for but a moment before leaving. Minutes later, Tiamat and the rest of the drakes burned Delthurk to ash.

As weeks went by, the dragons that had come to Zipacna for the battle began to leave. Others went with them, and Gradni supported their decision.

"We have to reclaim this world, and show them that we are not what they think," he said to them. It was nothing that they did not know; many of them had experienced more visions from funeral pyres than Gradni had. Gradni watched a group of longues float casually away toward the east where they had come from, when he saw a faint spark hanging over Zipacna. It had been there for more than a month, haunting Gradni each time he saw it. After seeing it every day and every night between watching his friends leave, he flew up toward it.

The Fire Spirit was skeletal. There was barely any fire surrounding his frame.

"What are you doing here, Ta'ar? Your quest is over."

Ta'ar spoke. His voice which was barely a whisper was offset further by his defeated tone. "As long as I am here, you will all one day be destroyed. I killed Zahk. I will kill you too."

Gradni looked him over. The thin fires were dimming even as he spoke. Soon there would not be enough to sustain him. Gradni pitied the Fire Spirit, but not enough to care what happened to him. He fluttered his wings and flew back down to his home. Chimera leapt at him as he landed.

Taken by surprise, Gradni playfully threw her off. Sirrush unexpectedly rose up from the flat rock he was on and joined in against Gradni. They leapt at him again and again, Sirrush somewhat viciously. Gradni occasionally let them tackle him so he could taunt them with his strength by tossing them away. They carried on for a while, until Gradni conceded defeat and let them topple him onto his back. When he looked up toward the sky, Ta'ar had vanished.

CPSIA information can be obtained
at www.ICGtesting.com
Printed in the USA
FFHW02n1610201018
48894566-53125FF